AF226261

Prince John's
Lost Love

Visit Jo Cook's website and subscribe to her newsletter to receive a FREE novella, A Rose for Carter, as well as news about upcoming releases.

AuthorJoCook.com

Also by Jo Cook

World of Eoroe: Bryten series:

A Rose for Carter (novella)
Prince John's Lost Love
The Guarded Heart

Prince John's Lost Love

World of Eoroe: Bryten
Book One

Jo Cook

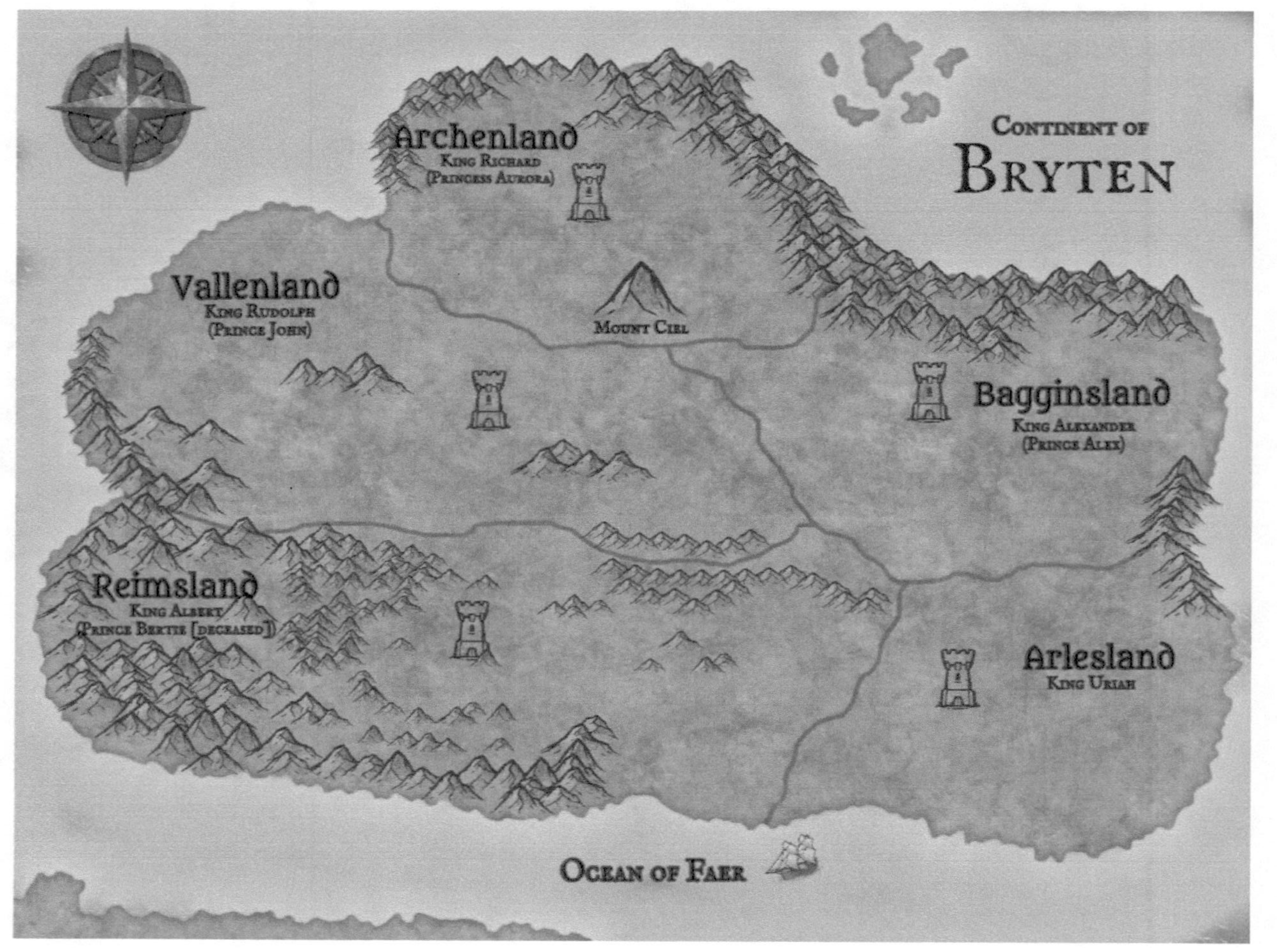
Continent of
BRYTEN
Archenland
King Richard
(Princess Aurora)
Mount Ciel
Vallenland
King Rudolph
(Prince John)
Bagginsland
King Alexander
(Prince Alex)
Reimsland
King Albert
(Prince Bertie [Deceased])
Arlesland
King Uriah
Ocean of Faer

Prince John's Lost Love

Table of Contents

Dedicated to Shirley Douglass, a fellow bibliophile who was like a second mother to me.
She is gracing Heaven now, and will never be forgotten.

13

Once upon a time in the world of Eoroe,

On the continent of Bryten…

Prince John's Dearest Wish

As the crown prince of Vallenland rode through the early morning mist, his thoughts weighed heavy. With his mother and sister, he'd returned late the night before from Archenland, the kingdom to the north. During the long carriage ride home, he'd been lost in contemplation, but fortunately the two women, full of chatter over everything that had happened at Princess Aurora's birthday ball, had been content to leave John to his thoughts.

He knew one reason they hadn't drawn him into conversation was because he'd finally asked Princess Aurora if she had feelings for him beyond friendship and she'd said no. His mother and sister thought he was crushed.

Prince John had spent the ride home contemplating why he *wasn't*.

Aurora was a beautiful woman and intelligent, and being with her had been restful. She was content to gaze out over the countryside if they were riding together, or sit quietly with a book if the weather kept them indoors. She didn't try to jolly him along, tell him to cheer up. She understood his sadness, because she was sad, too.

When they did talk, they discussed their respective kingdoms and the challenges therein. They didn't often touch on personal subjects, and John liked it that way.

Because every time he tried to talk about the thing that was most important to him on a personal level rather than as a future king, people got that look in their eye that said, *"Here he goes again…"*

Riding through the mist, his horse whiffling at the spring scents, John sighed.

Maybe everyone was right. Maybe he should just put it all behind him, accept that everything that could be done *had* been done. Move on with his life.

As a ruler, though, he was responsible for *all* his people. So surely, he should be even more responsible for finding the girl who'd once been a dear friend? John didn't think he'd ever be able to move on until he at least tried.

John knew his parents thought it was high time for him to get married, and he'd been prepared to do that if Aurora had had feelings for him. But she didn't, and John had been surprised to find that he'd felt liberated instead of devastated.

His mother had never thought Aurora was the right woman for him, so she'd been hinting about another girl for years. John had to admit Lady Maureen was a lovely woman, and in time he could easily see himself married to her.

But before that, before he settled down to having a family and taking over more of the duties of the kingdom …

He had to try to find Ceci. He'd never be able to get her off his mind if he didn't.

John took a deep breath, feeling like it was the first clean breath he'd taken in years. He knew what he had to do, and he would let no one dissuade him this time.

Clicking his tongue, he turned the horse for home.

The Queen's Blessing

A few days later, Prince John announced to his mother and father that he was going to visit the Duke of Wallingford. John kept his eyes on his breakfast plate as he spoke, but he felt the sudden stillness of his family, and from the corner of his eye he saw his parents exchange a glance with his sister. A slight intake of breath let him know his mother was getting ready to speak, but his father reached out and touched her hand before she could do so.

King Rudolph said diffidently, "The duke? You haven't been to visit them in a long time. Why now?"

"Because I want to know if they've heard anything about Ceci." John's voice was steady, but his heart was racing. He'd always been willing to go along with what his parents wanted him to do before. How would they react?

There was silence for a few long minutes.

He finally looked up at his mother. "I know you don't want me to go. I know you think I need to just forget what happened, that we've done all we can to find Ceci. But I can't, Mother. It's been seventeen years and I still think of her every day, still wonder if she's alive. If nothing else, even if she weren't important to me personally,

I would feel like I failed as a ruler if I didn't make the effort. Her family needs us!"

He turned to his father. "I know you did everything you could at the time to find her. But if she's still alive, she's twenty-two now. Maybe she's started remembering her life before, maybe she's started searching for her family. Maybe we can find some trace of her now, when we couldn't before. I have to try, Father. I can't go on like this." He clenched his hand, desperate to convince them, but trying to control his emotions so he wouldn't frighten his mother.

Because no matter what they said this time, he was going to help the duke find his daughter.

John's eyes darted back and forth between his parents, while his sister Morgana watched them all.

Queen Valeria studied her only son. His dark hair, cut short, curled slightly over his forehead. The brown eyes he'd inherited from his father, the small dimple in his chin he'd inherited from her. He'd grown a short beard to hide the dimple, tired of people teasing him about how young it made him look, but you could still see it if you knew to look. The dark slashes of his eyebrows were drawn together with the intensity of his desire to do this thing she didn't want him to do. And so…

She sighed and relented on the stance she'd held for so long. "You should go."

Her husband and children looked at her incredulously.

Valeria gave a small laugh and smoothed the napkin in her lap. "Oh, don't look at me like that. I'm not an ogre. I don't want to stop you doing what you really want to do, John. I just want you to be happy and safe, but I know Ceci's disappearance makes you unhappy. So, go and do your best to find her, but if you can't…" She reached for his hand and gazed at him intently. "If you can't, you must promise to move on with your life. It's long past time."

John hesitated, his eyes jumping from her to his father and then to Morgana before he gave a reluctant nod.

His parents exchanged another glance, and then his father nodded. "Alright, son. I'll send a letter by pigeon to the duke to expect you, and you may call on any of the royal resources you need."

John gave them a brilliant grin, feeling joy and a sense of purpose rising in him like he hadn't felt in… oh, much too long! He sprang from his seat and circled the table to kiss his mother and Morgana, and shake his father's hand, and then left at slightly less than a run. He had many things to do!

Wallingford

When Prince John's entourage rode into Wallingford, everyone in the village was lined up to greet them. They cheered as he rode toward the castle that rose above the trees around the village, and John's spirits rose with their shouts.

Riding up the long drive to the castle, he could see the family gathered out front as they always had been for his once-frequent visits. Dogs of various sizes milled around, panting in the warm spring sun, a few feinting at the sheep that cropped the grass on the front lawn.

Drawing to a halt, he grinned at the cries of welcome from the family, then swung down from his horse and shook hands with the duke, who clapped him on the back and embraced him like a son. They were related through someone's grandmother's cousin, and the families had always been close. John had treated their home like his own when he was younger, staying for weeks on end, and looking on the duke's sons as his brothers, since he had none of his own.

"John," the duke said, pulling back from the embrace to reveal eyes wet with unshed tears. "It's good to see you, lad. It's been too long." The duke shook his head and pulled a large handkerchief from his pocket as his three sons crowded around the prince, clapping him on the back and ruffling his black hair affectionately.

John grinned at the brothers and tried not to remember a sweet, high voice calling his name as small legs propelled a sturdy little body against his ten-year-old frame. Ceci had always been the first to hug him when he visited and had rarely left his side during his stays. That was one reason he hadn't visited in so long. He couldn't bear seeing her ghost everywhere he looked.

He also couldn't bear the emptiness in her family's eyes, their obvious attempts to put on a happy face while feeling a bone-deep misery.

"John," a soft voice said as a hand plucked at his sleeve.

Turning from the duke's sons, Prince John saw Lady Coraline standing with arms outstretched, a faint smile on her face. The small blonde woman had once been beautiful, but the years of sadness and loss had caused her radiant skin to stretch taut over the bones of her face, throwing the sharp cheekbones into relief and making her dark brown eyes look like pools of emptiness. There were purple circles under her eyes, intensifying the effect of holes in the middle of her face. John saw the smile in her eyes battling against her customary despair, and his heart ached.

Her eyes searched his for a moment, and whatever she saw there gave her pause. She stilled a moment, then reached for him again. As she drew him into an embrace, she whispered, "You've come to find her, haven't you? You've come to bring her home."

His throat aching so he almost couldn't reply, John whispered as she clutched him, "I've come to try," and kissed her sunken cheek.

John gave news of his family as the brothers escorted him to his room, but in the back of his mind he was fighting an overwhelming dismay. When he'd left his father's castle, he'd felt invigorated and full of hope. Surely there was some clue that had been overlooked all these years! Surely now they would be able to pick up the trail that had gone so cold.

But the pervading atmosphere, the complete loss of hope, in the duke's castle was beating against his frail optimism. This family, these brothers, had given everything but their lives in search of their sister. How could he possibly think he could do any better? Was it arrogance?

When he was finally alone in his room, John fell to his knees and prayed for the strength to inspire these hopeless men once more.

The duke had decreed that there was to be no serious talk at supper that night, but he hadn't factored in his own susceptibility to alcohol. He was drinking deeply, and Prince John saw from the look on his sons' faces that it wasn't a surprise to them when the duke started telling stories about his young daughter.

"My girl," he wept, tears falling like rain down his face. "My sweet baby girl! Who did it? Eh? Who took her?" he cried, reaching out to clutch John's arm.

John could say nothing. After spending the day with the brokenhearted family, it was all he could do not to weep himself. He just held tightly to the duke's hand as the older man continued.

"Seventeen years, it's been! Seventeen years of not knowing, of worrying, wondering if it would be better if she were alive or dead! A man can't live like this, John, no man can. No *father* can. It's our duty to protect 'em!" His eyes were earnest as he stared at the prince.

At a signal from the duchess, the duke's oldest son, Harry, a bear of a man with black hair and a long, wild beard, stood up and approached his father, gently drawing the duke up from his chair, holding the weeping man on his sturdy chest, and leading him down from the raised dais where the family sat. His two remaining sons watched along with the duchess and Prince John as the men traversed the room and disappeared up the stairs to the living quarters.

"Well," the duchess said as she turned to John, her tone determinedly cheerful, "Now tell me how your parents are doing, John. It's been too long since we've seen them."

John complied, but he scarcely knew what he was saying. His thoughts followed the old duke through the halls and up to his chamber, then fled along the corridors to the nursery, last home of the girl they loved.

The Duke Steps Down

The next morning, Prince John was not looking forward to breakfast with the sad family. After just a few hours with them, he was seriously doubting his promise to bring Ceci home. He'd always looked up to the duke's two oldest sons, and he had the utmost respect for the duke. It was madness to think he could do more than they had.

As his man dressed him in a morning suit, John considered the situation. He wanted to ask the duke to do something, but worried about offending him. He had a strong feeling, though, that it was time to make some changes. Maybe those would bring about the success that had eluded them so long.

The duke and duchess were already seated and eating with their three sons when John walked in, but the duke stood and motioned Prince John to take the seat to his right. The duke served the prince himself, saying quietly as he forked cold meat onto the prince's plate, "I'm sorry about last night. Coraline tells me I made a fool of myself." He glanced up at John and shook his head. "Please pardon an old man's broken heart."

John smiled. "Not at all. I think all our hearts are still broken. I just hope we can start to heal them soon." He took a mouthful of food and chewed for a moment, then forced himself to speak. "Duke… you and the duchess have carried this burden for so long. I think it might do you good to turn it over to your sons and me now. I'm sure your sons know as much about it at this point as you do."

The duke stared at him for a moment, obviously taken aback, then glanced at the duchess, who nodded silently. "Well… it goes against everything my father's heart demands, but…" He sighed. "Maybe you're right. Maybe it's time to turn it over to the younger generation. Truthfully, I don't have the stamina for it anymore, for feeling like I'm dying all over again when we find no trace of her."

John reached across the table to take the duchess's hand and promised them both, "Don't worry. We won't stop until we find out what happened."

He hoped *this* was a promise he could fulfill.

The Brothers' Story

After breakfast, Prince John and the duke's sons retired to the library and seated themselves around one of the large tables.

"I'd like to hear about the previous searches, any clues you found." John nodded at the oldest brother. "Harry, why don't you tell me what you remember. You were, what? Sixteen when Ceci disappeared?"

"Fifteen," Harry corrected. "And Christopher was thirteen. We went with Father to try to find her that night."

Christopher, a slight man with his mother's pale blonde hair and dark eyes, nodded and said, glancing at his youngest brother, "Matt was too young, but Father thought it was important for Harry and me to help. But we didn't find out much." He shrugged and shook his head.

Harry nodded as he listened to his brother. "Right. All we learned was that no one knew anything." He sighed.

John said, "Take me through it step by step. What exactly happened that day?"

They all looked at Harry, who took a deep breath and said, as if he'd rehearsed it many times, "It was a regular day. We boys were busy with our tutor, but Ceci was too young, so she was running around wild like she usually did."

Matt corrected him. "Ceci never ran wild. She was a good kid." There was a world of hurt in his voice.

Prince John knew Matt had suffered especially when Ceci disappeared. He'd been only five years older than his sister and had been the most dismissive of her attention. Determined to prove himself to the older boys, he constantly evaded Ceci and played tricks on her. He'd seemed to take special delight in telling his sister exactly how she'd messed up whatever thing she was trying to impress them with.

Although they were the same age, John hadn't liked Matt much back then, but he'd grown to like him in later years, as he saw the changes that guilt wrought on the young man. Whenever John had visited in the years following Ceci's disappearance, Matt had always sought him out and anguished over all the times he'd pushed his sister away. He'd said, more times than John could remember, "If I'd only let her follow me around, she would've been with us that day!"

John had pitied Matt, so he'd stayed silent, but he secretly agreed. It wasn't the brothers' fault that Ceci had gone missing… but they could've been kinder to the child, and that might have made a crucial difference.

Harry nodded at Matt's words. "You're right. She was a good kid. But she did run around the grounds as much as she wanted to, and none of us much minded where she was or what she was doing."

Christopher interjected, "Well, Nanny should've been watching her, but she was too old. We'd worn her out over all those years of trying to keep tabs on us, so she pretty much let Ceci do whatever she wanted."

"Like she did when you were here visiting," Harry said to John, the hint of a laugh in his voice, "Because all Ceci wanted to do then was follow *you* around."

John laughed, pleasure crinkling his eyes. "I never had a moment to myself, but I never minded. She was a cute little thing, and she always made me laugh."

Harry nodded. "You had time for her, or made time for her, which none of the rest of us can say." Deep regret tinged his voice and he fell silent.

John broke into his thoughts. "Tell me about the undergardener who disappeared the same day as Ceci. What was his name?"

"David." The middle brother, Christopher, cleared his throat. "His name was David. I saw his family about two years ago. Father found out pretty soon after we started the initial search that David was from a small village in Reimsland."

Reimsland was the kingdom to the south of Vallenland.

Christopher continued, "As soon as Father realized Ceci was gone and David had disappeared at the same time, we sent runners to Reimsland. The head gardener knew that David was leaving that day to visit his family for a month, and he was driving a wagon when he left. It would've been so easy for him to conceal Ceci among the trunks and boxes in the wagon if he wanted to kidnap her for a ransom. Even more importantly, Ceci was friends with David, had been following him around for weeks, so she might have gone with him willingly."

Christopher took a deep breath and continued. "But we found no trace of the wagon or David, other than the innkeeper just a few miles down the road who remembered David coming in briefly that evening. Father sent a pigeon to King Albert of Reimsland, telling him what had happened and asking him to search the village David was from, Greenbriar Village. King Albert…" Christopher's voice trailed off and he shook his head, brown eyes rueful. "Well, you know what he's like."

John nodded and pursed his lips. King Albert had a reputation for being argumentative, no matter the situation.

"Well, he refused to let Father cross the border to search for Ceci. Said he'd do it himself, that we had no business questioning his subjects. I'll tell you, I thought Father might go mad. For a while, he was convinced that Albert had ordered Ceci's kidnapping himself, that it was some kind of plot to start a war with Vallenland. That's when he got King Rudolph involved, right?" he asked John.

John nodded. "Yes, that's when Father sent a pigeon to King Albert demanding that he allow your father to journey to Greenbriar to question David's family. I think he had to threaten to break our treaty with Reimsland to get Albert to agree, but he did finally give in."

"Yes, but that was months after Ceci disappeared, and Father and Mother were almost out of their minds. King Albert claimed he had sent soldiers to Greenbriar Village as soon as he heard Ceci was missing, but we never really believed him."

Harry took up the story. "But neither could we find any trace of his involvement in the disappearance. We couldn't find anything at all. Beyond that one innkeeper, no one had seen David or the wagon, and no one had seen a child fitting Ceci's description."

John interrupted. "What was she wearing when she disappeared?"

Harry said, "A green linen dress, one of the old ones that she used for playing."

"So it wasn't clothing that would immediately alert someone that she was from a noble family?" John asked.

"Right. She could've easily passed for a child from the village in that dress. Her stockings and shoes… everything was old, worn-in. It was good quality, but nothing fancy."

John asked Christopher, "What did David's family say, the two times you visited them?"

"Oh, we didn't just visit them those two times!" Christopher hastened to clarify. "We've seen them many times over the years. Father…" He shook his head. "David's family was the only lead he had to hold onto, the only hope. So every time it got to be too much, he would set out to see them again, or send me or Harry to them. We've gotten to know them well over the years." He hesitated, then said, "Father never made any secret of his belief that David had taken Ceci with him, and his family seemed anxious to do anything that would clear David's name, so they were very helpful."

Harry said dismissively, "They didn't know anything about Ceci's disappearance. We're sure of that. There's never been any hint that David actually arrived there, and they've always been willing to let us into their houses, let us search all their buildings. King Albert was a nightmare to deal with, but the people of Greenbriar Village were very kind."

John said intently, "So what do you think happened to Ceci, then?"

Harry leaned forward and anger colored his voice as he spoke. "He kidnapped her! I'll never believe anything else. David kidnapped Ceci, and planned to hold her for ransom. He was a scoundrel through and through. He owed money, gambling debts, and he was going to use her to pay 'em off. That's what Father discovered. Now, something must have happened to change the plan, and I don't know what it was. All I can hope is that Ceci got away and managed to get somewhere safe and she's still alive. But I fear…" His voice broke and he dropped his head into his hands.

Matt said with a tremor in his voice, "We fear there was an accident and they were both killed. It just doesn't make sense that we've not been able to find any trace of either of them, unless something bad happened. Why bother to kidnap a child, risk imprisonment, if you aren't going to ask for a ransom? There's no other reason to kidnap such a high-ranking child of the nobility. He must have known we'd stop at nothing to find her… so what was his plan?" He shook his head in frustration.

John asked, "Do you think the men to whom David owed money might have attacked him?"

Christopher shook his head. "No, we talked to them several times that first year, and we're convinced they didn't know anything. He did owe money, that's true, but it wasn't very much money, not enough to risk a good job here at the castle." Christopher glanced at his brothers, then said abruptly, his eyes intent on John, "I don't think David had anything to do with Ceci's disappearance. I think it was just a coincidence that they both disappeared that day. Ceci was adventurous, and I've always been afraid that she may have gone exploring in one of the caves on the estate or drowned in the river. But we've done a thorough search of the grounds many times over the years, and never found anything. There's just literally no trace of her."

Silence again.

Frustration.

As the silence drew out, Prince John realized the brothers were waiting for him to say something, come up with a plan… looking to him as their leader. He wasn't entirely comfortable with that, having expected Harry to lead the search, but in a way it was a relief. Listening to the brothers recall how the duke had gone over the same ground over and over had frustrated John, made him want to try something different.

"Well," he said, "After hearing everything you've said today, it seems to me that it's too much of a coincidence that Ceci and David, a man that she liked and spent a lot of time with, disappeared on the same day. We know that David was seen driving his wagon that night on the road to Reimsland, so I think we should take that same journey, but this time we need to search for the adult Ceci rather than focusing exclusively on finding clues from seventeen years ago." John looked carefully at the brothers, who slowly nodded in agreement.

He continued, "We'll make sure we hit every house, every village, every cave where someone may be living between here and David's home village, in case she managed to escape from David, or they had an accident and someone took her in, not knowing who she was. My father has put the full power of his soldiers at our disposal, and fortunately we won't have to deal with King Albert now that he's so ill. His son Bertie is much more reasonable, and he's already given us permission to go into Reimsland to look for Ceci.

"We'll be looking for a woman of twenty-two years, but we have to remember that if she has any memories of her life here, they'll be the memories of a five-year-old child. I know the duke had a portrait of Ceci that he carried with him on his searches…"

Harry nodded. "Yes, it was the last portrait of her that was done. We also had the original artist make charcoal sketches of it on parchment that we left in all the major villages, but it's too much to hope that any of them are still in existence in the villages."

John said, "Well, that's alright because this time I think we should take the last portrait that was done of the whole family."

The brothers looked at him in shock and Harry protested, "But that portrait is five feet across if it's an inch!"

John shook his head. "No matter. Ceci knew your faces better than she knew her own, so she's more likely to recognize *them* than a sketch of herself."

The brothers nodded thoughtfully.

John stood up. "Now let's see that portrait."

The Trunk

For the rest of the day, John thought about how to lead the search. He'd been responsible for certain duties in his father's kingdom since he was fifteen, his tasks gradually increasing as he conquered one after another, so he felt comfortable leading other men. But he'd never led a search party.

He'd been too young to join the searches when Ceci first disappeared, and by the time he was old enough, the lack of information and the time that had elapsed had convinced his father that there were no clues to be found, so he'd steadfastly refused John's requests to join the duke's annual searches.

Looking back on it, viewing his parents' actions through adult eyes, he realized now that his mother had probably influenced his father. Anyone who would kidnap the child of a duke would think they'd landed a major plum if the king's son wandered into their territory. The hesitation with which his father had refused his last few requests, and the way in which he'd glanced at Queen Valeria before giving a firm denial, made John sure his mother had been the force behind the refusals. He couldn't blame her, especially after seeing the devastation wrought in the duke's family.

What did they need the most, in order to start the new search? Information about David, assuming he was the key to Ceci's disappearance. The duke had already worn out every avenue relating to David's family, according to the brothers, so maybe they should focus on what was known of David while he worked at the duke's estate.

John sought out the head gardener, Henrik. The old man had been groundskeeper on the estate as long as John could remember, so he had to be seventy years old if he was a day, but he was still strong and vigorous, digging holes for new bushes when John finally tracked him to the enclosed rose garden.

As he caught sight of the prince, Henrik stopped working and bowed his head briefly. He'd known John since he was a toddler, so they didn't stand on ceremony. "Your Highness," the old man said, removing the cap from his mostly bald head and wiping the sweat off his brow. "How are you? And the king and queen?"

They chatted politely for a few minutes, then John said, "I guess you've heard why I'm here."

Henrik peered up at him and nodded with a slight frown, his heavy eyebrows drawn together. "Yes, sir. You're looking to find Lady Ceci." He sighed and shook his head.

John, curious about his reaction, asked, "You don't think there's any point in continuing to look?"

"Well, sir, it's not so much that, as it is that I hate to see someone else forgetting about the people who're still with them because they can't let go of the one who's gone."

"Ah," John said, nodding. "Well, you're right that this is something that's weighed on all our minds for years. Maybe this time we'll get some information that will finally ease our hearts, though."

"Yes, sire," Henrik said, but he looked dubious.

"Now, what can you tell me about David? Was he a good worker? Did he seem honest?" John asked.

Henrik nodded, "Yes, Your Highness, he did. I know the duke would have it that he kidnapped the little girl, but I never could believe it myself. He was so kind to the child, and I never had a problem with him, which usually I do have problems with the new boys because they have their minds on something other than work, girls mostly. But David wasn't like that. From the first day, he was always punctual and worked hard, instead of me having to keep on him to get the job done. I can tell you, it was a relief to me to have one young man I could depend on."

Surprised, John asked, "And what about his gambling? Did you know anything about that?"

Henrik huffed and took a handkerchief from his back pocket to wipe his face as he replied. "Gambling debts! He didn't have any gambling debts! Those were rightly Paul's debts!" He saw the confusion on John's face. "Paul was one of the other undergardeners. Started about the same time as David, so they became friends, but I think Paul just used David, got him to do his work so he could leave early. Things like that. And he took David with him when he went down to the pub at night. That's where the gambling took place, and Paul was the one who did it! Then he up and ran off one day, after he'd racked up too many debts, and some of the people he owed started trying to get the money from Paul's friends. David, being a better friend than Paul deserved, told them he'd pay for a certain number of Paul's debts. *That* was the gambling debt he supposedly owed."

Frowning, John asked, "Why did the duke think that David owed it, then?"

Henrik waved his hand in disgust. "Those men, Paul's gambling friends, they told the duke that *David* owed the money. I only found out what they'd said years later, and I tried to tell the duke, but..." He shook his head and sighed. "I think the duke needed to blame someone for Miss Ceci's disappearance, and if David wasn't the one who took her, he wouldn't have anyone to blame."

John nodded thoughtfully, understanding how the duke could have subconsciously felt that way, but feeling a twinge of frustration if it meant clues had been missed that would've led to the truth. He asked, "What do *you* think happened to Ceci?"

Henrik sighed and shook his head. "I don't think she ever made it off the estate. You know there are caves underground all over the place. I think she fell through the top of a small one, and..." he shook his head. "It's the only thing that makes sense to me, the only reason they never would've found a trace of her for all these years."

John's heart sank. He talked to Henrik for a few more minutes, but there was no more information about David that seemed to be helpful for their search. Henrik knew David had been going home to visit his family, but couldn't remember why.

John left the rose garden. As he started up the path to the castle, he heard a hesitant voice behind him.

"Uh, Your Highness, sir?"

John turned to see a young man in his early twenties bobbing his head in an awkward bow as he held a rake in his hands. A quick glance at the young man's clothes placed him as one of the undergardeners. John smiled and said, "Yes?"

"Begging your pardon, Your Highness, but I heard what you was saying to Mr. Henrik, asking about Mr. David and the trip he was taking all those years ago…"

John's attention sharpened. "Yes? Do you know something?"

The boy hesitated. "Well, I don't know as I know anything about Miss Ceci's disappearance…"

John's heart sank.

"…but I do know why Mr. David was going home."

John raised his eyebrows. "Oh?"

"His sister had gotten engaged, and he was taking her the wedding present he'd made."

John was flummoxed. He'd never heard anything like this. His eyebrows snapped together. "What's your name?"

"Michael, sir," the boy said.

"Michael, how do you know that?"

"Well, I was just a little squirt back then, and Ma wanted me out from under her feet while she was working, so she'd shoo me out the door. She worked in the duke's kitchen, see?" He was earnest in his explanation, but John just wanted to know about David.

"Yes, yes, and how did you know about David…?"

"Well, I spent time hanging around on the estate, and Mr. David never seemed to mind if I followed him around…"

John's attention drifted for a moment as he thought about how Ceci had followed David around, too.

"… and one day I went to see Mr. David on his lunch break, and he was carving a big wooden trunk. He said it was a present for his sister's wedding."

John's attention sharpened again. "And he took this trunk with him the day Ceci disappeared?"

Michael nodded eagerly. "Oh, yes, Your Highness! I helped him load it. Well, I helped him and another one of the gardeners load it. I was too little to help much." He grinned.

John smiled back, but his attention was on the trunk. "Can you describe it?"

Michael's eyes lit up. "I can do better than that, sir! I can show it to you!"

"Show it to me?" John asked, confused. "But you said David took it…"

"Oh, yes, he took the trunk with him. But I thought it was beautiful, and I'd watched him carving it for about a month, so when I got old enough I made a small chest like it and gave it to my Ma for her birthday. She still has it."

"She lives here on the estate?" John asked, his heart pounding. A clue! Finally, a clue… something that might help track Ceci down.

"Yes, Your Highness. On the second floor of the castle." Michael started toward the castle, then paused, holding up the rake awkwardly. "Uh, maybe Mr. Henrik wouldn't want me to go…"

John promptly walked back to the rose garden and called, "Mr. Henrik? I need young Michael to help me with something, so I'm going to take him from his duties for just a moment."

Henrik peered at him in puzzlement for a moment, then nodded and turned back to his digging.

Michael's mother was flustered when her son showed up at her door with Prince John in tow.

"Oh, dear, Your Highness, you're much welcome, I'm sure, but I wish I'd had a moment to tidy up," she said breathlessly, darting around the room straightening things that were already straight.

John smiled at her a little distractedly, having no attention to spare for anything except the small chest that Michael picked up and held out to him.

The chest was about a foot long, but only six inches deep and tall. It was carved all over with an intricate array of flowers, leaves, birds, and butterflies.

"How closely would you say this resembles the one David made?" John asked.

"Well, except for the size, it's very close. Look," and Michael reached for the bottom of the chest, drawing out a piece of paper that had been folded and tucked into a recess in the bottom. "This is Mr. David's original drawing. He said I could have it, and even told me he'd help me make one when he got back from the trip." He looked up earnestly at Prince John. "He was a good man, sir. I can't believe he would've hurt Miss Ceci." He finished opening the folded paper and held it out.

John sucked in his breath. The drawing was beautiful, and the trunk it portrayed was similar to the one Michael had made, but much more intricate. He'd been about to ask Michael how big David's finished trunk had been, but the dimensions were right there on the paper: two feet long, eighteen inches tall and wide.

"And he painted it blue, Your Highness. The prettiest shade of blue I'd ever seen. Mr. David said it matched his sister's eyes, sir." Michael smiled.

John, his thoughts whirling and excitement making his breath catch, said, "Michael, you've been an immense help. I need to keep this drawing so we can ask people about it when we go look for Miss Ceci, but I'll get it back to you."

"Thank you, Your Highness. I'd appreciate that, but you keep it as long as you want," Michael said.

John turned to go, then turned back as a thought struck him. "Michael, why didn't you tell someone about this before now?"

Michael shrugged. "I thought they knew. Twasn't until I heard you asking Old Henrik questions today that I realized he didn't."

John mused, "And no one ever asked you questions…"

"Because I was so little," Michael nodded.

John stopped thinking about the ramifications of what Michael had told him long enough to thank Michael fervently and say goodbye to his mother, who was still straightening things, and then John was out the door and running toward the main part of the castle.

Dinner that night was a celebration. Not only did they have the drawing of the trunk, but Prince John had also found an old man in town who said he'd sold a mantle clock that David had bought for his mother.

David and Ceci may have disappeared all those years ago, but there was a chance the things David had loaded into the cart had survived and could be found… and might lead them to solve the mystery of Ceci's disappearance.

So they celebrated. It had been too long since real laughter and joy had filled Wallingford, and John was glad to be there to witness its return.

Forward into Hope

A week later, Prince John and the three brothers rode out with Section Captain Arne of the King's Royal Army and a contingent of twenty guards. The guards would help them spread the word about the search to neighboring villages and outlying houses. Prince John was determined that this time, there would be no chance of missing any witnesses. He was determined to start the search anew, instead of relying on possibly wrong information from previous attempts.

After hearing how well-liked David had been, John was willing to do what the duke had been unable to consider all those years: believe David had been innocent of any nefarious actions regarding the young Ceci. If David was innocent, John thought it was possible Ceci had stowed away in the wagon of her own free will. John clearly remembered a few times when Ceci had tried to secrete herself in *his* carriages after his visits, so it made sense she might have tried the same trick with her gardener friend, not realizing he was setting out on such a long journey.

And, due to the complete lack of evidence that David had ever made it to Reimsland, John thought it possible the wagon had been attacked along the way, and young Ceci had gotten separated from

David. John thought it possible David had been killed, so he was approaching the problem as if the only clues they had to go on were the contents of the wagon, which the thieves might have disseminated amongst themselves, and the unpredictable actions of a small girl who found herself unexpectedly on her own.

But if Ceci had survived an attack by thieves, John couldn't figure out why whomever she'd managed to find refuge with hadn't returned her to the duke, who would've compensated them well. John's worst fear was that Ceci and David had both been killed in an attack, but he didn't figure there was much point in alarming her family with that possibility, so he kept it to himself.

For the search, they had brought along watercolor sketches of David's carved blue trunk, as well as charcoal sketches of the mantle clock he'd bought from the old man.

As for the large portrait of the duke's family, painted just a few months before Ceci disappeared, it had been mounted on the side of one of the supply wagons that was traveling with the company, and covered with a loose cloth that would keep the road dust off, but allow them to uncover it as needed.

As the large company rode out, the mood was full of nervous energy and optimism. The optimism was because of the fresh eyes looking at the old problem, as well as the changes in what they knew, as far as the clock, the trunk, and David's possible innocence. The nervousness was based on all the failed searches in the past seventeen years, many of which had started with the same optimism.

Prince John recognized all that as he rode at the head of the party with Harry. He felt the weight of leadership on such an important mission: the weight of knowing failure would have dire ramifications for friends he loved, especially the duke and duchess, whose health declined with each new heartbreak.

John tried to focus on a good outcome, but in the night, in the dark, he'd found himself imagining having to break the news of a dead child to the duke and duchess, or (possibly worse) the news of another failed search.

As they rode out, he allowed himself one more doubt: should they make this trip at all? Or learn to live with not knowing? This was the one moment when they could turn back, turn away from possibly worse knowledge than what they'd had for so long.

But, as he'd known it would, the moment of doubt was swallowed in the need to know whether, if he gave it everything he had, he could finally bring his old companion home to the family that loved her.

He had to try.

So… forward into hope… and the unknown.

Lady in Hiding

Their first stop on the journey was the inn where David and his wagon had been spotted that fateful evening seventeen years ago. When Prince John's entourage rode into the yard, the innkeeper and his wife hurried out to greet them and escort them into the best parlor.

John and Harry set about questioning the innkeeper closely about that night, but he was unable to give them much information, other than the fact that David had stopped to water his horses and partake of some small beer, giving out the information to the innkeeper's wife that he worked at the duke's estate and was traveling home to see his family.

"I'm so sorry, your Highness and my Lords," the innkeeper said, glancing around as they all sat in the parlor. "I didn't pay much attention, being as we were busy that evening, and of course we had no idea then that the young lady was missing."

"Well, now, how could you?" said the innkeeper's sister, who was sitting beside him. "It was a frantic evening, it was. I remember it well… all the bustle and everyone wanting their supper ten minutes before it was ordered." She shook her head in remembered annoyance and folded her arms importantly.

John was confused. "It sounds like you were here that night," he said. "But I thought you lived elsewhere?"

The woman nodded. "Oh, I do! Live up north, we do, but we was down here visiting that month. We've only visited here… what's it been, Oliver?" She turned to the innkeeper. "Twice in the past twenty years?" She turned back to the prince with a smile. "Just pure luck that you've caught us here again!"

Pure luck. John stared at her and glanced around at the brothers, who had gone very still.

John asked, "Who was with you that other time?"

"Just my son, Mark," she replied, looking puzzled.

"How old is he?" John asked.

"Why, he's just turned twenty-four!" she answered, smiling. "And a fine man he is! Makes his mama proud!"

John asked, "And he's here with you again?"

"Oh, yes!" She turned toward the door and called, "Mark! *Mark!* Come here, boy!"

Footsteps were heard outside the door. A young man with a shaggy head of light brown hair came into the room, bowing when he saw the noble guests.

The innkeeper said, "The prince is helping the duke's sons search for their lost sister, little Lady Ceci. You remember the little girl who disappeared when you were here last?"

"Oh, he wouldn't know anything about that!" Mark's mother insisted. "He was dead asleep that night from eight o'clock on!"

John and Harry turned to look at Mark, who glanced from the men to his mother, hesitated, and then asked, "What did she look like?"

Christopher said, "We've got a portrait outside," and stood up to lead them all out to the wagon.

Out in the sunlight of the yard, Mark stared at the portrait of the family for a moment, then glanced at his mother and uncle. "I saw her," he said finally. "There was a tarp over the back of one of the wagons, and I saw her peek out from under it. I remember because her hair looked so bright in the torchlight, like the moon had come down from the sky. I'd never seen hair like that before."

They all glanced back at the portrait, where the platinum blonde hair of Duchess Coraline, young Lord Christopher and the child Ceci stood out so clearly against the dark hair and clothes of the other family members.

John looked at Mark's mother, who was staring at her son, mouth open in shock.

The woman said, "But… how did you see her? You were asleep!"

"I'm sorry, Ma. But I wasn't asleep." He shuffled his feet as his mother sputtered, but continued with determination. "I used to sneak down to the yard so I could see the horses. I heard you talking about the missing daughter of the duke, but I thought the girl I saw was just a village girl. I never would've thought one of the nobility would be hiding in the back of a wagon."

John heard a strangled sound from behind him and turned to see Harry staring straight up at the sky, his throat working as tears rolled down his cheeks.

Christopher was affected, too. His glazed eyes met John's as he softly said, "She was here. She really was here."

John said, "And she was *hiding*. David didn't know she was in the wagon. He never would've stopped here and left her alone if he'd been kidnapping her, so it must have been one of Ceci's tricks that went badly wrong."

"Oh!" Christopher exclaimed in dismay, then turned away as his emotions overcame him, his hands fisting at his sides.

Matt stepped forward and shook a surprised Mark's hand, staring at him with tears in his eyes. "Thank you," he whispered. "You've given us the first bit of hope we've had in almost twenty years."

To celebrate the news, Prince John invited the innkeeper and his family, especially his nephew Mark, to take a break from their work and enjoy some small beer, cheese and bread with them. John hoped they might learn something more from Mark, but all the young man could remember was seeing Ceci's bright hair for a few moments in the darkness. The innkeeper, his wife and sister were able to assure them that David hadn't seemed nervous or memorable in any way.

"Never would've remembered him if the duke hadn't come looking for him a few hours later. He was a quiet young man. Ordered his beer and bread while the horses were being watered, paid and then he was on his way. No reason to remark him." The innkeeper shrugged as his wife and sister nodded agreement.

"Did you ask him where he was headed?" John asked.

"Yes, Your Highness, but he just said over the border of Reimsland to his home. Didn't ask him where that was, since it wouldn't have meant anything to me."

The innkeeper and his family had no further news for them, but John told himself not to be greedy. They had hope again, and that was enough.

For now.

A New Direction

As they rode away from the inn, Christopher turned to Prince John.

"Another child," Christopher said, amazement in his voice. "We never thought to question the children before, and the only portraits we had of Ceci were the charcoal sketches. Nothing that showed that blonde hair of hers. We told the adults she was blonde, of course, but that wouldn't mean much to the children. They need to see something to understand it. We could've told them she had hair like mine, but it never occurred to us. All the years we wasted!" He shook his head in dismay, his fingers clenching on the reins.

"Don't do that to yourself," John said sharply. "Don't second-guess what happened back then. You did the best you could. No one is responsible for this, except maybe Ceci, but I know you don't blame her, so don't blame yourself. She was a child, and you were working without all the information. Just focus on being glad that we have new information, and hope that it will help us find her. Don't look backward, only forward." He reached out to clasp Christopher's shoulder briefly.

"You're right." Christopher nodded and dashed away the tears on his cheek with a rough hand. "You're right. Thank you." He cleared his throat.

John turned the conversation to something else, but internally he was thanking God that he hadn't had to live under the stress the brothers had lived with for all those years. He had never stopped thinking about Ceci, but at least her disappearance wasn't the primary event that defined his life or the life of his immediate family. He hadn't faced the day-in and day-out grief her family had felt.

He wondered if that was what made the brothers instinctively look to him as a leader. His hope was still intact, not bogged down by the cruel silence of the years like theirs was.

He had to remain strong for the other men, no matter what happened.

John firmed his jaw and sat a little straighter, taking their burden as his own.

As they rode along, Christopher said, "We know she was in the wagon as far as the inn, but we've never been able to turn up any information about David or the wagon past that point, so I think we have to assume something happened between here and the next inn, which is eight miles down the road. His family told us that's where David usually stopped for the night. For years, we always thought David skipped that inn because he was anxious to get to wherever he was taking Ceci, but now it must mean that something happened before he made it there."

Matt interjected, "We did consider the possibility that something had happened, though. Remember Father sent all those runners to the robbers' villages?"

"Robbers' villages?" John repeated.

Harry sighed. "This stretch of road has had more than a few attacks over the years by robbers. It's usually the same families that do the robbing, and we know where they all live, so after every robbery we track 'em down and lock up the attackers. After Ceci was kidnapped," Harry shook his head in frustration and corrected himself, "after she *disappeared,* Father sent runners to all those villages and put the fear of God into them, trying to make them confess, but they all claimed they had nothing to do with it."

John thought a moment and then mused, "What if the attackers came from Reimsland?"

"What?" said Harry in disbelief. "They wouldn't dare come over the border into Vallenland. They know your father's laws are much stricter than King Albert's."

John said, "They've been attacking Bagginsland for years," (Reimsland shared its northern border with Vallenland and Bagginsland) "even though King Alexander is just as strict on criminals as my father is, so they could've been operating here, too. If you're sure the attack didn't come from any known criminals in the area, then outside attackers have to be considered." He glanced at Harry, whose eyebrows were drawn in thought.

Harry said, "We did consider that they may have been attacked by men from Reimsland, but we thought it might have happened *after* they'd crossed the border into western Reimsland. We never thought about an attack by men from eastern Reimsland."

John said, "And if the attack came in the next eight miles, before David and Ceci made it to the next inn…"

Matt said softly, "The robbers might have taken them down the Highland Road."

Harry and Christopher exclaimed as John nodded.

The Highland Road wound through the mountains of southeastern Vallenland where it bordered Reimsland, and, most importantly, it went in the opposite direction of Greenbriar Village, David's home, where previous searches had always focused.

Harry said soberly, "Father sent runners down the Highland Road in the beginning, but he never seriously considered it as an option." He took an unsteady breath and then let it out in an anguished prayer. "Oh, God! The mistakes we made!" He beat his fist against his thigh in frustration.

John cautioned, "We still don't know that's what happened. Don't let yourself be overwhelmed by what you might have done in the past. Just focus on the possibility of finding her *now*."

Harry nodded, but his face was drawn in grief.

When they reached the point where the Highland Road split off from the main road, Prince John, his guards, and the brothers dismounted to water their horses at a stream. The men refreshed themselves with water and food from the supply wagon and discussed the feasibility of continuing toward Greenbriar Village, which had been their initial plan.

Christopher shook his head. "I think Prince John's reasoning is sound. We've been searching the road to Greenbriar Village for twenty years and never turned up anything about David or Ceci. It makes sense to me that they were attacked, and that the attackers may have come from eastern Reimsland, not western like we've always thought. I say we take the Highland Road."

Matt asked, "Do you think we should split up? Half of us go the Highland route and the others take the Greenbriar Road?"

Harry shook his head vigorously and said, "We've had our first bit of luck in years with all of us together, so I don't think we should split up. I'm not a superstitious man, but something feels different this time. I feel good for the first time in a long time, and I felt that way before we arrived at the inn this morning. Prince John, you're good for us, I think. I want you to know I appreciate you encouraging us not to give up hope." He reached out and shook John's hand, then pulled him in for an unexpected hug.

Christopher and Matt agreed with Harry's decision. One thing they couldn't quite agree on, though, was whether to let their parents know what they'd found out about Ceci being seen at the inn, and their decision to go down the Highland Road instead.

John and Matt thought they should keep the duke and duchess informed, but Harry and Christopher were adamant that it would cause unnecessary pain if they got their hopes up only to have them dashed.

"You weren't there for all those years," Harry reminded John. "You didn't see Father's heart get broken over and over, didn't see the hope in Mother's eyes change to despair every time we came home without Ceci. Right now they have a small bit of hope, but it's tempered with realism because they have seventeen years' worth of bad news in their minds. If you give them new hope, it might truly kill them if we don't find Ceci this time. No, I say we don't tell them anything until we know what happened, or we decide there's no use continuing."

John nodded slowly. "You're right. There's a high potential for grief if we give them news too early. Waiting might be hard for them, but at least it won't be painful. Protecting them should be our first priority until we know something definite."

Christopher nodded. "And if Father thinks we're on our way to Greenbriar Village, he won't expect any news for a couple of weeks anyway."

So they put away the food and water, pulled the horses from their grazing, and headed down the Highland Road.

The Highland Road

As he rode along the Highland Road two days later, Prince John was beginning to wonder if they'd been ridiculously optimistic. No one they talked to at the inns along the road remembered seeing a young girl seventeen years ago with pale hair like Ceci's. On the Greenbriar Road, the people had been questioned within days of the event, and then questioned regularly in the following years, so their memories years later were still reliable, but the people on the Highland Road hadn't been questioned about young Ceci since that first year. No one they'd talked to so far had been able to shed light on the whereabouts of the missing girl.

They'd made good time since they'd crossed the Reimsland border, and now they were nearing the kingdom of Arlesland. John was starting to lose hope because it seemed too far-fetched to think that Ceci would've ended up in Arlesland, two kingdoms away from her home.

If she had… they'd have to have the devil's own luck to find her. Arlesland was not an ally of Vallenland, so getting permission to enter it and search for Ceci would involve tricky negotiations between the kings, and King Uriah of Arlesland did not have a reputation as a willing negotiator.

John's only real hope lay in finding something from David's wagon, something the presumed thieves had sold afterward, so he was glad they'd thought to bring the sketches of the clock and the hand-carved trunk.

Then, on their second day in Reimsland, they found hope again in a small village.

Matt was showing a drawing of the clock to the men gathered in a local pub when a grumbling voice drew their attention to a table in the corner.

"Eh? What's that you said?" the question came again.

When they glanced over, they saw an old man peering at them. He stood up and shuffled to the bar, his beer sloshing to the edge of his tankard with each step. John and the brothers watched it with fascination, wondering when it would spill over.

Unable to bear the suspense, Matt jumped up and rescued the drink from the man's trembling hands, courteously pulling out a chair as he set the tankard down on their table.

"What's that you said?" the man asked querulously.

John replied politely, "Do you mean our conversation about the clock and blue trunk we're searching for?" He pushed the sketches toward the man, careful to avoid the puddle of damp that was forming around the beer.

The old man peered down his nose at the sketch of the clock. "Yep. Yep, that's it," he mumbled, then suddenly looked up at them suspiciously from under bushy eyebrows. "What you want with it?"

John glanced at the brothers, who looked as surprised as he felt. "I'm sorry… do you recognize the clock?"

"Yes, yes, of course I recognize it," the man answered impatiently. "Stared at it for the past…" he paused to consider. "Eighteen years? Yeah, that'd be about right," he nodded.

"Might it be seventeen years?" Harry asked.

The old man glared at him, annoyed at being corrected, but after a moment said reluctantly, "Yes, I guess it might be. What be you wanting with it, I asked?" He retreated behind ferocity again.

John took over. "These items disappeared the same night that the daughter of a duke in Vallenland went missing. These men are her brothers, and we're seeking knowledge of the clock and trunk."

The old man shook his head. "Oh, I don't know anything about a girl or a trunk. But I know that clock! Given to my brother Jedediah, it was, by his son. Didn't come from no duke, though. Given to him by his son, it were."

John's eyebrows drew together. "And the clock looks like this drawing?"

"That's what I said, innit?" The old man's eyebrows drew together ferociously.

John realized he was taking the wrong tack. "Forgive me, sir. I neglected to introduce myself and my companions. I'm Prince John of Vallenland, and this is Lord Harry, Lord Christopher and Lord Matthias, sons of the Duke of Wallingford."

"Your Highness, Your Lordships," the man acknowledged with a slight nod of his head to each of them, obviously unwilling to be cowed by their nobility. "Amos Anderson at your service."

"Mr. Smith, it's a pleasure to meet you," Prince John said. "I wonder… would you introduce us to your brother?"

Amos tilted his head graciously. "Certainly, gentlemen." He peered down at his beer. "Although it might be nice to have a little more refreshment first…"

John hid a smile and beckoned the barkeep.

The Clock

As their horses pulled up in the farmyard, the door of the house opened and a white-haired couple stepped outside. When they spotted the simple crown on Prince John's head, they immediately bowed and curtsied, looking surprised and flustered.

"Good day to you, sir, ma'am," John said with a smile, nodding at the couple. Wilbur Smith had decided not to accompany them out to his brother's farm when he found out they didn't have a well-sprung carriage for him to ride in. Instead he'd given them rather rambling directions, full of helpful hints like "look for the tree split by lightning two years ago on the farm that Widow Hensley used to own." Despite this, John and the brothers had somehow found the place.

John introduced himself and the duke's sons to Jedediah and his wife, then handed them the sketch of the clock. "We think you may be in possession of this clock, and wondered if you could tell us how you came by it."

Jedediah nodded. "Oh, yes, sir! That's the clock our son bought us quite a while ago! I'm sure he spent more than he should have on it, but he was so proud of it that I couldn't criticize. It's had pride-of-place in our house ever since. You'd like to see it?" he asked, motioning them to come inside.

The prince and brothers followed the man inside, his wife silently bringing up the rear. There, in the cramped sitting room, was the clock, on the mantlepiece above the neat fireplace.

Harry made a sound low in his throat and rushed to compare the clock with the sketch. The details weren't perfect, which wasn't surprising since the sketch was based on the clockmaker's memory, but when Harry turned the clock over they could see the clockmaker's initials carved into the bottom, just as he'd told them they would be. Harry turned his back to the rest of them as he placed the clock back on the mantle, and remained standing that way for a moment.

John turned to the old couple and asked, "Your son … do you know where he got the clock?" John liked the old couple, and hoped their son hadn't been one of the men who'd stolen the clock from David Lane.

The man squinted at him, lips pursed as he tried to remember. "Well now… let's see… I don't believe…"

His wife moved forward from where she'd been standing in the back of the room. "Your Highness, he said he got it from some travelers in the local pub. They had several items they were selling, I believe."

Christopher's eyes lit up. "Did he say what any of the other items were?"

She thought for a moment. "I don't remember, really, except he said they were carrying everything in a big blue trunk."

Matt exclaimed and a strangled cry came from Harry, still standing with his back to them. When John glanced at him, he saw Harry's hands were clenched on the mantle, the knuckles white.

John said as calmly as he could, "Did your son mention whether the travelers had a little girl with them, a girl who had blonde hair like Lord Christopher's?" He motioned toward the second brother, who was gripping Harry's shoulder as he stared at the couple.

The man and wife shook their heads, clearly puzzled.

John explained quietly, "The young sister of these men disappeared seventeen years ago, and we have reason to believe she may have ended up in this area of Reimsland. We're searching for anyone who may have seen her. The man she was originally traveling with had this clock, and the blue trunk was also his."

The man and his wife exclaimed in surprise and offered their condolences to the brothers, then the wife said, "My son said he told the travelers they'd have better luck selling their items in some of the larger villages farther down the Highland Road, and they said that's where they were headed."

John and the brothers exchanged glances, asked a few more questions of the couple, and took their leave, politely declining Mrs. Jedediah's offer to stay for supper. John surreptitiously left some gold coins on a table as they left.

As they rode back to the village, John called the section captain of the guards forward.

"Arne, what do you know of the larger villages ahead of us?"

The older man wrinkled his forehead and sighed heavily. "Not much, sire. There aren't too many between here and the Arlesland border, though, so they should be easy to check."

"Good," John said with a nod. "We leave at first light."

He could only pray that signs of Ceci would turn up before they reached Arlesland, so they'd never have to enter it.

Brigands from the East

The mood was glum at breakfast two days later as John and the brothers sat in the private parlor of an inn close to the Arlesland border. After their great luck finding the clock, they hadn't found any more clues along the Highland Road. Their newfound hope was so precarious that it could fall back into despair with very little provocation, so John was facing an uphill battle to keep everyone's spirits up.

The innkeeper was serving them that morning, and John, grasping at straws, started a conversation with the man as he heaped cold meat and warm biscuits on their plates.

"Mr. Brown, as you know, we're searching for Duke Wallingford's lost daughter, whose portrait you saw last night."

"Ah, yes, Your Highness. Such a tragedy," the man sighed, shaking his head as he handed the empty serving platter to a maid and turned attentively back to the prince. "I wish I could help you in your quest, but…" He shook his head again.

"Can you tell us what life was like in this area seventeen years ago?" John suggested, forking a piece of meat. "You never know what information might help."

"Well, yes sir! I can do that. Let's see, seventeen years ago… ah, yes! That's when we were having the big drought and the farms were struggling so bad." He nodded sagely. "Had lots of people trying to feed themselves with little food available, so more people were stealing." He shook his head in dismay.

John asked, "Was it mostly people from this area who were stealing, or did you also have people from other areas of Reimsland coming into this area to steal?"

"Oh, mostly from other areas, Your Highness. We try to take care of our own here, as much as we can, so it was brigands from the east coming in."

"From the east? Do you know where?"

"Most of them were from Arlesland. The border is only about a day's ride from here. Rumor was they were attacking travelers all throughout Reimsland and even into your kingdom, too." He nodded emphatically.

"Arlesland…" John whispered the name in dismay. Glancing around, he saw the same speculation in the brothers' eyes as he knew must be in his. After questioning the innkeeper a few more minutes about the brigand attacks, he dismissed him.

As soon as the door closed on the innkeeper, Christopher said, "If the thieves who attacked David's wagon were from Arlesland, we should be asking questions at the border. If they escaped there with Ceci and David after the attack, that would explain why we've never found a trace of them."

John cautioned, "Since we don't share a border with Arlesland, my father doesn't have any kind of treaty with King Uriah, so we can't cross the border without risking war."

Harry grunted, while Christopher and Matt made faces to show how little they cared about treaties when their sister's life was at stake.

John smiled faintly and said, "While I agree with you in spirit, I can't risk war. I'll send a pigeon to my father, asking his advice. King Alexander of Bagginsland might be able to offer some insight as well, since he *does* share a border with Arlesland."

John called the innkeeper back into the room. "What can you tell us about Arlesland?"

The innkeeper shook his head, raising his eyebrows. "Oh, Your Highness! If you can avoid going there, I would highly recommend you do so! That's a lawless place, it is! King Uriah…" he shook his head again. "Well, let's just say he's not a good king. He forces the people to pay taxes they can barely afford and throws them in jail for the slightest offense. Then, of course, he has fewer people to work the farms, so that causes even more problems. The people there are known to be shifty and untrustworthy, but you almost can't blame them when you know what their daily lives are like. If you do cross the border, make sure you're alert at all times, because that royal crest on your wagon could make you a target!"

The innkeeper left and John looked at the glum faces around him. Distaste and worry were apparent in each brother's eyes as they considered their little sister growing up in such a kingdom.

John said, "I'll send a letter to my father immediately."

The brothers finished their breakfast in silence.

From the inn, the pigeon with the letter to King Rudolph would have to travel to one of the larger towns, where the message would be sent on via another pigeon that was trained to take messages to a town in Vallenland, where the message would be conveyed by yet another pigeon to King Rudolph's castle. The king's reply would travel back the same route, so they couldn't expect to receive any reply for at least a day, and most likely two or three days, since the king would probably want to consult (via more pigeons) with King Alexander in Bagginsland.

Therefore, the prince and the brothers informed the delighted innkeeper that they would be staying for a few days, and settled in to make the most of their time there.

Martha's Trunk

Over the next three days, the men spent their time riding to neighboring villages and solitary homes in the area. They asked the same question at each place: whether anyone remembered seeing a small girl with white-blonde hair. Remembering young Mark, the innkeeper's nephew whose seven-year-old self had spotted the stowaway Ceci, they were always careful to ask the question of anyone who might have seen her, no matter how young they'd been seventeen years ago.

But no one could recall having seen the young lady… until one day, they finally had a break.

While talking to the barkeep at their inn about the search for the blue trunk, John pulled out the watercolor sketch of the trunk to show him.

Martin, the barkeep, studied it a moment, then said, "That's Martha's trunk. She lives right around the corner, but they're out of town right now. I know all about how she got it, though… more than her husband knows, actually."

Shocked that they'd finally found the trunk, John raised his eyebrows and motioned for Martin to have a seat at their table.

Martin began, "What you need to understand is that old Wilbur Smith had been after Martha to marry him for years. He doesn't look it, but he has a lot of money squirreled away, so he's quite the catch. But Martha was hankering for a man her age named Elijah. He was a bad 'un, though, Elijah was, and Martha's first husband died young and poor, so she'd been fighting for security for her and her kids for a long time. She wasn't fixing to tie herself to a man who couldn't support her.

"Elijah, though, he seemed to really love Martha, and he tried to prove that he would change for her. One day, after Wilbur had been courting Martha pretty regularly, Elijah shows up in here with that blue trunk in the back of his wagon, telling me it's a gift for Martha, something to show her once and for all that he's ready to settle down. So off he went to Martha's house with that trunk, and he came back an hour later with his tail between his legs. Said he'd given her the trunk and she'd loved it… but when she found out how much he'd spent on it, she flew into a rage. Told him she'd never marry a man who spent money on foolish things, and she didn't ever want to see him again. He rode out of town that night, and Martha and her blue trunk married Wilbur. From what I've heard, Martha lied to Wilbur about how she got the trunk. She wanted to keep it, but she also knew Wilbur never would've let her, if he'd known it came from Elijah."

John and the brothers were nodding, slightly confused by Martha's machinations but understanding the main point: she had David's blue trunk. John asked, "Do you know where Elijah got it?"

"Well, he had dealings with a lot of unsavory people. He told me he got the trunk off one of his acquaintances who was known to work the Highland Road."

Harry frowned. "By 'work' do you mean…"

Martin said bluntly, "Steal."

John leaned forward. "Do you know the name of the man he bought it from?"

Martin shook his head. "No, all I can tell you is that he was from Arlesland. From what Elijah told me, the man would come into Reimsland and spend a few weeks going up and down the Highland Road, taking what he could, and then slip back over the border when people started hunting for him. Heard he even slipped into Vallenland a few times, actually."

John and the brothers stared at each other. No question about it; they had to go to Arlesland.

John asked abruptly, "Do you know if a message has been delivered for me?"

Martin said, "I saw the maid going up to your room earlier with something that looked like a pigeon tube in her hand."

John and the brothers went flying for the stairs.

A Royal Summons

When John ran into his room, he saw the pigeon tube laying on the small table next to the bed. Unfurling the note tucked inside, he quickly scanned the random phrases on the page, all part of his family's secret language.

Finishing, John looked up at the brothers. "Father says he and King Alexander of Bagginsland have arranged safe passage into Arlesland for us, but he wants us to proceed with great caution. He doesn't trust King Uriah, but a condition of our safe passage is that we must visit the king's castle before we do anything else." He made a small face. The Arlesland king's castle was located a couple of days' ride from the border, so if they had to go straight there they wouldn't have the luxury of the time they usually spent showing the portrait to people in the villages they rode through and asking them whether they'd seen Ceci.

Matt suggested, "We could send the guards ahead of us to let people know we're coming so they can gather in the center of the villages and see the portrait as we ride through. We'll have to stop to water the horses, anyway, so we can just time the stops to coincide with the villages."

Harry clapped him on the shoulder. "Good idea, little brother!"

"Little brother?" Matt exclaimed and stood on tiptoe to loop an arm around Harry's neck and ruffle his hair vigorously. "I'm not so little! Unless you're talking about stomach girth! Then I'd have to agree with you…" and he looked down pointedly at Harry's waistline.

Harry roared in mock anger and put Matt in a headlock of his own.

John and Christopher grinned and exchanged glances, both glad to see this new lightness between the other two. Finding the blue trunk had definitely re-invigorated them… even though it was leading them to Arlesland.

The lightheartedness continued through the rest of the afternoon, and the evening meal found them laughing and joking around almost as if they didn't have a care. They planned to leave early the next morning so they'd have time to spend a few minutes in each village on their way to King Uriah's castle. Some of Prince John's guards had already left to alert the villages.

John knew, however, that beneath their excitement the brothers recognized the same danger that concerned John: if someone in Arlesland were found to have hurt the missing girl, it could have significant political repercussions for both kingdoms, whose relations were already strained.

Prince John could only pray they would find her alive and well.

King Uriah

When Prince John and the brothers rode into King Uriah's courtyard, their emotions were raw. Their ride through Arlesland to get to the castle had been overwhelming. The people who lined the roads in the villages were dirty and too thin, cheeks drawn with hunger below the suspicious golden eyes and dark hair they shared.

Realizing a king could be so careless of the people he was charged to protect was appalling to both the prince and the duke's sons, but even more distressing was the fear that Ceci, if she had grown up here, might have become a narrow-eyed, tight-lipped version of her formerly open and sunny self.

Prince John especially felt the pressure of the hungry eyes on him as they rode through the villages. He tried to smile and greet the people, but it felt disrespectful as he rode past them, as if he didn't care enough to help them when they so obviously needed it. His father had always drilled into him the sacred responsibility he had to take care of his subjects, to make their lives better even at the cost of his own, and John fully believed that was his life's purpose. There could be no higher calling than to be a protector to simple people who wanted to live their lives in peace, with full bellies and a little bit of leisure time to enjoy life.

These people looked like they had to fight their neighbors to survive, and it left John feeling stricken and helpless. He wanted to give them money, since he could do nothing else, but he didn't have enough with him to make a dent in the need he saw. Besides, if Uriah found out he'd done such a thing, the king would undoubtedly take it as an insult. John's anger grew as they rode, until he was seething with it as the king's castle came into view.

John didn't think he could clench his jaw any tighter than it already was after the stress of that ride, but he found he was wrong when the person who came to greet them was not King Uriah, nor even a member of his family or court, but his captain of the guards.

Looking down from his horse at the man who waited with a row of soldiers behind him, John rightly took the insult as a show of intimidating strength from their host. The captain and his soldiers were unsmiling, golden eyes narrowed like those of the villagers.

John glanced sideways at the brothers and saw they were as tense as he. Harry gave him a long look, silently asking if John wanted to make some kind of challenge now to prove their own strength. John had to admit he was tempted. Everything about the Arlesland king, whom he hadn't even met, raised his hackles, and his instinct was certainly to attack the hidden threat he could sense. But John's training as future king stood him in good stead, and he gave a small shake of his head. Their mission was too precious to risk it.

John dismounted, not bothering to hide the frown on his face.

"Your king is not coming to greet us?" he asked the captain.

"No, Your Highness." The captain made no excuse for King Uriah, for which John was begrudgingly grateful. If the knives were to be out, he wanted them in full view, not hidden behind polite lies. "I'll show you to your rooms, and then escort you to the king."

John nodded curtly and followed the captain inside.

When John and the brothers had refreshed themselves, they met back in the corridor where the captain waited. "Your guards are settled in the barracks," the captain said as he led them down the hall.

"Thank you," John replied. He was uneasy with his guards so far away from him in a hostile environment, but as they separated in the courtyard he'd given the secret signals to his section captain to put him and the other guards on high alert. It was imperative that John gain King Uriah's support for the search for Ceci, so he had to do everything he could to accomplish that goal, even if it put himself in a dangerous situation.

All that mattered was Ceci.

King Uriah was seated on a throne on a raised dais, his legs sprawled open and chin on one hand in a deliberately disrespectful pose. John stopped at the bottom of the dais and studied the man who was staring at him with open hostility.

"You think someone in my kingdom kidnapped your little girl," King Uriah sneered.

John thought fast. The king was taking the search as a personal insult. He had to make Uriah understand that it was in both their interests to find anyone who disrespected the borders between kingdoms.

"It's possible that someone has laid a false trail of rumors to make it look as though an Arleslander is guilty," John said smoothly, hoping to focus the king's anger toward the unknown "someone" rather than on John and the brothers.

King Uriah's golden eyes narrowed, and John knew he'd caught his attention.

"That person may have brought the Lady Ceci into Arlesland in an effort to foster animosity between our great kingdoms. If that is the case, I appreciate your willingness to help us rout this scoundrel and his accomplices so we may continue our relationship of cooperation."

Then John broke protocol and dipped his head in a slight bow to King Uriah, not enough to indicate subservience, but enough to show he was willing to let the other king take the lead. For now.

The scowling king regarded them for a long moment, his eyes sliding to each of the brothers. "Where do you think this person has taken her?"

John breathed a little easier. "We don't know, Your Majesty. We need your help to find her. I assure you, if we do find her here, and find the person responsible, we will dispatch him to you for punishment."

The king studied him, then signaled to his captain, who directed servants to place a chair beside the king, and three more chairs at the foot of the dais. King Uriah motioned for Prince John to join him.

As he sat down, John said, "Your Majesty, I bring you greetings from my parents, King Rudolph and Queen Valeria." He motioned toward the brothers, who were still standing respectfully. "I present to you Lord Harry of Wallingford, and his brothers Lord Christopher and Lord Matthias."

Harry bowed to King Uriah and said, "Your Majesty, I bring you both greetings and heartbroken thanks from the Duke and Duchess of Wallingford, and extend the same from myself and my brothers. We are most grateful for any help you can offer." He gave another low bow, joined by Christopher and Matt.

After surveying them thoroughly, King Uriah motioned for the brothers to be seated and turned to Prince John. "I saw you once when you were a small boy," he said, an unexpected smile playing over his lips.

Feeling deeply relieved that the king's mood had changed in their favor, John smiled back and asked, "When was that?"

"Queen Valeria's twenty-fifth birthday party."

"Ah!" John nodded. Turning twenty-five was a big milestone in their world. It signaled the transition from childhood to full maturity, especially for royalty. Unless the need was dire, a king or queen was never crowned until then. By that age, his mother had already been married to his father for six years, though, so John himself would've been five years old.

The same age Ceci was when she went missing. John felt a brief pang but forced himself to focus on what Uriah was saying.

"… don't usually leave my kingdom, but it was my first opportunity to attend a royal event in another land. My father had always refused invitations from other royals and insisted I do the same, but he was bedridden at that time and had turned much of the running of the country over to his advisors and me. So I made the decision to go and didn't tell him until it was time to leave." The king laughed, surprising John with the carefree sound. This was a completely different man than the one he'd been talking to just moments ago.

"But that was my only journey outside the kingdom," Uriah said, a scowl appearing on his face again. He signaled for a servant to bring wine, although it was still fairly early in the day. "Your parents were kind to me on that visit, which is why I granted you an audience today."

"I appreciate that very much," John assured him, taking a small sip from the wineglass the servant offered him.

Uriah drank deeply from his. "Tell me about this missing child."

John motioned toward Christopher, who stood and told the king everything they knew or surmised about Ceci's disappearance. Taking his cue from John, Christopher made it seem as though they believed the thieves who had attacked David's wagon had been working to cause friction between the kingdoms.

John, watching Uriah's face, was sure that the king was aware that brigands from Arlesland had been operating in Reimsland and possibly even Vallenland. He showed no surprise or consternation at that part of the story, only a slight furrowing of the brow as he considered the motivation Christopher and John had assigned to the attacks, obviously realizing it was to his benefit to go along with their story.

After about an hour of discussing their search, the king released them to rest before supper. The brothers followed John out to the barracks, where he took a moment to talk to his section captain, then the four of them strolled around the grounds, supposedly admiring the trees (no flowers dared bloom at Uriah's castle) but really discussing their impressions of the king.

John said, "I told Arne to find out everything he could about Uriah. I heard some story about him years ago, but all I have is a vague remembrance of a tragedy… no details."

Supper that night was a bit of a trial. John had attended many dinners with royalty, but nothing like this. For one thing, there was no entertainment. No musicians during the meal, no recitations of poetry or dancing displays afterward. And for another, Uriah was a miserable conversationalist. After his brief lapse into levity earlier that day, he'd regained his surly demeanor in time to make the meal a misery.

The worst part came afterward, though, when the brothers wheeled in the family portrait depicting the young Ceci.

King Uriah rose from his seat to stand before the portrait, ordering servants to bring the lanterns closer so he could see it clearly. He leaned close and studied the young Ceci's face as Christopher pointed out the hair that was so similar to his, then he shifted to peer at the painted smile of Duchess Coraline.

He glanced at the brothers as he straightened. "A beautiful woman, your mother. I danced with her at Queen Valeria's birthday ball. Ceci seems to have inherited her mother's looks. You must promise to bring her here if you find her in Arlesland." The king turned and walked back to his seat, giving John and the brothers time to exchange startled glances.

King Uriah was interested in Ceci.

John couldn't imagine a worse fate for Ceci than to be queen of this miserable kingdom, and he could tell her brothers felt the same. There was a small silence as the king settled himself while they all tried to think of a way to dissuade him.

"I do most sincerely hope we will find Ceci soon, but I think you would enjoy meeting her more after she's had some time to spend at home," John said smoothly, smiling politely. "She's been away from noble surroundings since she was five years old, so it's more than we could possibly hope that she's retained the manners you are used to." John thought he was laying it on rather thick, since the king had demonstrated appallingly bad manners himself. "Ceci will need time to re-learn all the social graces that a noble needs." He glanced at Harry.

"Yes, Your Majesty," Harry hastened to add. "Our parents wish us to return with all speed if we find her, but we would welcome a visit from you afterward." Harry hoped the king would continue his custom of never leaving his kingdom.

Uriah waved his hand. "That doesn't matter. I'm sure she can learn all she needs to know very quickly. Yes, I would indeed like to see her. Bring her to me when you find her."

The brothers smiled at him weakly and John hastened to change the subject.

After Uriah dismissed them that night, John returned to his room, where a servant assisted him in undressing. When the servant left, John locked the door, then stepped quickly to the bed where he slipped his hand under the pillow and, as expected, found a folded piece of paper. SC Arne had checked his room earlier and surreptitiously left a note.

Sure there was at least one spyhole in the room, John waited to unfold the letter until after he'd retired for the night and drawn the curtains around the bed. He could barely read it by the light of the guttering candle in the lantern hanging above his pillow, but he managed to make out the coded words. When he finished, John crumpled the letter into a ball, drew back the bed curtain and tossed it into the fireplace, then lay awake thinking.

Brown as a Nut

John waited until they'd taken their leave from King Uriah and were well on their way down the road to the next village before he called his section captain to the front of the group of guards where he and the brothers rode.

"Tell the duke's sons what you learned last night," he directed SC Arne.

"Many years ago, before Uriah took the throne," Arne began, his voice taking on the singsong quality of a minstrel, "he was a young man, unfettered by the responsibilities he would later bear, and somewhat careless as young folk are. He was well-liked in the kingdom, but known to have a temper.

"One night, not long after he returned from his journey to Vallenland for Queen Valeria's birthday ball, he was out drinking with friends at a local pub. An assassin burst into the pub swinging an axe, and Uriah's guards leapt to defend him, as did his friends. Before the young prince's horrified eyes, the assassin's axe cut off the head of a young man who had been his bosom companion from childhood.

"They say after that night, he turned in on himself, becoming bitter, morose and suspicious," Arne continued. "It's said he believed he'd brought a curse on the kingdom because he disobeyed his father's orders not to travel outside the borders of their land. Now, he seems to find joy in humiliating the nobles who seek his favor, and punishes his people for crimes far beyond what they deserve. He is a hard king, unmerciful and spiteful. They say to cross him is to sign your death warrant."

John felt the brothers' eyes cut over to him and he glanced at them, answering the unspoken question. "We can't let him meet Ceci until she's back in Vallenland. There she'll have the protection of my father, but here we're terribly vulnerable. I'll think of some reason we can't return to King Uriah if we find Ceci, something plausible."

The brothers nodded, but John could tell by their silence that they were uneasy.

It was in the third village they visited after leaving King Uriah that John and the brothers found the first person who might have seen Ceci since they'd left Vallenland.

As had become their custom when they arrived at an inn, they spoke to the innkeeper and asked him, his family and staff, as well as any guests staying there, to view the portrait of the duke's family. As the crowd stared at the huge portrait in awe, Lord Christopher told the sad tale of his missing sister and how they'd traced David's belongings along the Highland Road.

They'd chosen Christopher as the spokesperson for two reasons: one, he was naturally dramatic and could bring people to tears with the story; and two, the hair color he shared with his missing sister. His hair was a little darker now than it had been as a child, but it was still much paler than people in those parts were used to, and the brothers wanted to burn the image of that hair into people's minds so they would immediately think of the duke's family if they ever saw it again.

Christopher got to the part of the story when he always stepped away from the portrait so the crowd could see the painted young girl behind him. As he stepped aside, a gasp went up from a young woman in the audience.

"It's the girl in the tinker's van!" she exclaimed, pointing at the portrait.

"What?" cried the innkeeper's wife. "The tinker's daughter? Why, she's got hair as brown as a nut, she does! What do you mean, saying that's her?"

"No! Not the tinker's daughter!" the girl said. "At least... I don't think that's who it was. It was just a girl... I don't know who she was..." Her voice faltered and stopped.

"Hmph!" snorted the innkeeper's wife, turning back to Lord Christopher. "She doesn't know what she's talking about! Why, all those years ago, she was just a child herself!"

John and the brothers glanced at each other.

"But you think you saw a girl with hair like this?" John motioned to the portrait.

"Yes," the girl said hesitantly. "But I just caught a glimpse of her for a moment, then she ducked behind a curtain. The only reason I remember is because I'd never seen hair like that. And I haven't seen it again until today." She glanced at Christopher.

"You only saw the girl that one time?" John asked.

She nodded.

"But the tinkers had a daughter, you said?" John turned to the innkeeper's wife, who sniffed.

"That's right, Your Highness! But her hair was brown as a nut, just like a hickory nut."

"Well, she wasn't really their daughter, Your Highness," her husband interrupted. "She was their niece, I believe. She came to live with them when she was about six years old."

"Yes, that's right," his wife took over again. "Six years old and hair brown as a nut!" She glared at the young woman who'd dared suggest otherwise.

"And you don't remember them ever traveling with a girl who looked like this?" John motioned toward the portrait again.

"No, sire, that I don't," said the innkeeper, as his wife shook her head vigorously.

John studied the young woman who thought she'd seen Ceci. "If you think of anything else you believe can help, please let me know," he said. "We'll be staying here this evening."

After supper, John invited the innkeeper and his wife to join them, motioning for the servant to pour glasses of small beer for them.

"Ah, thankee kindly, Your Highness! Hits the spot, that does!" the innkeeper said, smacking his lips after a long swallow.

"You're welcome," John said with amusement. "Now, tell me about this tinker and his daughter."

"Oh, you don't believe that tale Agatha was telling earlier, do you?" the innkeeper's wife pooh-poohed. "She's a silly girl, Agatha is. Now if she'd been telling you what a young gentleman looked like, I might believe her, because she does spend a lot of time studying the boys!" She laughed and took a swig from her mug. "But something that happened that long ago? Agatha can't remember an order I gave her five minutes ago, much less something from when she was a child!" She sniffed.

John shrugged. "Tinkers travel all over, so they might have other information we could find useful. It wouldn't hurt to talk to them."

"Well, you can't do that, Your Highness!" the innkeeper's wife said, as her husband shook his head sadly. "The tinker and his wife, they died… oh, I guess it's been five years now?" She looked to her husband for confirmation.

"Yes indeedy," he sighed. "Bad accident they had. Cart went right off the road at the worst spot, right where it drops off real steep-like, and turned over several times. Broke both their necks, they did."

"And was their daughter with them?" John asked, holding his breath.

"Oh, no!" the wife scoffed. "She was already off and married by then! Married young, she did! Must've been… what, seventeen?"

Her husband nodded.

"Seventeen," she confirmed. "And had a child a year later. Her parents never even got to see the baby." She sighed at such misfortune.

"And does the child have brown hair like her mother?" Christopher asked, hoping against hope.

"Yes, indeed she does!" The wife nodded. "Brown as a nut! Just like her mama's!"

John felt a deep disappointment. His heart had leapt in his chest this afternoon when Agatha had identified Ceci immediately. He'd been hoping somehow the girl she'd seen would turn out to be Ceci and they could track her down. But it seemed this was another dead end.

As John sat alone by the fire in the common room that night, staring into it and wondering whether they'd run out of luck, he heard the soft scuff of a shoe behind him. Turning his head slightly, he saw the young woman who'd claimed she'd seen Ceci standing hesitantly beside his chair.

"Agatha, isn't it?" John said genially.

"Yes, Your Highness," she replied, bobbing a curtsy.

John smiled and turned back to the fire, but she still stood there, rubbing her hands together as if trying to work something out in her mind. Puzzled, John turned back to face her.

"Did you think of something else you wanted to tell me?" he asked.

"No, sir… not really, but…" She hesitated.

John watched her for a moment, then abruptly stood. "Forgive me, Agatha. Would you like a seat?" He drew up another chair close to his by the fire.

"Oh, thank you, Your Highness!" She perched on the edge of the chair, her hands still wringing together and a hesitant smile on her lips. "It's just… I'm sure I saw that little blonde girl in the back of the tinker's wagon!" she said in a rush, leaning toward him. Her hands were still now, gripping the edge of her seat. "She had hair just like in that portrait you showed us, and she looked about five years old, which is how old I was, too. But I never saw her again after that."

"You only saw the tinker's daughter or niece or whatever she was with the tinkers after that?" John asked, frustrated.

"Yes, sir… but I didn't see *her* that first time. I don't think she started traveling with them for maybe…" she squinted in thought. "It must have been about a year later, because the first time I remember seeing her was after my sixth birthday. My ma had said she'd buy me a treat for my birthday the next time the tinker came through, and that's the first time I met the tinker's daughter. She had a little cornhusk doll she was playing with, and I told Ma that's what I wanted for my birthday present. So Ma bought me one and we played together until it was time for the tinker to leave."

"I don't suppose there's any way they could've been one and the same girl?" John asked, grasping at straws.

Agatha hesitated. "Well… I didn't get a very good look at the blonde girl, and I guess they might have dyed her hair…"

John frowned. "You mean change her hair color? It's possible to do that?" He'd never heard of such a thing.

Agatha's eyes lit up. "Oh yes, Your Highness! Some of the older ladies in the village dye their hair darker. Don't like looking old, you see, so they cover up their gray hair."

John raised his eyebrows and nodded. "That's very interesting." He frowned. "How do they dye it?"

Agatha shrugged. "I'm not sure, sir, but I know there are different herbs you can use, and I think they even use walnut hulls." Her eyes lit up as her mouth quirked in a smile. "Maybe *that's* why the tinker's daughter's hair was brown as a nut."

John laughed in delight.

As he made his way to his room that night, his mind was racing. They'd been confident that one of the identifying characteristics for Lady Ceci was her distinctive hair. But what if whoever had taken her had also dyed her hair?

He shook his head in frustration. That would make their search so much harder.

But surely… surely, if Ceci were still alive, she wouldn't still be dyeing her hair. And even if she were, *she* at least would know her hair was actually a different color. They just had to pray that word of their search would get to her, and she would come forward.

Cesily

The next day, Prince John told the brothers about his conversation with Agatha the night before, and especially about the possibility that Ceci's hair had been dyed.

"Dyed!" Harry exclaimed, clapping a hand to his forehead. "I didn't even know that was possible!"

Christopher laughed. "Shows how much you know about women, brother! Mrs. Hennessy dyes her hair, I'm pretty certain." Mrs. Hennessy was the duke's cook.

Harry's mouth fell open, making the other men laugh.

"So," John summarized, "It's possible that the blonde girl Agatha saw turned up a year or so later with dyed hair, and grew up as the tinker's daughter. If so, there must be quite a story there to explain how Ceci got from David's wagon to a tinker's wagon. Or, the alternative is that Ceci was briefly in the tinker's wagon but didn't stay with them, and their 'daughter' really was one of their relatives."

"We need to find the tinker's daughter!" Harry exclaimed.

John nodded. "I agree that should be our first priority. Even if she's not Ceci, she may know about a blonde girl who traveled briefly with them."

They sought out the innkeeper, feeling fortunate to find him without his wife, who was sure to argue again against Ceci being the tinker's daughter.

"The tinker's daughter? Well, like we told you yesterday, she got married and moved away. About all I know is that she had a daughter. Don't even know what town she moved to."

"Is there no one here who would know?" Harry asked desperately.

The innkeeper saw their dismay and shook his head in apology. "No, sir, no one I can think of. The tinkers only came through here about once a year, once every six months at the most, so we saw 'em when we saw 'em, and forgot about 'em the rest of the time." He shrugged.

John and the brothers stared at each other, trying to think of some way to find Ceci.

Matt asked, "What was their normal route?"

"Oh, they went round about Hampton Village and Yaegertown, I believe. Not sure where they went after that, though."

Yaegertown was where they'd been headed anyway. There were only a few small villages between the one they were currently in and the larger town, so it would be easy to check them on the way.

John called SC Arne to get the guards ready to ride. They should make the next village by the noon hour, and hopefully be in Yaegertown tomorrow. As John turned to follow the brothers upstairs to pack their things, he thought of something.

"What was the name of the tinker's daughter?" he asked the innkeeper.

"What's that, Your Highness? Oh, her name? Cesily, sir, it was Cesily…" the innkeeper's voice trailed off as he saw the way the prince stared at him.

From the corner of his eye, John could see that Christopher, who'd been going up the stairs in front of him, had come to a dead halt. John turned and saw that Harry and Matt were also staring down at him, the same frozen look on their faces that he was sure must be on his.

Cesily. It couldn't be a coincidence.

Could it?

Second Chance for Miscreants

In the parlor of the inn, two men had been listening closely to the conversation between the prince, the duke's sons and the innkeeper. They had been present the day before when Christopher had told the story of Ceci's disappearance, and since then they'd been skulking around the prince's party, listening at doors whenever possible.

As John and the brothers ran up the stairs, the men put their heads close together.

"It's her! It's got to be her!" one man hissed to the other.

"We searched that tinker wagon from top to bottom!" the other hissed back, his face red with frustration.

"Well, they must have had a secret compartment, then. You know how those tinkers are… always hiding something from the king's men. Wouldn't be no problem to hide a kid, too, I suppose." He took a drink from his tankard, wiping his mouth on the back of his hand. "Well, there's no use worrying about it now. Besides, if we'd sold her back then, we wouldn't have made nearly as much money off her as we can now. Can't believe we had a high-born noble and didn't know it." He shook his head in disbelief, then narrowed his eyes. "But we'll make up for it now."

His companion scoffed. "And how do you reckon on doing that?"

"I'll tell ya." He leaned forward, his eyes darting to the window to greedily watch the fine horses and wagons that made up the prince's entourage.

A Lady by Any Other Name

At Hampton Village's only inn, Prince John and the duke's sons learned that the tinkers had usually spent every winter there, so it had been the closest thing to home for them. The innkeeper also told them that Cesily had married a man who had grown up in Hampton Village.

"Ah, yes!" the innkeeper said. "I well remember him, and his wife Cesily, and their daughter Mary. Mr. Walker's dead now, of course. Died, oh I guess it's been four years now."

John felt an odd leap in his stomach. When the man had said Cesily was married, he'd had a hard time wrapping his mind around the idea of Ceci with a husband. It didn't seem right for some reason… and now he felt relieved, which made even less sense. If Ceci had found someone she loved, he should be happy for her, and sad that her husband had died.

Shouldn't he?

"Did Cesily remarry?" he asked.

"Don't know. Haven't seen her since her husband was laid in the ground. Ran off to town, she did. Said she could make a better life for her and her child there."

Harry groaned and dropped his head into his hands, clutching at his hair. Christopher clasped his brother's shoulder, strain on his face.

John sighed. Another delay. "What town?" he asked.

"Yaegertown. Sixteen miles down the road."

At that, the brothers perked up. Sixteen miles was nothing. Harry looked over at Prince John speculatively.

"No," John said with a laugh. "We're not going there tonight. It would be midnight by the time we arrive and we'd have to find another inn. We all need a good night's sleep, because tomorrow we'll have to ask around town to find Cesily."

Harry grimaced, then nodded.

The next morning, Harry had his brothers and John up before the rooster even crowed, and routed the innkeeper from his bed soon after to make them all breakfast. John added a small amount to the total of their bill in thanks, and followed Harry out the door with a sigh. He hoped this would not be another fruitless day.

After several hours on the road, they came up a small hill and spotted a wagon pulled over to the side of the road ahead. Seated disconsolately on the grass beside it was a young woman wearing a large hat, her head turned away, watching two men who were struggling with a broken wheel.

As the prince and brothers rode up the hill, the noise of their approach reached the small group at the top. The young woman turned her head and John heard Harry gasp.

Below her hat, the girl's face was round with the full cheeks of youth. Her porcelain skin was touched with the faintest tint of peach, and her mouth was a perfect rosebud, slightly open in surprise as she surveyed the handsome men riding toward her. Her eyes were large and dark and fixed limpidly on Prince John as he rode at the head of the company, his small crown catching the sun's rays. As she caught the prince's eyes, she gave a shy smile that made his heart beat faster.

She was a lovely girl. But it wasn't her beauty that had caused Harry to gasp and every cell in John's body to tighten.

It was the flaxen curls that showed beneath the woman's hat.

They weren't as pale as Christopher's hair, but the curls were most definitely blonde, a hair color they hadn't seen since they left Vallenland.

John ticked points off in his head: she was the right age, right hair color, right eye color…

John glanced around at Harry, Christopher and Matt, his stern eye instructing them to let him do the talking.

The company drew up and Prince John and the brothers dismounted.

"My condolences on your misfortune, ma'am," John said with a smile. "Please allow my guards to assist you."

The girl smiled, revealing perfect teeth, and stood to curtsy. "Your Highness, I would be most delighted to do so." Her voice was low, with a hint of laughter in it that he found oddly compelling.

"Allow me to introduce myself. I am Prince John of Vallenland." He watched her carefully for a reaction, seeing a slight color rush to her cheeks, turning them from the delectable shade of a fresh peach to the perfect blush of a rose. "And these are my companions, the sons of the Duke of Wallingford. Lord Harry, Lord Christopher and Lord Matthias." He spoke slowly, making sure she heard all the names fully.

The girl stared at him, then stared around at the brothers. Her small, perfect hands clenched, gripping and releasing the small bag she held. "Oh!" she uttered, glancing back at the men with her, who were listening in silence. "Oh! Vallenland! Lord Harry! Christopher! Matthias! Oh! Why do those names cause my heart to race?" The girl seemed to be talking to herself, her words low and mouth barely moving as she stared at them, and yet they could hear her clearly.

She started forward, raising her hand toward Harry's face as if to touch it, then drew back as if the motion had startled her from some dream. "Can it be?" she murmured.

John glanced at the brothers and saw the looks of agonized hope on them. He stepped in front of Harry and said, "Ma'am, I'm afraid you find us at somewhat of a loss. May I enquire as to your name?"

"It's… oh! Can it be? It's… Cesily! That's the name I've used for so long!" Tears were brimming in the girl's eyes now. "But now, looking at all of you… hearing those names! I feel that I'm not Cesily anymore! I feel that I am…" she stopped, staring agonizingly from one brother to the next as a slow tear rolled down her perfect cheek. She drew a shuddering gasp.

Harry, tears in his eyes, stepped forward. His voice hoarse with emotion, he said, "Ceci? Is it you, my darling Ceci?"

"Yes, yes! It is I!" she burst out, the tears flowing freely now as she reached out to Harry again, cupping his face.

The oldest brother had tears pouring down his face, too, as he pressed her small hand to his rough cheek, turning his head to kiss the palm.

As if in a dream, Christopher and Matt drew closer, hesitantly reaching out to the girl. Christopher gently touched one of the curls that lay on her shoulder, and John knew that he was mentally comparing it to his mother's hair. Matt had broken down completely. Tears poured down his face as he kissed the hand she held out to him. "Ceci?" he whispered.

"Yes, my darling Matt, yes! It is I!" she sobbed.

John's eyes narrowed. His thoughts whirling, he turned to see how the repair of the wagon wheel was progressing. His guards had spliced the broken strut with a piece of wood from their supply wagon and were putting it back on the wagon now.

John thought quickly. Turning back to the girl, he saw that the three brothers had moved to encircle her and they huddled together, not talking, simply looking at each other. The girl turned from one to the other of them, her dark eyes wide and lips parted in amazement as she searched every inch of their faces, exclaiming over how much they had changed since the last time she'd seen them.

"Ma'am," John said, smiling as she turned to look at him. "I'm so sorry to interrupt, but your wagon has been repaired. I wonder if you would introduce us to your companions."

"Oh, certainly!" With a last lingering glance and sweet smile for each of the brothers, she motioned the men forward. "This is Henry."

The taller of the two men, who had black hair and piercing eyes, bowed to Prince John and the brothers. "Your Highness, my Lords. It is a pleasure to meet you!"

The girl continued, "And this is James."

The other man bowed as well but said nothing, merely smiling slightly.

"May I suggest that we continue to Yaegertown, where we can get rooms at an inn and continue our conversation in comfort?" John suggested.

"That's a wonderful suggestion!" she said with a joyful laugh, turning back to caress the cheeks of the brothers, a soft smile on her face. "Somewhere to continue our reunion!"

John, watching the duke's sons gaze at her with adoration, clenched his jaw and gave orders to his section captain to find a likely inn.

Even once they reached the hustle and bustle of Yaegertown, the brothers barely took their eyes off the girl riding among them, sometimes to the detriment of pedestrians who had to jump out of the way of the stallions bearing down on them. Yells and curses made no impression on the besotted sons of the duke, though.

At the first inn they found, John arranged for a luncheon to be brought to them in a private dining room, then he sat to the side of the tight group of brothers and the girl. His eyes flickered to the opposite corner of the room, where her two companions were relaxing in chairs by the fireplace, smiling as they watched their friend charming the duke's sons.

Her eyes were wide and limpid, her smile heartbreakingly sweet. "Oh, I can't believe you're finally here! You found me! I've dreamed of this day for so long!" She turned again to the wall where they'd propped up the family portrait, her slender hand going out to lightly touch the faces on it. "Mama! And Papa! How I long to see them again! Shall we leave first thing in the morning to return home? My heart will surely burst if we must wait longer!" A tear appeared in the corner of her eye and she sniffed, lifting her lace handkerchief to dab at the moisture, then gave them a radiant smile. "Oh, Harry! Christopher! And Matt." She cupped the cheek of the youngest brother. "I've missed you so much!"

Harry leaned toward her, catching her other hand in his. "How did it happen, Ceci? We know you stowed away in David's wagon, but what happened after that? Were you attacked by thieves?"

"Yes, yes! That was it exactly!" She dropped her head into her hands and shuddered. "Oh! It was horrible! Did you find David? Did he tell you about the attack?" she asked, raising her head.

Matt said quietly, "We've never found any sign of David, Ceci. You're the only one who can tell us about that night."

"Oh! Only I left, to tell the tale!" She dropped her head into her hands again and began to sob.

The brothers leaned in close and wrapped her in their arms, heads close to hers. She'd taken her hat off when they entered the inn, so her golden locks showed up well next to Harry and Matt's dark hair and the pale head of Christopher.

John leaned back in his chair and sighed.

After a few moments, the girl raised her head and said in a low voice thrumming with emotion, "Yes, it was horrible. They beat David horribly and then they must have killed him. I heard grunts and moans and screaming. Horrible, horrible noises!"

Harry moaned in distress and put his arm around her, sheltering her from the memories.

"And then the next thing I knew, I was trussed up in the back of a wagon, being taken far away from my beloved home! I must have been unconscious, because I couldn't remember anything about what had happened for a long time! Fortunately, the men who took me stopped to water the horses at an inn just as I managed to loosen the ropes around my wrists. I slid from beneath the empty grain sacks they'd thrown over me and ran to the back of the inn, where I met these two knights in shining armor!" She threw out her hand to Henry and James, who straightened up in their chairs and smiled lovingly at her, Henry's wide grin revealing some missing teeth.

"I didn't remember anything about who I was, but I knew I'd been taken from my loving family. Henry and James tried to provide a new family for me, hoping that one day I would remember where I'd come from so they could take me back. But until today, we had no idea who that family was." Her gaze softened and she leaned into Harry's embrace, reaching out to cup Christopher's cheek.

John cleared his throat and stood up, reaching into his inner pocket. He brought out Ceci's favorite locket, the gold pendant catching the sunlight as it dangled from the fine gold chain.

The girl gasped, hand going to her throat as she stared. "It's beautiful!"

John held it out to her. "Do you remember?"

Tears started to her eyes, and she stood up to take it from him, gripping his arm with her other hand. "Thank you so much, Prince John, for bringing me something so special!" She looked down at the locket for a moment, tears trickling down her cheeks, then reverently brought it to her lips and kissed it gently. She raised dewy eyes and whispered, "Will you put it on me, please, Your Highness?"

His mouth looked a bit grim but he smiled. "Of course."

When he'd settled the necklace around her neck and fastened the clasp, his fingers lightly brushing the back of her neck, she moved back to her chair with the brothers.

"It was your favorite locket, my dear! You wore it for a solid year, I think!" Harry said, smiling at her with love.

John touched Matt lightly on the shoulder. "Would you help me take these plates to the kitchen? That way we won't be disturbed by the innkeeper."

Matt raised his eyebrows in surprise, then glanced at where his brothers were talking in low voices to the girl, and stood, albeit reluctantly.

After they'd deposited the plates in the kitchen and assured the innkeeper that they didn't need anything at present, John drew Matt out into the yard.

"Can you believe we found her, John?" Matt breathed, throwing his hands up in relief, a grin on his face.

"No, actually, I can't," John said grimly.

Matt's hands fell and he frowned. "What do you mean?"

John sighed. "I don't think that's Ceci."

Matt stared at him. "*What?*"

"I don't think it's her," John repeated.

Matt's eyebrows drew together. "Why not? Her name is Cesily, and she's the only blonde we've seen the whole time we've been here…"

"What did she call you?" John interrupted.

"Matt." He shrugged, puzzled.

"Exactly," John said, eyebrows raised, urging Matt to make the connection.

Matt's face went blank. "Oh…"

"And what did she call your parents?"

"Mama and Papa…" his voice trailed off, dismay replacing the blankness.

"And she didn't remember the locket. She could tell she was supposed to, so she acted like it was special, but she treated it like a regular locket. Ceci *loved* that locket. She would remember it."

Matt was silent a moment. "But… the hair…"

John said, "I think it's a wig. When I put the chain around her neck, I saw the edge of it. It's a very good one, very professional, but I'm sure it's a wig."

Matt's face crumpled, pain and anger in his eyes. "Harry is going to be devastated."

"Yes," John said grimly. "He is."

They walked back into the dining parlor, John having assured Matt that he would handle the denouement, and settled into their chairs. Matt's face was carefully blank.

"My dear," John said to 'Cesily' at a small break in the conversation, "The chain of your necklace has a small kink in it. Allow me to fix it." He stood up and moved behind her to unclasp the necklace.

The girl started to protest but he was too quick.

As John lifted the necklace over her head, somehow the button of his sleeve got caught in her curls and tugged at them. "Oh, I am sorry, my dear!" he said, reaching to untangle her hair. But then the button on the other sleeve became entangled… and suddenly the lovely blonde hair slid right off the girl's head and dangled from John's fingers.

Harry and Christopher stared as she clasped her hands to her oddly flattened head.

"My hair!" she exclaimed, twisting toward John. She looked much less beautiful, the flaxen curls having been replaced by a tight-fitting skullcap from which tendrils of dark hair escaped.

John met her startled eyes with narrowed ones of his own, and for a moment their gaze held.

Then the girl laughed and said, "Oh, what a fright I must look!" She turned back to Harry and Christopher and clasped their hands where they lay limp in their laps. Her gaze went to Matt but skittered away when she saw his hard eyes. "You must understand… my hair got darker as I grew up. Now it's the same shade as *yours*, dear Harry! But I longed for the beautiful fair hair of my youth," she said as she reached up to stroke Christopher's hair where it lay against his neck, "so when I had the chance to purchase a blonde wig from an actress friend of mine, I couldn't resist. And I would say it's the best purchase I ever made, because it brought me to your attention, my dear brothers." Her eyes filled with tears and she gazed softly at Harry and Christopher, and even made another valiant attempt with Matt.

John laughed, impressed despite his anger. "That's a very good recovery, ma'am, but I'm afraid it won't do. You made some other mistakes that are less easily explained, and those, along with the hair, make me quite certain you are *not* the Lady Ceci."

Harry found his voice. "What are you talking about? What mistakes?" He twisted to look at John, consternation on his face.

John said, "I'll tell you later. I don't want to give these charlatans any more information than they already have."

"But…" Harry began to protest.

"He's right," Matt broke in. "He told me what he noticed, and he's right." His gaze cut back to the girl, disgust in his eyes. "She lied to us: a dirty, filthy, low-down lie."

The girl's eyelids flickered, but then she gave a little laugh and glanced at her accomplices, who had been watching the scene warily. "Well, boys, I think we're done for!" Her voice had become much less cultured and soft. Now it had a distinct Arlesland accent, and a shrillness that spoke of life in a large, noisy town. Her eyes hardened and the sweet curve of her mouth changed into a cynical smile. She stood up and motioned to her companions. "I know when to cut my losses, and you, sir," she tapped John's chest, "are not a man who is easily fooled." She took the wig from his hands and flipped it upside down, then tucked her head down and settled the wig on it. She looked into the mirror over the mantel and adjusted the curls, gave an insouciant grin to them and said, "Catch ya later, fellas," and left, Henry and James on her heels.

Harry's mouth was still wide open in confusion, but Christopher's lips had thinned. "How did you know?" he asked John through gritted teeth.

John glanced at Matt, who went to the door and looked into the hallway.

"They're gone," he reported, closing the door.

John explained what he'd noticed, softening his words as Harry's face crumpled. "They must have heard about our search and decided to try to pass her off as Ceci. I'm guessing she's an actress. She was very, very good."

"And we would've believed her, would've taken her home to Mother and Father!" Harry groaned.

"Well, I sincerely doubt the deception would've gone that far. That wig wouldn't have fooled a lady's maid, for one thing. I imagine the goal was to travel with us long enough to rob us blind, and then disappear in the night."

Christopher huffed in disgust, then dropped his head into his hands. Tears had started to run down Harry's cheeks.

"Don't lose hope," John urged him. "This was bound to happen. It's amazing no one has tried to pass themselves off as her before. It was a hard lesson, but we'll be much more wary of anyone else claiming to be Ceci."

Harry sighed and nodded, wiping his eyes. "You're right. But… for a little while, I was so happy. I hadn't realized how sad I'd become until I thought we'd finally found her. The relief… was overwhelming. To lose her again…" He shook his head. "I'm not sure how much longer I can bear this."

John put his hand on Harry's shoulder and squeezed. "We're all in this together, and we'll survive whatever happens. I promise you."

Yaegertown

Prince John and the duke's sons were gathered around the supper table at a quiet inn in Yaegertown, discussing what they should do next. They'd spent a few days in the town, asking if anyone knew a woman named Cesily, to no avail. The town was too big for one woman to stand out, but John had a feeling their lack of progress had as much to do with the open suspicion on the faces of most of the people they questioned as it did with any anonymity Cesily might have found. As John and the duke's sons made their way through the town, people turned to stare at their fine clothing and general air of well-being. The sunken cheeks and disheveled state of the people they'd seen in the villages was somewhat lessened here, since many of the people were employed on noble estates, but the look in their eyes was the same.

It was only when they'd thought to inquire at some of the larger estates that they finally made progress. At a small castle several miles outside Yaegertown, they found a housekeeper who stared at them with sharp eyes but finally said, yes, she'd had a kitchen maid named Cesily until a few weeks ago, but she didn't know where the girl had gone.

"Up and run out on us, she did! Left all her things behind, too! Not that she had much, mind you. The clothes on her and her daughter's back, that's all she took as far as I know. Thought she'd send for the few things she'd left behind, but she never did."

John asked, "But you're sure she's alright? Maybe she met with an accident."

"Nah!" the housekeeper said, waving a hand dismissively. "Not her! Saw her gettin' in a fancy carriage that day, one of the boys did, her and her daughter, too. She must've gotten a position good enough for her to just up and leave immediately." She sniffed at such effrontery.

"Whose carriage was it?" Christopher asked, hope flaring in his eyes.

The woman shrugged. "Don't know. Boy couldn't see the crest for all the people around it."

Another dead end.

So now they were trying to figure out in which direction to take their search. Consultation with the innkeeper had revealed there were three large estates within a day of Yaegertown: Bucksbury, Glastonheight and Heighlawn.

As he bent over the map spread out on the table, John traced the routes of both the roads under consideration and listened to Harry argue with Christopher.

"We know the Earl of Glastonheight has the largest castle, which means Cesily would've had an easy time getting hired on there. That's why it makes the most sense for us to go there next."

Christopher sat back in his chair and crossed his arms, sighing. He shrugged. "I can't argue against what you're saying. But I feel very strongly that we should go to Heighlawn instead. I can't explain why."

John was surprised when all three brothers turned to him. He laughed. "I don't know which way to go!"

Matt smiled. "Well, you're outside the family, so if you make a bad decision, we can be mad at you without it causing bad feelings for years to come."

John laughed. "Well," he turned the map around so they could see it better, "I think we should follow Harry's suggestion and visit the earl of Glastonheight first, because it's closer and there's a road near his castle that leads to Heighlawn, so we wouldn't have to backtrack if we don't find Ceci at Glastonheight." He paused. "Or we could split into three parties and check all the castles at once."

"No!" Harry shook his head. "We stay together."

Christopher nodded and said, "Glastonheight it is," he said, giving into defeat graciously.

Harry clapped his hands in relief. "Now, more wine!" He reached out to ring the bell.

Glastonheight

Prince John sent one of his guards ahead to Glastonheight to inform the earl of their incipient visit and ask if he could recommend a local inn for them. The earl sent back in invitation for them to join him at his castle instead.

As they rode into the earl's courtyard that afternoon, John was pleased to see the earl and his lady waiting to greet them with smiles. The courtyard, like the rest of the estate, was well-kept and the earl's people were neatly dressed and smiling. It looked like Glastonheight had somehow managed to avoid the blight of heartsickness that affected the rest of Arlesland.

John felt his stiff shoulders relax, and hoped Ceci had found a home here.

Introductions were made, and Lord and Lady Glastonheight escorted them inside while the guards settled in the barracks.

As they walked up the wide stairs to the open front door, the earl said, "We have some small rooms near yours where a few of your guards can bunk as well, if you like."

John nodded in relief and motioned to Section Captain Arne to follow them. He didn't have a bad feeling about the earl, but it was always smart to have a few guards around.

After they'd washed their hands and faces and changed from their travel-stained clothes, John and the duke's sons followed a servant down to a large room on the main level, where Lord and Lady Glastonheight awaited them with plates of cold meat and fruit. As they walked in, they saw that the Wallingford family portrait had been placed on an easel near the fireplace, where light from the windows illuminated it well.

"Now then," said the earl with a smile, "You must tell us what has brought you so far from your home, and how it relates to this portrait."

John motioned for Christopher to oblige, and the middle brother stepped up beside the painting. As he wove the tale, John watched the faces of their hosts. The earl looked intrigued, a slight smile on his lips until Christopher related Ceci's disappearance, at which point he looked suitably subdued. The countess listened with wide eyes, gasping in dismay, eyes tearing up when she heard how the duke and his sons had continued searching for Ceci for so long.

Christopher explained, "We thought our best bet of finding Ceci was her blonde hair, since it's so unusual here."

The countess murmured agreement.

Christopher continued, "But we realized recently that she may be dyeing her hair. We came across mention of a young woman going by the name of Cesily," he said, watching the earl and countess carefully but they gave no sign they recognized the name, "who has brown hair and a young daughter, and it's possible that she is our lost sister. We have information that she recently took a position with one of the large estates close to Yaegertown, so we hoped she was in your employ."

"Ah!" The earl shook his head. "No, I'm afraid not, my lords. We haven't hired any new staff in several months. Am I right, my love?" he asked his wife.

"Yes, darling. I haven't hired anyone since the new gardener came." She turned to John and the duke's sons, her eyes sad. "I'm so sorry, but I'm afraid we can't help you."

John and the brothers sighed, disappointed. John said, "Well, that marks one place off our list at least. But it's possible Cesily is not the missing Lady Ceci, so we'd still like to have Lord Christopher tell the story to all your staff, in case any of them might have seen her over the years."

"Certainly, certainly!" The earl was affable. "Let us partake of refreshment, and I'll arrange to have the staff assemble in the Great Hall afterward to view the portrait."

Prince John and the brothers held out hope that one of the staff members would have information about Cesily, but it was not to be. John and the brothers made plans to leave at first light the next day, and spent the rest of their day enjoying some hunting with the earl on his extensive estate.

Unexpected Guests

The Earl of Glastonheight chuckled over supper as he read the missive that his servant had just brought.

"Well, Your Highness, my Lords," he said, looking around at them, "you'll want to change your plans for the morrow, but the delay will help you in your quest! The Earl of Bucksbury and his family will be joining us at midmorning."

John and the brothers exclaimed.

"Yes, it's a bit of good fortune!" Glastonheight said. Looking down at the letter, he sighed and chuckled ruefully. "The earl can be quite entertaining, but his wife…" he chuckled again. "She can be a bit of a trial. Talks incessantly about the most trivial things, and expects you to care. His young daughter is charming, however. And, since the earl's estate is in the northern part of the kingdom but his country house is in the south, they do know everyone for miles around. They may be the perfect people to help you with your quest. I would suggest, however, not attempting to talk to Lady Bucksbury about your quest until after lunch, because she will completely ignore you in favor of telling all the news that she knows first, so you'll just be wasting your breath."

The men laughed and agreed to his plan.

"Darling, you mustn't tell Lady Bucksbury about the quest beforehand," the earl said to his countess. "Let Lord Christopher tell it."

"Oh, pooh!" she replied, waving her fork. "As if I could get a word in edgewise with Magdala!" She confided to Matt, who was sitting on her left, "Glastonheight claims that Lady Bucksbury is a trial to *him,* but the truth is that he and Bucksbury escape out of doors as much as they can, leaving me with all the work of acting polite while being bored senseless." She glared at the earl.

They all laughed, the good spirits of John and the brothers restored with the magic wand of hope.

Prince John and the brothers were out hunting doves when Lord Bucksbury's carriages pulled in that morning.

John and the brothers thought their best chance of catching sight of Cesily and her daughter, if they were traveling with Bucksbury's entourage, was during the arrival, when everyone would be in one place, so Glastonheight had a hard time convincing them to stay away from the castle during the arrival.

"No, no! I assure you," Glastonheight said, "it will be nothing but chaos and confusion, and if you do happen to spot your sister in the group, it will only add to the chaos! We'll never be able to make Lady Bucksbury understand what's happening if you don't prime her first with the story. If the girl is with her, you'll see her soon enough."

John and the brothers glanced at each other uneasily, all of them feeling a strong need to stay at the castle. But John's training in subjugating his own desires to the interests of diplomacy won the battle and, reaching out to squeeze poor Harry's shoulder in commiseration, he turned to the earl and said, "Thank you, my Lord. We would be glad to join you for some hunting."

Lady Bucksbury

Prince John and the duke's sons met the Earl and Countess of Bucksbury at lunch, which hadn't come soon enough for the brothers. Harry and Christopher were wound tight as piano wires by the time they returned to their rooms from the morning's hunt. Neither of them had hit a thing, and John had to admit his attention hadn't been fully on the sport, either. He'd never been much of a hunter, anyway, but John had learned to love the camaraderie if not the sport.

But that morning, only Glastonheight seemed to be fully enjoying himself.

Arriving back at the castle, the brothers and John quickly washed up, changed clothes and made their way to the dining hall. Entering, they saw Lady Glastonheight sitting on a sofa with an elegantly dressed woman with dark hair and sharp eyes, as a man looked on from a chair by the fireplace. Their hostess looked up in relief as they came in, interrupting the other woman to rise and curtsy to the men.

"Ah, here are the special guests I mentioned," she said to her newly arrived guests. "Prince John of Vallenland and his companions, sons of the Duke of Wallingford…"

At the word "Vallenland," the other man and woman made sounds of surprise. It wasn't often that they met visitors from other kingdoms, insular as Arlesland was.

Bows and curtsies ensued along with murmurs of "Enchanted!" as each of the duke's sons was introduced and bowed over the countess's hand.

John looked up from his polite bow to see the lady looking at him with calculating eyes.

"A prince of Vallenland!" she exclaimed. "Now, I wonder what you're doing here…"

Pleased that she had quickly expressed interest in their mission, John began to turn to Christopher to invite him to tell the tale, but...

"Ah!" Lady Bucksbury exclaimed, turning back to Lady Glastonheight. "I completely forgot to tell you about Lady Dewry's dress!"

Lady Glastonheight shot an apologetic look at John and the brothers as she sank in resignation back down onto the sofa.

Hiding a smile, John turned his attention to Lord Glastonheight, who had just entered and was greeting Bucksbury.

The meal that followed was a study in torture for the duke's sons, and afforded John some rather exasperated amusement. Lady Bucksbury was everything Lord Glastonheight had professed: self-absorbed, a chatterer, and silly in the extreme.

John had grown to like Lady Glastonheight the previous day, but he willingly sacrificed her on the altar of inanity, leaving her to listen alone to Lady Bucksbury's blatherings while he devoted himself to conversation with the men. He didn't feel too badly about it once he realized that Lady Glastonheight was daydreaming while the other woman chattered on. Amused, John watched them covertly as Lady Bucksbury talked to herself and the Countess of Glastonheight gazed out the nearby window, not even pretending to listen.

Finally, the time came when the last bite had been eaten. Lady Bucksbury put down her fork and, as if a spell had been broken, turned to John and continued as if she'd never interrupted her own train of thought. "Now, tell me why you're here."

"I would be very pleased to do so, but Lord Christopher does it much better than I," John said, turning courteously toward the duke's son.

Lady Bucksbury listened more carefully than John had expected, her sharp eyes locked onto Christopher's face. Christopher told how Ceci went missing, the years-long search for her, and what they'd found out on this most recent search that had led them to Arlesland. Unlike Lady Glastonheight, Lady Bucksbury didn't exclaim or get teary-eyed. Her eyes narrowed slightly as she took in one point or another, but otherwise her face remained impassive.

In fact, the only hint of emotion John could discern was merely a further freezing of her features at one point.

When Christopher told how they'd found out about the tinker's daughter named Cesily, John was watching Lady Bucksbury and saw her sudden stillness. Christopher continued speaking, but after a moment John stopped him.

"Forgive me," John said to Lady Bucksbury, smiling his most charming smile. "Did that name, Cesily, mean something to you? It's our belief that she and her daughter went to work for one of the large estates near Yaegertown, and we were hopeful she might have ended up here at Glastonheight, or possibly at your estate."

Lady Bucksbury pursed her lips slightly, then shook her head. "No. No, I don't believe I know anyone of that name. It's unusual, and I'm sure I would remember it. It rather reminds me of..." and Lady Bucksbury went off into one of her nonsensical stories, leaving John frustrated. He'd been sure he saw a spark of something in her eyes, but this woman didn't have the brains of a gnat.

But for a moment, the feeling remained that she might not be as foolish as she appeared.

A Missing Maid

That afternoon, the Earl of Bucksbury called his staff into the Great Hall to listen to Lord Christopher tell the tale of the lost Lady Ceci. As with Glastonheight's staff, the men and women listened silently, eyes wide and heads turning in unison as Christopher motioned to the painting beside him, but none of them had any information.

Supper that evening was another trial for Prince John and the brothers. Their nerves were raw with the back-to-back disappointments of finding that no one in either of the noble households, two out of their three top choices of where Cesily might have ended up, had news that could aid them in their search.

As Lady Bucksbury poured out one of her monologues to a vaguely listening Lady Glastonheight, John and the duke's sons discussed their plans with the earls.

"I suppose our next stop will be the Earl of Heighlawn's estate," John said to Glastonheight. "His seems to be the only other large estate near Yaegertown, so it's the next logical choice of where Cesily might have gone for work."

Glastonheight nodded. "Heighlawn is a good man. He'll help you if he can."

John hesitated, his eyes darting between the earls.

Bucksbury smiled at him curiously. "What is it, Your Highness? You may speak freely here," he said, glancing to the other end of the table, where the countesses, one paying attention to nothing but her own words and the other paying attention only to her food, sat.

John trusted his instincts about men, and he liked both these earls. "I have to admit I feel some confusion. You both seem to be good men, and the village around Glastonheight seems prosperous. The people look happier than those we saw on our way to Yaegertown…" His voice trailed off, not sure how to broach the subject that was really on his mind.

Bucksbury glanced at Glastonheight, who held his gaze for a moment, then Glastonheight leaned toward John and the duke's sons and said quietly, "We play a long game here, Your Highness. Our king is not a man we respect, but he has the backing of powerful people. We must walk a very careful line between serving him, and serving the needs of our people. Unfortunately, some of the other nobles in our kingdom aren't as dedicated to their people as we are, and they follow the example of their ruler. We had high hopes of Uriah at one time, but…" He sighed in regret.

John, his curiosity stoked, nodded quickly. "We heard something of how the king's behavior had changed after some kind of attack?"

Bucksbury nodded. "Yes, an attack in which an assassin killed his dearest friend. Uriah was an intelligent boy and although he had his faults, he did seem to want to be a good leader. But something broke in his mind that day, I think. He became paranoid and suspicious of everyone. They say his mistresses lead a terrible life, but the man holds some kind of sway over them, so they refuse to leave him."

Harry growled low in his throat. "He told us that if we find Ceci, he wants to meet her."

The earls raised their eyebrows and grimaced.

Harry nodded. "We think he may want to marry her."

His pained look deepening, Glastonheight said, "It would certainly be an advantageous match for him, but I would not want it for any sister of mine."

"Nor do we," interposed Christopher, mouth grim. "He's demanded that we bring her back to him, so we would grievously offend him if we don't."

Glastonheight pondered a moment. "If you find her, keep it quiet until you can get her across one of the borders and pretend you found her there."

"That's a good idea," John agreed, glancing at the brothers, who nodded. "Thank you for the suggestion."

"Not at all," Glastonheight smiled. "I hope that if we ever need your help, you will assist us as well."

John smiled, but refused to commit to what Glastonheight was hinting at without knowing more about the situation in Arlesland. "I assure you, I and my father will always do what is best for our people, and if we can assist in making life better for yours as well, we would be glad to do so."

Glastonheight nodded, looking a little disappointed.

"So you'll leave for Heighlawn tomorrow?" the earl asked, turning his attention to the cheese and fruit the servants were placing before them.

Later that evening, when they were all watching Matt soundly trounce Harry at chess, something in Lady Bucksbury's monologue caught John's attention. He turned toward where she sat on the sofa with Lady Glastonheight.

"… I've searched all over, but there's not a sign of her!" Lady Bucksbury was obviously peeved, her mouth pinched, eyes narrowed in disgust.

Lady Glastonheight was frowning. "That is very odd. You said she told no one she was leaving?"

"Not a soul! I can't understand it! She had very little money with her, just the few coins I had given her for the two weeks she had already worked, so where in the world could she be planning to go?"

John interrupted. "Is someone missing?"

Lady Bucksbury waved her hand dismissively. "Just a silly servant girl. Although you'd think a woman with a child would have more sense."

John frowned. "A woman with a child? Do you mind if I ask her name?"

Lady Bucksbury's face froze just as it had earlier that day during the story about Ceci, but then it relaxed and she answered him easily. "Cora. She's one of my maids, not a very good one, I might add, but her child was a companion for my daughter." She sniffed, playing with the tassle on the arm of the sofa.

Cora. Not Cesily. John glanced at Lady Glastonheight and saw she was smiling at him in kind understanding. "I wondered the same thing when I met her today," she said, "but she's not your Ceci. It's too bad because her daughter was adorable."

John sighed and turned his mind to this new mystery, glad to have something else to think about. "Are you sure she left? Maybe something has happened to her."

"Oh, no! She definitely left. One of the castle boys saw her and her daughter hopping into a wagon at the castle gate around noon, free as you please!" Lady Bucksbury's hand waved up, up, imitating the flight of a bird. "She's gone, leaving me with no companion for my dear Ana." She sighed.

John smiled in sympathy and turned back to the chess game, thoughts of the missing maid fading from his mind.

An Invitation from "Friends"

A note was delivered to Prince John a few days later while he sat at breakfast with the Earl and Countess of Heighlawn. He and the brothers had arrived there the previous day, and were planning to leave that afternoon, although they weren't sure where to go next. They'd found no clues to Ceci or Cesily at Heighlawn, and were swiftly running out of places to search.

John's sudden stillness as he read the note in his hand made Lord Christopher ask, "What is it, John?"

John looked up as quiet fell over the other brothers and their hosts. His face was blank for a moment, then he said with a small smile. "Oh, nothing much. One of the village men has heard about my father's farming techniques and wishes to ask me some questions. He's asked me to meet him at the village inn this morning."

The duke's sons looked puzzled and glanced at each other. Vallenland farming techniques?

John continued, "I do apologize, Lady Heighlawn. Perhaps I could leave Lord Harry and Lord Christopher here to entertain you this morning while I go on this errand?"

The countess looked surprised, and Harry and Christopher gave him startled looks as well. The men had no idea what to talk to the countess about, and the countess had no particular wish to spend an hour or more alone in their company, but Prince John had put them all in the awkward position of not being able to say so.

So they all murmured assent while not meeting each other's eyes.

"Good!" John said. "And Heighlawn, perhaps you would come along with Matt and me this morning."

The earl agreed immediately, glad he wasn't relegated to stay home with the others.

When John, Matt and the earl were mounted on horseback and headed for the village inn, John told them what the note had really said.

"Someone claims to have found Ceci," he said grimly, glancing at Matt with raised eyebrows.

"Ohhh," Matt said in understanding.

John looked over at Heighlawn. "Some men tried to pass an imposter off as Ceci when we were in Yaegertown," he explained. "Harry and Christopher were especially upset when they found out the girl was a fraud, so I don't want them to know anything about this yet."

Heighlawn nodded, sympathy on his face.

Matt's face was like a thundercloud. "If it's another imposter… How anyone could think to make money off another's misfortune is beyond me. Who sent the note?"

John shook his head. "No name. It was signed 'From an Interested Friend.'"

Matt huffed in annoyance. "I'll *bet* they're interested… in making money!"

"Well, at least we're on our guard this time," John said, his lips thinning.

John, Matt and the earl were shown into the inn's large dining room and they headed straight to the fireplace to warm their hands, which were chilled from the ride in the cool morning air.

When the door opened, they turned as one to see a young woman and child being ushered through the door. The woman had a kerchief over her long brown hair, which was a shade darker than that of the child whose hand she held. Her wary eyes darted over the three men, and lingered in puzzlement on the thin crown John wore.

John's heart began to thump. This was no wig-wearing imposter, at least. Could it be Cesily? He glanced at Matt and saw the same hope on his face.

Then the woman stepped all the way into the room, and John saw the two men slinking in behind her, wearing rather shamefaced grins and bowing obsequiously. The prince felt a surge of anger, but before he could speak, Matt had stepped forward, his hands curling into fists.

"You!" he growled at the men, teeth bared. "How dare you!"

Henry stepped forward, shoulders hunched and a determined smile on his face, rather like a disobedient dog trying to slink its way back into its master's good graces. "Now, now, my Lord, don't hold that little incident against us! I assure you, this is no trick!"

John's furious eyes went from oily Henry to James, who also had an ingratiating grin on his face and seemed to be trying to simultaneously bow and hide behind Henry. John turned his eyes on the woman.

She was staring at him, dismay and confusion on her face as she looked from him to Henry. She had pulled the child tightly against her side.

Henry continued, "This time, we've actually found the girl you wanted! Gentlemen, may I present to you: the Lady Ceci!" With a flourish, Henry stepped forward and yanked the kerchief off the woman's head, displaying… dark brown hair.

The woman went pale and gasped, turning to yank the kerchief away from Henry. "How dare you!" she hissed. Her hands shook as she tried to put it back on.

Henry, to John's surprise, looked completely dumbstruck. He was staring at the woman's head, peering at it closely as if looking for something. "What have you done, you stupid girl?" he hissed, grabbing her arm and shaking her.

"Here now!" the earl said with anger. "There's no need to handle her so roughly!" He raised his walking cane and whacked Henry's forearm, knocking it away from the girl.

Henry howled and forgot himself enough to glare at the earl, then turned his glowering eyes on John. "I assure you, Your Highness, that woman's hair is actually blonde! I saw it myself, just a day ago, and so did James! I swear upon my life's honor!" Henry placed his hand over his heart and tried to look pious.

John regarded him. "Your life's honor?" he asked with derision, then turned to the earl. "Heighlawn, these are the very same men who tried to pass the other imposter off on us weeks ago." He turned back to Henry and James. "You would've been much smarter to get someone else to bring the girl to us. We might have believed *them*."

Henry was sputtering. "But, Your Highness, I swear, as God is my witness, she had blonde hair not two days ago! She's dyeing it, just like the girl you seek!" He snarled at the girl, "What did you *do?* Oh, you wretch! You've ruined everything!"

Matt had been watching in silence. Now he leaned toward John and whispered, "He seems truly upset. Do you think he's telling the truth?"

John studied the young woman. She was still staring at him, but the dismay on her face had been replaced by something else. What was it?

Fear. She was terribly afraid.

Cora tried to slow the pounding of her heart and her panicked breathing. She had no idea what Henry and James had led her into, but she had to be calm and get herself and Mary out of the room quickly.

The prince spoke, his eyes and mouth stern. "Why are you with these men?"

Cora stammered a little as she answered, "B-b-because they told me there was a job for me at Heighlawn. I need work, sir, to feed my daughter." Surely they would have mercy on a woman with a child to feed. Another wave of fear ran over her and she bent to pick up Mary, holding her close on her hip.

Mary, picking up on the tension, hadn't said a word. When Cora glanced at her, she saw the child's eyes were wide.

The prince glanced at the girl, too, and his eyes and mouth softened. "Hello, little one," he said gently. "That's a pretty dolly you have."

Mary just stared, clutching the doll tighter.

The prince said to Cora, his eyes sharpening again, "You had no idea these men were going to pass you off as the woman we've been searching for?"

"N-no, Your Highness. I'd never want to be caught up in something like that."

"What do they mean by saying you had blonde hair two days ago?" he asked.

Cora glanced at Henry, then said firmly, "I don't know, Your Highness. I suppose they must've been drunk."

Henry hissed, "You lying tramp!" and turned on her with fury, raising his hand to strike her.

With a gasp, Cora turned away, huddling protectively around Mary, but the prince grabbed Henry's arm.

The earl strode to the door and called the innkeeper. "Call the constable to come get these men immediately!"

"Yes, milord, right away!" Eyes wide, the innkeeper whistled for his hulking son, who grabbed Henry and James by the back of their shirts and hauled them protesting out the door.

As Henry was being dragged away, he called back, rage distorting his voice, "She answers to the name Cesily!"

Cora's heart almost stopped. She hugged Mary closer, burying her face in the child's hair for a moment to hide her fear.

When she looked up, the prince was watching her. "My apologies. I haven't introduced myself or my companions. I am Prince John of Vallenland, and this is my friend Lord Matthias of Wallingford, and our host, the Earl of Heighlawn. May I ask your name?"

Cora's heart had started beating furiously when she heard the name of the young man with him, and she suddenly felt dizzy. She quickly lowered Mary to the floor and crouched beside her, pretending to adjust the child's dress while she regained her equilibrium. Then she stood and curtsied, saying, "My name is Cora, Your Highness, and this is my daughter, Mary."

John asked, "Does the name Cesily mean anything to you?"

The little girl suddenly raised her doll and offered it to the prince, but Cora pulled the girl's arm back and whispered, "Quiet little mouse."

Mary subsided, watching him silently.

"No, Your Highness, it doesn't," Cora said, smoothing Mary's hair nervously.

John said, "We're searching for a girl who went missing seventeen years ago, the sister of Lord Matthias. Her name is Ceci, but we believe she may have changed her name to Cesily, and that she might be dyeing her blonde hair brown. Do you know of such a woman?"

Cora could barely hear him over the roaring in her ears. She felt like she was going to faint, but managed to shake her head.

A speculative gleam had come into John's eye. He'd just remembered something. "Cora… did you happen to work for Lady Bucksbury until a few days ago?"

Cora stared at him for a heartbeat or two, her mind working furiously. She couldn't understand how he would know that, and had no idea whether it was dangerous for her that he did. Lady Bucksbury knew nothing about her previous life, though, so Cora decided truth was the best policy in this instance. The lies were getting hard to track. "Yes, Your Highness, I did."

John turned to Matt. "Remember Lady Bucksbury was annoyed because one of her maids ran off? She said the woman had a little girl." He turned back to Cora. "That was you?"

"Yes, Your Highness."

"You left what must have been a good-paying job, and now you're out of work?" he questioned.

Cora flushed. "Yes, Your Highness."

John didn't say anything, just watched her curiously.

Cora reluctantly explained, "Lady Bucksbury wanted me to marry one of her tenant farmers. I'm determined never to marry again. Her insistence made it impossible for me to remain with her."

John said slowly, "I see. You'll need a good job, if you plan to provide for your daughter all alone."

"Yes, Your Highness." As if she didn't know that to the very marrow of her being. She'd never have trusted Henry and James to help her find a job otherwise.

John studied her. He found himself drawn to her and her daughter, whose big brown eyes had remained fixed on him the entire time he questioned her mother. He believed the young woman when she said she'd had no idea what Henry and James had been planning. The shock on her face had been real, and now she was in a strange village with no work prospects.

Oddly, he felt responsible. And he was learning to trust his instincts on this trip.

He turned to the earl. "Heighlawn, might I impose upon you to take in Cora and her daughter this evening, since she's in this situation because of us?"

Cora gasped.

Heighlawn was shocked that the prince would ask him to host a servant as a guest, but after studying John's face a moment, he turned to Cora. "Please do me the honor of being my guest tonight. Do you and your daughter ride, or would you prefer that I send for a carriage?"

Cora at Heighlawn

When Cora and Mary rode into the courtyard of Heighlawn, Cora was seated in the innkeeper's wagon, while Mary rode seated on the saddle in front of Lord Matthias.

When Prince John had made his surprising request of Lord Heighlawn, Cora had protested, knowing how untoward the suggestion was.

"Indeed, Your Lordship, I couldn't begin to intrude on you in such a way! Mary and I will be perfectly fine on our own," she had insisted.

The earl had glanced at the prince, secretly agreeing with her and wondering why the prince had put him in such an awkward position.

Prince John had said smoothly, "Ma'am, I feel responsible for those men bringing you here. Please allow me to assuage my guilt by providing you with a safe place to sleep for the night and arranging for your travel back to Yaegertown tomorrow."

"Oh, but we would be perfectly safe here at the inn, if you would but arrange for a room!" she'd protested. It went against her instincts to allow him to pay for even that much, but the truth was that she and Mary were in a pickle, so she would once again do what was necessary to make sure her child was safe. It went beyond anything to think that they needed to be put up by Lord Heighlawn, though.

Prince John had known the earl thought he'd lost his mind, but he'd also known the man would do what he wanted, so he'd merely shook his head at Cora's protest.

Matt, listening with one ear while making silly faces at Mary, had said with a laugh, "Well, I must agree with Prince John and insist that you come back to Heighlawn with us so I can spend more time with my new friend!" He'd chucked the girl under her chin, making her giggle.

Cora, seeing she was outweighed, had hesitated and then reluctantly agreed to accompany them. Lord Heighlawn had offered to get a horse for them both to ride, but Cora had quickly demurred, saying, "Thank you, milord, but I'm not dressed for riding."

The innkeeper, anxious to please Heighlawn and the foreign prince, had then offered up his wagon for her, and Matt had offered to take Mary up on his saddle. Cora was about to say no when Mary turned to her with shining eyes and begged, "Please, Mummy, please!"

Lord Matthias had smiled at Cora and said, "Don't worry. I'll take good care of her. I used to know a little girl who was afraid of horses, and I wish I'd taken the time to help her get over that. Your daughter will be very safe with me."

So Mary had ridden in delight on top of the tall stallion, Matt telling her how to pull on the reins to direct the huge horse this way and that.

When they stopped in front of the castle, Prince John jumped down to help Cora from the wagon, then lifted Mary off Matt's saddle.

"Oh, Mummy! That was wonderful! Can we get a horse?" Mary asked, staring up at the animal.

Matt dismounted and laughed. "I do apologize. I may have started a lifelong passion." His eyes twinkled at Cora.

Cora smiled and looked down at Mary. "No, love, I'm afraid I can't buy you a horse. But maybe wherever we end up will have horses you can visit sometimes."

Mary pouted for a moment, until Matt lifted her up to pet the horse's nose. "Mummy, it's just like velvet!" she said, turning her head to look at Cora, a beaming smile on her face.

Cora turned to where Prince John waited patiently to escort her inside. "The earl has gone ahead to order a room prepared for you and Mary," he explained as she hesitantly took the arm he offered.

Cora thought about protesting again, but instead smiled faintly and tried to keep her knees from wobbling as she walked up the stairs with him and entered the Great Hall, where Lady Heighlawn waited to greet her.

She and Mary would spend the night, which would give her time to think up a new plan for them, and then they would get as far away from Prince John and his friends as they could.

When Lady Heighlawn rejoined the men in the drawing room after settling Cora and Mary in their room, John and Matt were regaling Harry and Christopher with the tale of the second attempt to fool them into accepting an imposter as Ceci.

Harry said in disgust, "The same men?"

Matt nodded his head vigorously. "Yes! The same ones! And they didn't even do a decent job of coming up with a story." He laughed and flung himself down on a chair, shaking his head.

Christopher asked in confusion, "What was the story again?"

John said, "Something about her hair being blonde two days ago, but overnight it turned brown." He shrugged.

Christopher said, "What made you bring the girl back with you? I would've thought you'd want nothing to do with her."

John hesitated, looking at Matt. "I'm not sure. There's something about her, though. I don't think she was involved in the plot to fool us. She seemed just as stunned as we were when those men announced her as Lady Ceci."

Matt nodded. "I agree. She seemed to want nothing to do with them after she realized why they had brought her there. My impression was that she's a good mother who just wanted to provide for her child. She seems to be afraid of something, though."

John said, "I noticed that, too. She mentioned that the reason she ran away from Lady Bucksbury was because they wanted to marry her off, so maybe she's nervous that we'll deliver her back to Bucksbury."

Harry snorted. "No fear of that! I'll happily live the rest of my days without meeting Lady Bucksbury again!"

Cora walked into the drawing room alone, the maid having explained that Cook was expecting Mary to come to the kitchen to help her roll out some cookies for afternoon tea. "We'll take care of her, ma'am, don't you worry," the maid had said comfortably, leading Mary off to the kitchen after leaving Cora outside the drawing room door, where the butler ushered her inside.

The men and Lady Heighlawn smiled as she walked in, and Prince John introduced her to Lord Harry and Lord Christopher. Cora gave her curtsies with a polite smile, but looked uneasy.

"Come sit with me," the countess said, patting the sofa cushion beside her. Lady Heighlawn, a romantic at heart and a fierce proponent of elevating the lower classes, was convinced the prince had fallen in love with Cora at first sight, and that was why he'd taken her under his wing. She was looking forward to watching the two of them together.

Cora settled a little uneasily on the cushion, feeling nervous as the others watched her.

"You're all settled in?" Lady Heighlawn asked.

"Oh, yes, milady, and Mary is in love with the room," Cora said with a quick smile.

"Oh, dear," Matt said, eyes twinkling. "First I made her fall in love with horses, and now Lady Heighlawn has made her fall in love with lush furnishings."

Cora said, "I'm afraid our regular life will be sadly flat for her after this little adventure."

Lady Heighlawn patted her hand and said, "Well, I'm sure you make her life the best it can be. I only wish we could offer you a job. The earl said you had expected to find an opening here?"

"Yes, milady." As she glanced around, she saw they were all curious about how she'd come to be at the inn the day before. After the care they'd shown to her and Mary, it was a small thing to satisfy their curiosity. She took a deep breath. "After I left Lady Bucksbury,

I took Mary to Yaegertown, hoping to find a new job. That's where I met Henry and James. Henry pretended to know me and tricked me by saying he had connections here at Heighlawn who would help me get a job."

John mused, "I wonder why Henry approached you…"

Cora flushed. "I don't know, Your Highness. But I was glad to take the chance of getting such a good position."

"Oh, how shameful those men were!" the countess exclaimed. "How cruel to raise your hopes, as well as those of the duke's sons!"

"Yes, milady," Cora said quietly, wishing someone would change the subject.

John saw her distress and said, "Well, that's all over with now. Let's talk about something much more interesting: the meal Cook has prepared for lunch! What might we expect today, Lady Heighlawn?"

As the countess launched into a recitation of the menu, Cora glanced around at the prince and the duke's sons. She was still wary of them, wary of the search they were conducting for a girl with blonde hair.

But she couldn't help liking them a little.

After lunch, Cora collected Mary from the kitchen and took the girl up to their room so they could both rest for a while. She didn't want to be a burden on her hosts, didn't want them to feel like they had to entertain her. The situation was embarrassing to Cora, but Mary would have good food for another day and a warm, comfortable bed for another night, and that's all that mattered.

Cora lay on the bed with Mary, whose chatter about all the things she'd done in the kitchen was slowing into mumbles as she fell asleep, and tried not to worry about their future.

Down in the drawing room, a different conversation about Mary's time in the kitchen was going on.

Lady Heighlawn had gone to the kitchen to check on the plans for that evening's meal, and came back to join the men with a frown on her face.

The earl said, "Why the long face, dear?"

The countess glanced around at the prince and the brothers. "I don't wish to tell tales on our new friend, but Cora's daughter Mary told Cook some things…" her voice trailed off and the frown deepened.

When she didn't speak again, the earl prompted, "What things, dear?"

"It sounds like she and her mother are well-acquainted with hunger. Mary said that before her mother got the job with Lady Bucksbury, they sometimes only had one meal a day. Cora told Mary that the cook at their old estate would only provide the midday meal, and Cora had to use money from her meager earnings to buy any other food, so they usually went without."

The earl gasped in dismay and the other men frowned.

"Is that normal in Arlesland?" Lord Christopher asked.

The earl raised his eyebrows and sighed. "Well, it's not normal in *this* area of Arlesland," he said. "Glastonheight, Bucksbury and I try to make sure our people always have enough to eat. We know the better we feed and educate them, the better the land will fare. But in other parts of Arlesland, I'm afraid a much more short-term way of thinking prevails. Some of the nobles act very *ignobly* and work their people hard for little reward. Do you know where Cora lived before she worked for Bucksbury?"

"Yaegertown is what Mary told Cook," Lady Heighlawn said. "So it makes sense that's where Cora would go after she ran away from Lady Bucksbury. Mary said they slept in a stable for two nights, and that the stableman gave them some food the first day, as well as some eggs for breakfast the next morning, but the only other food they ate the second day was what those two men fed them at supper that night."

"Ah. That's probably why Cora was so willing to trust them," Matt mused. "They'd taken care of her when they didn't have to, and they were promising her a life that would allow her to take care of her daughter."

"Why did she leave Bucksbury? Magdala isn't the easiest person to get along with, but it would've been a good place for Mary to grow up." Lady Heighlawn asked.

John answered, his voice thoughtful, "She said Lady Bucksbury was trying to force her to marry a farmer, and she's determined never to marry again."

"Oh, dear," Lady Heighlawn said. "Why doesn't she want to marry again?"

"She didn't say." John asked, "You're sure you don't have any positions available for her here?"

Lady Heighlawn exchanged a glance with the earl, then both slowly shook their heads. The countess said, "We really don't. I suppose we could make up a position for her, maybe add a kitchen maid?" She glanced again at Lord Heighlawn, who was shaking his head vigorously.

"Now, you know Cook said there was barely enough room for her and the workers she already has! If we bring another on, we'll have to make a bigger kitchen, and I'm not spending money to hire another maid *and* build a new kitchen! Besides, we don't have anywhere for her to sleep! That's why she's in the guest room now!"

Matt suddenly leaned forward. "What if we took her with us?" he asked Prince John.

John and his brothers frowned.

Harry said, "With us? To do what?"

Matt said, "Well, not to *do* anything in particular. But we've been talking about going south to the other large estates to search for Ceci, and then we'll be turning north to search the estates in the eastern part of Arlesland. If we take Cora with us, she can look for work on the other estates, and if she doesn't find it there… well, she can come to Vallenland with us and *we'll* find a position for her." Matt sat back with a slightly mulish expression. He hadn't really intended to say the last bit, but now that he had, he thought it was a good idea. His heart had been touched by Mary that morning as she rode along in front of him on the horse.

As his brothers glanced at each other, and then at Prince John, Matt burst out, "She's the same age Ceci was when she went missing!"

"What?" Harry asked. "Who is?"

"The little girl! She's five years old. And if I can't help my sister, at least I can help another little girl who needs it!" He jumped up and stalked toward the fireplace, putting his forearm on the mantle and staring into the fire, back stiff.

John glanced at Harry and Christopher, who shrugged and nodded. Harry said, "If that's what you want, little brother, that's what we'll do."

John added, "As long as Cora agrees, of course. Because if we tried to force her…" his mouth quirked.

"She'd just run away," Harry and Christopher finished, rueful grins on their faces.

Matt looked at them over his shoulder, a reluctant grin on his face as well. He kicked one of the unburnt logs at the edge of the fire and turned around, shoving his hands into his pockets. "Well, good, then. That's settled."

"You can talk to Cora about it at supper tonight," Prince John said.

Matt nodded, already thinking of ways to broach the subject.

In the end, it was Mary who accepted Matt's invitation, not her mother.

Mary had come downstairs with Cora before supper so she could say thank you to the earl and countess for their kindness, and say goodnight to the prince and the duke's sons. Matt, wisely choosing to appeal to Mary rather than Cora, crouched down and said, "Mary, we're going to be leaving tomorrow to continue our journey…"

Mary asked, "On the horses?"

Matt smiled. "Yes, on the horses. And we were thinking that if you and your mother wanted, you might come along with us…"

"Oh, Mummy! Can we? Can we please, Mummy?" Mary pleaded, leaning against her mother and looking up with wide eyes.

"Oh, no, certainly not!" Cora said, appalled. "We can't intrude on your plans any further, and I certainly couldn't accept…"

Lady Heighlawn interrupted, reaching out to take Cora's hand. "My dear, I think you should listen to what the men are proposing. They have a very good plan." She nodded at Prince John, who leaned forward, elbows on his knees.

John said, "Cora, we would be glad to have you join us. As you can tell, Lord Matthias is quite taken with your daughter…"

Matt reached over and tickled Mary's belly, making her giggle.

"… and we'll be visiting several other estates in our search for Lady Ceci. If you ride with us, we can offer you protection on the road, and give you the opportunity to visit all the large estates south and east of here to look for a job. We have a wagon you can ride in, and plenty of food, so it won't inconvenience us at all. And I can assure you, now that Matt has the idea in his head, we will never hear the end of it if you don't go with us!"

Cora glanced at Lord Matthias, who was grinning.

Matt looked down at Mary and confided, "It's very true. I get whiny when I don't get my way."

Mary giggled, "Mummy says I do, too!"

Cora glanced around at the brothers, then back at John. She started to shake her head, determined not to accept any more help from these men she barely knew, who were searching for a blonde woman.

Matt said, "And if you don't find a job here in Arlesland, we would be pleased for you to go north with us to Vallenland, where I can assure you we *will* find work for you."

North. They wanted to take her *north*.

She opened her mouth to speak, then closed it and looked down at Mary's head, stroking the girl's hair.

John said, "Well, you don't have to decide tonight. We'll be leaving after breakfast in the morning, so you can tell us your decision then."

Cora nodded, glancing up at him for a moment, then dropping her eyes and leaning down to kiss Mary's head.

That night, Cora lay awake long after Mary had fallen asleep, thinking over Lord Matthias' proposal.

Part of her longed to take Lord Matthias up on his plan. She was so tired of fending for herself, of worrying whether she and her child would have enough food while she tried to save enough money so she and Mary could travel north to Bagginsland, where she hoped to find the pine trees and mountains she'd dreamed about for so long. Cora wasn't sure where Vallenland lay, but Lord Matt had said they had to go north to return home, so it was a golden opportunity. Traveling with the prince would ensure her and Mary's safety, as well as providing them with food.

But she'd been determined to have nothing to do with these men.

Now that she'd met the prince and the brothers, though, she was beginning to regret her flight from Lady Bucksbury. The men obviously didn't think she was the woman they were looking for, so she'd had nothing to fear from them that day. Working for the earl had been a good-paying position, and she probably could've stayed there for another three months before Lady Bucksbury would've become adamant about her marrying that farmer. She could've saved so much money in that time!

But now she was almost penniless, in a part of the kingdom where she had no connections and no prospects, and a prince was offering to make her life easier.

There had to be a catch. Cora had been raised to be suspicious, and usually her fears had been borne out.

But it was different here. Lord and Lady Heighlawn weren't like Lady Bucksbury. They were kinder, more thoughtful. They actually seemed to care about her and Mary.

And Prince John and the duke's sons… they weren't like Cora had expected them to be that day she'd fled. She'd expected hard men, angry men, like her pa. But they were the complete opposite.

They laughed at everything, joking around and smiling for no reason. Cora couldn't remember ever being around people who smiled all the time. Usually when someone smiled, it was because they were trying to trick you. She wished she'd remembered *that* when Henry had given her such a big, toothy (and toothless) grin that day in Yaegertown. Kindness meant trickery.

So what was the trick here? Maybe there wasn't one…

Wouldn't it be nice if there were people whom she could trust? People who would help her, rather than hurt her?

She was so tired. It would be nice to give the burden to someone else, at least for a little while.

Joining Forces

As she walked down to breakfast the next morning, Mary's hand held firmly in hers, Cora's heart pounded.

"Can I tell them, Mummy? I want to be the one to tell them! Lord Mattus will be so excited!" Mary said.

"Yes, darling, you can tell him," Cora said, her smile a little tight. She was second-guessing her decision, but she couldn't go back on it now, not without risking terribly disappointing her little girl.

She just hoped she was making the right choice. Her pounding heart told her it wasn't.

But it *was* the best thing for Mary, the safest option she could provide as a mother. She was sure of *that*.

And Mary was the most important thing.

Mary dropped her mother's hand and went running to her new best friend as soon as they entered the breakfast room. "Lord Mattus! Lord Mattus! We're coming with you!" she cried, long hair bouncing as she ran.

Matthias' eyes widened and he scooped her up in his arms, holding her as he turned to Cora. "Truly? You're coming with us?"

Cora smiled, the fear in her heart easing as she saw how happy Mary was with the young lord. "Yes, milord. Truly."

"Yay!" Matt cheered, with Mary joining in. He went dancing around the room with her, making her laugh. When he circled back to Cora, he placed Mary on the ground again and said to the child, leaning over to look her earnestly in the eye, "And I think you'd better just call me Lord Matt."

"Lord Matt," Mary pronounced solemnly. Then she squinted at him. "May I ride on your horse, Lord Matt?"

He chuckled. "You certainly may, milady," he said, sweeping into a low bow.

"Yay!" Mary cheered again, jumping up and down, making them all laugh.

Run! Hide!

Cora's heart was calm when she rode out with the prince's large entourage that morning. Now that they were on their way, she felt like she'd turned their fate over to a force bigger than herself, one that she hoped could do a better job managing their lives than *she* had thus far.

Their journey that day seemed to bear out her optimism. The prince and the brothers were wonderful traveling companions, not expecting her to talk, but including her in their conversation so she didn't feel left out. When they weren't talking, they sang as they rode, Harry's bass voice booming out over the plains they crossed and echoing off the rock walls of canyons.

But at the inn where they stopped that night, doubts crowded her heart again.

After supper, Prince John and the duke's sons went out to the yard where their wagons were parked. As had become their custom, they'd had the innkeeper send word out to the villagers to come view the portrait of the duke's family.

Cora and Mary followed them out into the yard, which was full of villagers. Christopher walked to the wagon and uncovered the portrait, his brothers and Prince John lining up nearby. Since they were at the back of the crowd, Cora lifted Mary to stand on the back of a bench so she could see over the people in front of them.

As Christopher began to talk, Cora stared at the portrait. This was the first time she'd seen it since that day at Glastonheight, when she'd fled in terror. It had been in the hallway when she arrived with Bucksbury's entourage, but it had been covered with a cloth. It was only later, when Lady Bucksbury's young daughter Ana had disobeyed orders and pulled off the cloth, that they had seen the striking portrait of the family. A servant standing nearby had told them about the lords who were looking for the little blonde girl in the painting…

And Cora's blood had run cold as Ma's voice screamed through the roaring in her head, *"Run! Hide!"*

She'd fled straight up to their room, hastily packed their clothes in a satchel, and run out the door with Mary on her hip. She'd spotted a wagon heading out the gate and convinced the driver to take her and Mary with him, and as she'd turned for a last look, she'd seen the earl and four men ride into the courtyard.

She'd thought she'd escaped… only to be delivered to two of those same men a few days later by conniving Henry and James.

The fear that had driven her that day at Glastonheight was one she was long acquainted with: fear that the bad men would find her, the ones Ma had told her about.

But the men were here, and they weren't bad at all. Maybe it wasn't her they were after? Maybe there were other men she still needed to fear? As the familiar panic started to rise, Cora forced her thoughts back to the present.

Standing tall in front of the crowd of villagers, Christopher was talking about his sister Ceci, and how she'd loved to explore the estate. He talked about them searching for the little girl, and the fear of his parents and brothers as they realized Ceci wasn't anywhere on the estate.

As she listened to Christopher, the portrait seemed to grow in size until it filled Cora's vision. She could picture the little girl playing on the estate, could picture exactly what the house looked like, because of course it would look like the house she'd told Ma about all those years ago, the one Ma had said she'd dreamed up. She could picture the mother and father's anguished faces as they searched for their child, the brothers' bewilderment when they couldn't find her in the usual hiding places.

As Christopher talked about all the searches they'd conducted over the years, a roaring filled Cora's ears, just like it had the first time she'd seen the portrait.

But this time she heard horses' hooves pounding over a dirt road as a wagon raced through the night.

Cora felt a soft touch on her arm, and heard her name, but she couldn't break the spell that held her.

"Mummy! Mummy!" It was Mary tugging on her hand that finally recalled Cora to her surroundings. She stared down at the child in confusion.

"Are you alright, Cora?" she heard a voice say, felt a hand laying warm on her arm.

Giving her head a shake, Cora blinked and looked away from Mary to see Prince John looking at her with concern. "Are you alright?" he repeated, and she realized he'd already asked her that once.

Looking around, Cora realized the villagers were all gone. The duke's oldest sons were wrapping up the portrait in the traveling cloths, but Matthias stood behind Mary, his hands on her shoulders as he watched Cora.

Cora tried to smile, although her face seemed frozen, and said, "Yes, of course I am," even though she felt far from alright.

John silently handed her a handkerchief. Surprised, Cora took it. He said, "You were crying."

Cora put up a hand and realized tears must have been pouring down her face, judging by how wet her face and chin were. "Oh, I'm so sorry," she apologized, mortified. "I don't know what happened. I must be very, *very* tired." What in the world had led her to such a display?

John studied her a moment, then smiled in understanding. "It has been a long day. Let's get you and Miss Mary to bed." He chucked the little girl under her chin and motioned toward the door, watching Cora carefully as he followed them into the inn.

Christopher was an effective storyteller, and many people (especially the women) were brought to tears by the tragedy of the lost Lady Ceci, but he'd never seen anyone get totally lost in the story like Cora had.

It was odd. And it wasn't the only odd thing about Cora. There was definitely a deeper mystery there.

And John was determined to get to the bottom of it.

After that night, Cora made sure to stay inside whatever inn they were staying at while Christopher told the story of the missing child, but Mary usually went outside with the brothers. Christopher had even managed to work her into the story, saying, "Our sister Ceci was only five years old, like Mary here, when she disappeared." Then he would pause for a moment while Mary beamed up at him, so the audience could appreciate her helplessness and innocence, and picture another little girl just like that who had been torn from her family.

Prince John had taken to staying inside with Cora most evenings, even though she'd begged him not to change his routine on account of her.

"They don't need me while Christopher is telling the story. I'll go out when he's done and answer any questions the villagers might have. Most of them just want to indulge their curiosity while pretending it's sympathy." He gave her a rueful smile.

"Well, a lost noble lady is a rather dramatic story, you have to admit."

John nodded. "It is. I also have to admit that we're starting to lose heart these past few days. We seemed to have quite a great run of luck up until Yaegertown, and then… the luck just dried up."

"Yaegertown is where you heard about Cesily and thought she might be Lady Ceci?"

"No, Yaegertown is where we heard she had gone off in a carriage from one of the big estates. It was one of the small villages where we first learned about Cesily, and that she might be dyeing her hair brown, which is why Henry thought he could pass you off as her, apparently," John said, his mouth twisting as he remembered the trick that had brought Cora into their lives.

"What made you think she was dyeing her hair brown?" Cora asked curiously.

"Well, there was a girl in the village, a woman, really, about your age, who said she'd seen a blonde girl in the back of a tinker's wagon seventeen years ago. She said she never saw the girl again, but the next year the tinkers showed up with a girl they were calling their daughter, but the girl had brown hair."

"And that was Cesily," Cora said.

"Yes, Cesily was the tinker's daughter, or niece or something."

"But they might have been totally different girls…"

"Yes, of course, and at first we thought they were, until we found out the girl's name was Cesily. That seemed like one coincidence too many," John said.

"Because Ceci sounds like Cesily?" Cora asked. It was highly unlikely that a tinker's daughter could be a lost noble, so it seemed like a bit of a stretch to her.

"No," he said slowly. "It's because Ceci's name is actually *Ceci Leigh*," John said carefully, his eyes steady on hers.

Ceci Leigh.

Cesily.

The roaring was filling Cora's ears again, and the room faded until all she could see was Prince John's face. He was still talking, but the only reason she knew was because his lips were moving.

All she could hear was the weeping of a little girl, alone and scared.

John saw Cora's face go blank, slackening until there was no life in it except her eyes, which widened as if she were staring at something horrible.

John leaned forward, grasping Cora's hands in his. They were icy cold. He chafed them, trying to warm them.

"Cora? Cora! What's wrong?"

She continued to stare at him, unmoving. He wasn't even sure she was breathing.

"Cora!"

No response.

Heart pounding, John scooped her up and carried to her to the chair closest to the fire, then knelt to throw more wood on it. He laid his hand on her cheek. Icy, just like her hands. He grabbed a blanket from the basket by the chair and threw it around Cora.

As he did so, Cora looked up at him vaguely, then her eyes cleared and she glanced around at the fire and down at the blanket.

"Are you alright?" John asked, frowning slightly as he crouched down beside her. He picked her hands up and rubbed them.

"Yes… I'm sorry… what happened?" Cora asked.

"I don't know. I was telling you about Ceci's name, and you seemed to… lose yourself somewhere." He shrugged. "I don't know how to explain it. It was like you weren't there all of a sudden. Your eyes were empty. It was a little scary, honestly. Please don't do it again," he smiled at her charmingly, a small dimple appearing in his chin, barely visible through his short beard.

Cora stared at that dimple. She'd never noticed it before.

John squeezed her hands. "Hey. Stop it. You're fading out on me again."

She looked up, expecting to see the teasing glint in his eyes, but they were serious, intent on her, searching her face with concern. She forced a smile. "I'm fine. I must be tired."

"Hmm. You say that a lot. We may have to start making a pallet in the supply wagon so you can sleep while we ride," he said, the teasing light back in his eyes, although it was tinged with worry this time.

"Or maybe I shouldn't stay up as late at night." She smiled wanly, pushed the blanket off and stood up.

"You sure you're alright?" he asked, his hands hovering as if to catch her if she collapsed.

"Yes. Thank you, Prince John, I'll be fine. Good night." She walked as steadily as she could to the door, although in truth she felt quite wobbly.

John watched her go, questions swirling in his mind.

Cracks in the Facade

Mary unwittingly caused some consternation amongst the group one day while playing with her doll as she rode along in the supply wagon with Cora. They were making a new dress for the doll out of some scraps of cotton they'd picked up at the inn the prior night.

"But Mummy, Cesily doesn't want to wear that!" Mary said, pushing aside a piece of yellow ribbon Cora had been attempting to tie around the doll.

As one, the heads of Prince John and the brothers whipped around to stare at Mary.

Harry snapped, "What did you say?" as he rode over to them.

Mary, scared by his tone, shrank against her mother.

Cora's face flushed and she put an arm around Mary. "It's alright, love. Lord Harry didn't mean to scare you. He was just surprised by what you called your doll." She looked around at the men, her face calm, and smiled. "We've heard you talk about Cesily so much, you know." She shrugged, hoping the non-explanation would suffice.

Harry nodded a bit jerkily and gave Mary a smile, reaching out to stroke her hair. "Sorry, little one. I'm a bit jumpy today."

"We all are," John said. "It's been too long since we found any signs of Ceci or Cesily either one." He sighed and touched his heels to his horse to speed up and get next to Lord Harry.

That night, Cora had a terrible time getting Mary to calm down enough to go to sleep. The child was exhausted and whiny, but refusing to settle.

"Mummy," Mary demanded, "Tell me a story about Cesily!" She held her doll up by both arms, making the cloth legs dance across the bedsheets.

Cora was exhausted, too. She could feel her temper fraying and held onto it with desperation. "Which story do you want to hear?" she asked, her voice carefully even. Mary's favorite stories lately had involved horses, and Cora was sick to death of them.

Surprisingly, Mary said, "Cesily meets PJ!" and Cora gave a relieved sigh. That was a story she never got tired of telling, a favorite one she had made up as a child and used to tell herself at night when she couldn't sleep, either. Truth be told, she still sometimes told it to herself on long, lonely nights.

"Once upon a time," she began, pulling Mary close.

Three-year-old Cesily was running through the castle as fast as her short legs could carry her. She had been watching from her nursery window for the past hour, determined to be the first to see the entourage as it wound its way up the drive. As soon as the first horses appeared, she gave a squeal of delight and dodged around the arms of her nanny to go flying down the corridor.

Cesily didn't remember the boy who was coming to visit, but she'd heard her brothers talk about him. Cesily loved her brothers and followed them everywhere, but invariably, once they spotted her behind them, they ran away faster than she could follow, or hid until she gave up looking, or just slung her over their shoulder and carried her back to the nursery, where Nanny could scold her.

Her brothers talked about all the adventures they'd had with PJ, at their home and his, but they also somewhat derisively talked about other things. They obviously respected him, but they just as obviously couldn't understand why he preferred *watching* deer rather than riding out with the hunting parties, or how he could spend hours sitting on a rock beside a creek, observing the tiny insects and wildlife around it.

Cesily, having received similar criticism herself, was sure that in PJ she would find the bosom companion she'd always longed for. Being the only girl child in the family, and being the youngest, she was lonely much of the time, living in a world of invisible friends.

But sometimes she longed for a real person to laugh with and talk to her. Her mum said Cesily should make friends with one of the noble girls, but they just wanted to play with their dollhouses, which bored Cesily a bit. Having grown up with brothers, she longed for someone to run through the woods with her, climb trees and go wading in the creek. Nanny was too old to do those things, so Cesily wasn't allowed to do any of it without her brothers, which meant she spent most of her time *not* doing it.

Cesily was determined to make friends with PJ, and hopefully even lure him away from spending all his time with her brothers. To this end, she had found a special present for him, which was clenched in her small fist as she pelted down the last staircase and went flying across the front hall to the immense wooden doors.

Even though Cesily had run as fast as she could, her brothers had still beaten her to the driveway. When she arrived, panting, her brothers glanced at her for a moment, the oldest one taking the opportunity to say, "Your stocking is falling down, squirt," before they turned back to face the drive.

Red-faced, Cesily pulled up her long dress to see that, indeed, one of her stockings had come loose from the garter during her run through the castle and was now bagging around the ankle strap of her shoe. She glanced up to see that the horses had almost reached the house. Panicking, she ducked behind a large potted tree that stood at the bottom of the front stairs and frantically stuffed the stocking tighter around the ankle strap, not having time (or privacy) enough to re-attach it to the garter.

The entourage had reached the house. She peeked out from behind the pot and saw a boy the same age as her youngest brother descending from his horse. Cesily stopped messing with the stocking and stared.

He wasn't a particularly handsome boy, his face being rather nondescript, but he had a gentle smile, and his large, dark eyes were alive with laughter as he greeted her brothers. He was dressed in expensive clothes of silk, and wore riding gloves of leather with gold stitching. His riding boots were also of expensive leather, so although they were well broken-in, they looked almost new.

As he glanced past her brothers to her parents, who had just come out the front door and were walking down the stairs, he spotted Cesily. For a moment, he looked surprised that she was hiding behind a pot, then the gentle smile broke on his face once more and his eyes began to dance.

"And who do we have here?" he asked.

Her brothers turned around and the youngest said dismissively, "Oh, that's just our little sister! She's *supposed* to be up in the nursery because she's still a *baby*."

Stung and embarrassed, Cesily jumped out from behind the pot, the recalcitrant stocking forgotten. She said, with fisted hands and furious eyes, "I am not! I'm three years old!" She glanced at the visitor and her lip trembled as tears of mortification began to pool in her eyes. She'd so wanted to make a good impression on him and now her brothers had ruined it, just like they ruined everything!

"Oh, definitely not a baby," the boy said, still smiling. "This is a Lady in training, if I'm not mistaken, and a true *gentleman* never insults a lady." He darted a laughing glance back at her brother to take the sting out of his rebuke, then swept into a low bow, his leg extended gracefully. "My Lady, I am most pleased to make your acquaintance. Would you allow me to escort you inside?"

Cesily stared in amazement, then sniffed, gave him a wobbly smile, and carefully dipped into the curtsy she'd been rehearsing for weeks. "Yes, milord," she said, like she'd heard her mother do.

"You can call me PJ," he said as he tucked her small hand in the crook of her arm. "And what's your name?"

As she replied, Cesily decided that this boy was the true definition of a gentleman, unlike her brothers, and she firmly pinned all her affection to him in that moment.

They started up the stairs and Cesily remembered her special gift. She gasped and let go of PJ's arm abruptly, turning to descend two steps back to the potted tree. She found the gift where she'd dropped it during the stocking debacle and ran back to PJ's side.

"Here," she said breathlessly, embarrassment making the words stick in her chest. "It's my special rock."

The bit of quartz was pale pink on the outer rim, with a darker pink center. PJ stared at it a moment, then turned it this way and that, the sunlight sending a shimmering ripple across the many facets.

Cesily waited with bated breath for his reaction. She could hear her brothers snickering behind them, laughing at the gift she'd thought was suitable, but she had faith in her new friend.

"It's beautiful," PJ said, looking down at her with his kind smile. "Thank you for trusting me with it. And I think…" he put one hand in an inside pocket of his coat, "I might have something for you, too. I was going to give it to you later, but…" He drew out a pouch of dark red velvet and laid it on his hand beside her piece of quartz. His fingers gently pulled the end of the bow that bound the velvet pouch and it gaped open. "Go on," he said, offering it to her.

Cesily, heart racing, put a chubby finger inside the pouch. She felt something small and slippery and managed to hook it on her finger and draw it out. A gold chain, finely wrought. Dangling from it was a flat, gold pendant with an elaborate letter C in the middle.

As Cesily gasped and looked up at him with shining eyes, her brothers got bored and ran past them up the stairs to the breakfast that was waiting within. PJ turned his head to watch them go, then carefully placed the piece of quartz in his pocket and reached for the necklace.

He whispered, "It has a secret." He slowly pushed on one side of the pendant, which slid over and rotated ninety degrees, revealing an interior surface with the same elaborately carved C, but this one was turned backward. PJ turned the pendant slightly and Cesily gasped. The Cs carved on the interior and exterior surfaces now combined to form the shape of a butterfly, with the curlicues of the C making its wings.

Cesily couldn't speak, could only stare at the butterfly. He'd had this beautiful thing created just for her.

Suddenly she realized PJ was gently wiping her cheek with his handkerchief. She looked up at him, her eyes swimming with tears. "Don't cry, little one," he said.

Cesily threw her arms around his waist and hung on for dear life.

Cora finished the story and looked down at Mary, whose eyes were closed, mouth ajar. Cora had known she was asleep soon after she started the story, but she'd continued talking, the familiar sentences soothing her.

She kissed Mary's forehead, then reached out to turn down the wick in the lamp and slid under the bedspread, falling asleep immediately.

Cora awakened in the middle of the night to tears streaming down her face and a cry about to break free from her lips. She sat up in bed and buried her face in her hands as the sobs shook her. Another bad dream. She'd been having them more and more frequently, although she could never remember the details, just the sense of loss and loneliness.

When she was finally awake enough to stop crying, Cora climbed out of bed and put on her robe, then walked to the window to stare out at the moonlit yard. The wagon with the duke's family portrait mounted on it was parked under her window. Two guards were posted nearby, but the portrait was on the side of the wagon next to the inn, while the guards were standing on the other side, talking in low voices.

Staring down at the wagon, Cora was seized by an impulse. She glanced at Mary, whose breathing was slow and deep. They were in one of the smaller villages, so the prince's party was the only one at the inn. Mary would be completely safe by herself, and there were guards in the hall who could come get Cora if she should awaken.

Cora tied the robe tightly around her, slipped on her shoes, and tiptoed to the door, easing it open.

The hallway guards sat up straight in their chairs when she came out. She carefully closed the door and whispered, "I have a cramp in my leg. I'm going to walk it off."

The guards nodded and settled back.

Downstairs, Cora eased open the outside door and walked into the moonlight. She could hear the guards in front of the wagon talking as she walked slowly and carefully across the hardpacked dirt to the portrait. When she arrived at the wagon, she paused, listening for any sign that the guards had heard her.

Nothing.

Slowly, she untied the rope that held the cloth cover.

The moonlight bleached all color from the portrait, so it was a study in darks and lights. The faces of the duke, Harry and Matthias were hard to see, but those of the duchess, Christopher and young Ceci could be seen clearly, their painted white hair glowing and illuminating their faces.

Cora stared at the painting a long time, dimly aware that she was growing cold, but unable to leave. There was a growing pressure in her throat, pushing up from her chest. She stared at the faces, feeling as if something important were about to happen, as if she were on the verge of a discovery, but feeling so confused and upset that she wanted to run away.

The pressure built as Cora stared at the painting, and finally… it broke. Tears ran down her face, and she leaned against the painting as she wept silently, sobs shaking her body. She pressed her lips together desperately to keep from crying aloud.

After an age, the emotional storm passed, and she pulled back to look at the painting again. The moonlight had grown brighter and now all the faces stood out in sharp relief.

The confusion inside Cora's mind cleared, and her finger moved to the duke's face, where she lightly touched the painted smile, and whispered a name.

A Revelation

As they rode along the next day, Cora was silent. She smiled when Mary or one of the others talked to her, but didn't volunteer any conversation herself.

Prince John was careful not to let her notice, but he was watching her closely. She looked dreadful, dark circles under her eyes, and her shoulders hunched as if she were frightened. He and the duke's sons had been careful to make her and Mary feel welcome in the group, and he would swear that Cora felt safe with them.

So what was wrong?

John set the problem aside for the moment, and let his mind worry over the more pressing issue.

The men were putting on a good face for Cora and Mary, but they were all frustrated. No further progress in their search for Ceci, and no job prospects for Cora, made them feel like they were completely wasting their time, although John had a sneaking suspicion that Matt had been quietly making sure none of the estates they visited offered Cora a job. Matt was completely taken with Mary, treating her like the little sister he'd lost, but giving her the love he'd withheld from Ceci. John couldn't blame him, and it did all of them good to have Mary's joyful presence on their journey.

But her mother… she was even more fearful and worried than when they'd met her, which didn't make sense.

Another source of tension came late that afternoon, when the supply wagon that Cora and Mary were riding in hit a rock and broke two of the wheel struts, bringing their progress to an abrupt halt.

After conversing with his guards and the brothers, John came over to the verge where Cora and Mary were playing with Mary's doll.

"How bad is it?" Cora asked, searching John's eyes.

He sighed. "We won't be able to fix it today. The sun is going down and we're all tired. If you want, we might be able to make the next village before it gets too dark. There will be a full moon again tonight, so we should be able to see the road fine. You would have to ride, though…"

Cora tried to stop herself, but her head was already shaking as soon as she heard the word "ride." Cora had finally admitted to the men that she was scared of horses a few days into their trip. She knew her fear of horses was irrational, and she'd been trying to overcome it, even going so far as to feed the horses lumps of sugar each morning before they got on the road. But the thought of riding one of those giant beasts… she couldn't.

John studied her for a moment, then smiled and nodded. "Alright. We'll camp here tonight. You'll have to sleep a bit rough, but we'll make you a pallet in the wagon and you can stare at the stars all night. You'll be perfectly safe," he reassured them.

Mary sat up straight, staring at him with her mouth open. "The stars? We're sleeping outside tonight?"

"That's right!" John grinned at the dawning excitement on her face.

"Mummy! Sleeping under the stars!" Mary's eyes were shining, and then they got even bigger. "Just like the fairies, Mummy! We'll be just like the fairies!"

Cora laughed and agreed, and John was relieved to see that she didn't seem concerned by this change in plans.

In the end, though, Cora and Mary didn't sleep in the wagon. When Mary realized that the brothers and Prince John were sleeping on pallets arranged around the fire, nothing would do but for her to have a pallet amongst them, and Cora joined her somewhat begrudgingly, knowing the ground would be hard and cold. John soon put Mary to work gathering soft grass and leaves to make a bed for her mother, though, and Cora had to admit that, while not as soft as the featherbed they'd slept on at Heighlawn Castle, it was much softer than most of the others they'd slept on over the years.

"It's so *elegant*," Mary said with a wide grin as she stroked the blanket she was lying on, making the men laugh.

"That's one of Lady Ana's favorite phrases," Cora explained.

"Well, I would have to agree, Miss Mary," Prince John said. "This is a very fine bed you have, and a wonderful view." He turned his gaze upward, where the stars glittered in the crystal-clear sky, darkest blue to the east and pale blue to the west, where the sun had died only a little while ago.

Cora, staring upward, agreed with him.

The guards around the camp talked in low voices, as did the prince and the brothers, making a deep background sound to the croaking of the tree frogs around them. Cora lay down next to Mary and stared at the heavens until her eyes drifted shut and she dreamed.

She was running toward the barn, trying to keep up, but her brothers were running faster, their longer legs stretching out as they disappeared into the darkness. Her sturdy legs carried her through the vast doorway and she stopped, looking around in the dim light, trying to discern their hiding spot.

Suddenly, objects pelted her, hurting her briefly before cracking and oozing onto her dress.

Eggs.

Her brothers were throwing eggs at her, and, as the horrible smell made clear, they'd planned the attack weeks ago, hiding the eggs away to turn putrid.

Mouth open in surprise and dismay, she looked down at her pretty dress, the one Nanny had warned her *not* to get dirty, which was now covered in the stinking mess. Anticipating the scolding to come, tears stung her eyes and she began to wail.

Laughing, her brothers sprang from their hiding place and ran past her out the door.

Forgetting the state of her dress, she ran after them, determined to keep up this time. But it was no use. As they disappeared into the woods, the youngest one yelled back at her, "Go back to the nursery, baby!"

She fell to the ground, panting and sobbing. "Please! Please wait!" She cried and cried, calling out their names, but they kept running.

"Cora! Cora! Wake up!" Strong arms were shaking her so that her head wobbled on her neck, the movement making her wince. She opened her eyes, the firelight flickering so at first she wasn't sure what she was looking at.

Prince John and the duke's sons were gathered around, staring, as John held her with hands that hurt. She winced and tried to pull away.

John's grip slackened, but his voice had the iron that his fingers now lacked. "Cora, what did you say just now? You were dreaming and you called out a name…"

Cora stared, the dream wisping through her mind. She could almost catch the memory, but it drifted just out of reach. She squinted at John, her eyes losing focus as she looked inward.

John urged, "Try, Cora, try to remember. You were saying, 'Please, please wait. Please wait…'"

Cora's gaze turned to the youngest brother, whose eyes were agonized. A heartbeat, and she spoke.

"Please wait, 'Tias," she whispered, and he broke in front of her.

"Ceci," a deep voice rasped, drawing her attention from Matthias. She looked at Harry, who had tears streaming down his face. "You're Ceci, aren't you? No one else called him that, ever."

Cora stared at him. It wasn't possible that she could be a lost noble, the daughter of a *duke*, from another kingdom. Things like that didn't happen.

It would be wonderful if it were true.

But wonderful things didn't happen, at least not to her.

Cora stared, unable to speak, emotions roiling through her body, overwhelming her.

John let go of Cora's arms, afraid he was scaring her. He was shocked by what had happened. He and the brothers had been talking around the fire, keeping their voices low to avoid waking Cora and Mary, when they'd heard Cora talking in her sleep.

When he'd heard her mumbling and glanced over his shoulder, he saw her head turning back and forth as if she were in distress, her lips moving, but not making understandable sounds.

Then suddenly the words had come clearly, ringing out through the night, a plea in a child's voice. And then that name that had brought them all to their feet in shock, sent them running to Cora, fearing that they'd misheard…

Hoping desperately that they hadn't.

Now she'd confirmed it, and changed their world completely.

John sat back on his heels, making way for the brothers to crowd around her. As he'd done with the imposter weeks ago, he moved away and watched, eyes intent on her face.

His immediate reaction had been joy when she'd said Matthias' nickname. Joy and overwhelming relief. He'd been drawn to her from the beginning, and this must be why.

Then a small doubt had crept in. Maybe Henry and James were more cunning than he'd given them credit for. They might have had someone in the yard at the inn that day, when he was telling Matthias how he'd deduced that the first "Cesily" was no such person. They might have heard him pointing out that Cesily had used the wrong nickname for Matthias, the wrong names for the duke and duchess. "Mama" and "Papa" were indeed what most noble children called their parents. But Ceci Leigh had been no ordinary child. She'd had her own special names for those she loved.

As he watched, Christopher stood and pulled Cora up with him, leading her over to the family portrait. He unwrapped it and whispered, "Do you remember? Do you remember this day?"

Cora hesitated, then shook her head sadly.

Harry grabbed a lantern from one of the guards and brought it over to the wagon, holding it so the soft glow fell full on the painting, lighting up the happy family. Harry asked, voice trembling, "Do you remember Mama and Papa?"

John's eyes narrowed, waiting.

Cora took a small step forward, her shaking hand reaching out to lightly touch the face of the duchess.

"Mummy…" she murmured.

The brothers inhaled as one.

John cautioned himself that it might be a fluke. It was a common nickname, even if somewhat uncommon among the nobility.

Cora's hand moved to the duke's face. John held his breath and knew by their stillness that the brothers were doing the same. He'd never heard anyone but Ceci use *that* nickname.

She said, a sob catching her breath, *"Diddy."*

The brothers exhaled.

They'd found her.

John heard one of the duke's sons sob as they moved in to hug Cora. Harry's body shook and he murmured Ceci's name over and over. Tears were still pouring down Matthias' face, and Christopher had joined him in an unchecked release of pain.

John let his head drop. It was *finished.* Relief flooded him, making his knees weak for a moment.

Harry suddenly raised his head and stood back from the huddle around Cora. "I just realized…" He turned to his brothers, a grin lighting his face through the tears. "What does Father always say to Mother?"

Christopher and Matt broke into grins, then turned amazed eyes on the girl beside them, remembering their father's booming voice as he teased Lady Coraline.

The brothers said in unison: "Cora, I adore ya."

"Cora," Christopher breathed, reaching up with both hands to cup her face.

She stared at him, scared to believe, then finally whispered, "After my husband died…" Her voice trailed off for a moment. "I wanted a fresh start, and somehow that name came to me. It… soothed me." She shrugged, not sure how to explain it.

Christopher wanted so desperately to believe, but the woman who had impersonated Ceci weeks ago had left a strong impression. His hand went hesitantly to the kerchief Cora was still wearing. "You never take this off," he whispered, and gently tugged the end so it slid down…

… to reveal a distinct line of pale hair at her brow.

"Ceci," he whispered, tears starting to his eyes again as he brushed his thumb across the blonde roots. "It *is* you." He tried to smile, but it was a shaky effort.

His sister's face puckered and she began to cry deep sobbing breaths that shook her body.

The Locket

The next morning, John awoke and rose from his pallet to see the guards standing around waiting rather than packing up the camp for departure like they'd planned. He saw them casting glances at the wagon, and turned to see Cora… *Ceci* and the brothers, *her brothers,* seated on the ground, sound asleep as they leaned against one of the wheels, blankets packed well around them. Ceci sat in the middle, with Harry and Christopher huddled against her on either side. Ceci's head was on Harry's shoulder, and a peaceful smile showed through his wild beard as he slept.

Matthias was leaning against the side of the wheel by Christopher, sound asleep like the others. But in his lap, cuddled against his chest, her head barely visible above a muddle of blankets, was Mary.

John stood and stretched, smiling down at them, then said to his waiting section captain, "Let's plan to move out at noon. Get out the maps so we can plot the fastest course for home, and make sure it goes nowhere near King Uriah's castle."

"Yes, Your Highness," SC Arne said, a grin breaking across his face. "And may I offer my congratulations to you and the lords?

We overheard a little of what happened last night, but weren't sure if we'd understood."

"Thank you," John said, smiling contentedly. "Yes, this is the Lady Ceci. I'm sure we'll all hear her story when she wakes. Last night we were overcome with exhaustion and didn't do much talking."

"That's understandable, sire." Arne nodded, his face serious once more. "The strain the duke's sons have been under is immense, and you shouldered a lot of that burden yourself on this trip."

"True, but not nearly as immense as the one Ceci must have been under for the past seventeen years," John mused.

His curiosity wasn't much slaked when Ceci and her brothers finally awoke, since Ceci had again convinced herself she *wasn't* who they thought she was.

"But how could I possibly be your sister?" she asked. "I don't remember anything about running away or being kidnapped. I grew up with my parents, the tinkers. I *know* that. I remember *that*. So how could I possibly be your sister? *From a kingdom so far away?* It doesn't make sense."

Watching her as he ate his breakfast, John suddenly remembered something. Without saying a word, he put down his plate and walked over to kneel beside Ceci where she sat on a log with Mary on her lap.

John put his hand into his coat and pulled out the locket, dangling it in front of them.

With a soft cry, Mary reached out and took the pendant in her hand. She looked at it, then gasped and craned her head to look up at her mother. "Mummy, look!" she said. "It's just like the locket in the story!"

Ceci, eyes wide and face white, slowly reached down to take the locket from Mary. Her other hand crept up and, fingers trembling, she slid the front of the locket to the side and down.

Mary laughed in delight and looked up at Prince John. "It's the butterfly! Just like in the PJ story!"

John sucked his breath in, then asked quietly, "What do you mean, the 'PJ story'?"

"It's the story Mummy always tells about PJ! He was Cesily's best friend, and he gave her the secret locket!" Mary rattled off, taking the locket from her mother's hand and showing it to John. "See? The C stands for Cesily!"

"For *Ceci Leigh*, yes it does," John agreed, looking up at Ceci.

Her eyes were troubled and for several moments she couldn't speak. "But… I thought it was just a dream I used to have! The locket is real?" She looked down at it in wonder, then back up at Prince John. "But PJ gave it to Cesily… to Ceci Leigh," she corrected, then shook her head in confusion. "Why do *you* have it?"

"Because you, Ceci Leigh," he said, his mouth twisting sadly, "left it behind the day you disappeared. I brought it along to help you remember me." His smile grew warm, his eyes steady on hers.

Ceci's face was blank as she studied him, trying to figure out what he meant, why he was looking at her like that.

Then his face faded away, but his eyes remained, teasing her, laughing *with* her, not *at* her, and the soft, round face of young PJ, Cesily's best friend (*her* best friend?), appeared, his eyes laughing into hers.

"*You're* PJ," she whispered. "PJ stands for…"

"Prince John," he agreed. "Your brothers thought calling me that would take me down a peg or two, since it was hard to properly roughhouse with someone they had to call 'prince.'"

Ceci giggled as a tiny remnant of the old joy, carefree and effortless, welled up as she looked into those laughing eyes she'd loved so much.

He was PJ. *Prince John* was the boy who'd visited her in her dreams for so many years. It was the memory of *his* kind eyes and easy smile she'd clung to during the hard times.

Ceci couldn't wrap her mind around it. It was another stunner in a day (and a night) full of them.

John asked, "Would you like me to put the locket on you?"

Ceci shook her head. "No. No, I'd like to look at it some more," she said, feeling a bit shy. But looking at the locket made it all seem somehow real to her, as if a piece of her dream had solidified. If the locket was real, then the rest of it might be as well.

"Is your house made of stone?" she asked abruptly of the brothers.

They paused in eating their breakfast.

Harry swallowed and said, "Yes, it's made of local stone, beautiful pink quartzite."

"Does it sparkle in the sun, like it has tiny diamonds in it?"

Harry laughed. "Well, I never thought so, but you did always talk about the diamonds in the stone."

"I remember a big house that sparkled," she said. "And does it sit on a hill, with the village below it?"

They nodded, smiling.

"That's the house. That's the one I used to dream of." Her breath caught in her throat for a moment. "Mountains. Are there mountains around the house?"

Grins broke out on the brothers' faces.

Christopher confirmed, "Yes, beautiful mountains, with snow on the peaks no matter the time of year."

Ceci's nose prickled as the tears welled up. "Ma said I made it up," she whispered.

Mary turned to look up at her, confused.

"But I didn't," Ceci whispered to her, smiling through the tears. "It was all real." She suddenly hugged Mary. "And you have a grandmother and a grandfather!"

At her words, the brothers stared at each other, stricken. They'd been so focused on the miracle, on the end of the long search, that they'd forgotten even their parents.

Harry turned to John. "We have to let Mother and Father know we've found her!"

John cleared his throat, which had tightened as he listened to Ceci remembering, and said, "We need to get Ceci home as soon as possible, but we have to do it without alerting King Uriah before we can get back across the border. It will take us how many days to get to the border?" He turned to SC Arne.

Arne said, "Three days, sire, if you want to go north to Bagginsland, which is what I would recommend. It's only two days to go back to Reimsland…"

"But King Albert of Reimsland is a closer ally to King Uriah than he is to my father, so he might try to stop us," John finished.

"Yes, sire."

John turned to the brothers. "We should make for the Bagginsland border as quickly and quietly as possible, and send a pigeon to the duke from there. A pigeon could fall into the wrong hands, and we shouldn't do anything to alert King Uriah that we've found Ceci. In fact, I think we should send a few guards on to the village we had hoped to arrive at yesterday, with word to expect us in a few days. That way, if King Uriah is keeping watch on us, he'll be looking south while we're traveling north."

North. Ceci's heart leapt in her chest and she gave Mary another joyful squeeze. They were finally going north!

SC Arne said hesitantly, "There's one problem, though. We can't make haste with the supply wagons."

All eyes turned to Ceci. Her heart dropped into her stomach.

"Ceci," Prince John said.

She looked at him, fear on her face.

"It's time to get over your fear of horses."

Ceci's head began to shake, her lips quivering.

"You must, Ceci Leigh," he said, quietly but firmly. He held her gaze, the moments stretching out. "Your life, *Mary's life,* depends on it."

Ceci's eyes slid down to her daughter, who was watching her with wide eyes. She looked back up at Prince John and, slowly, she nodded.

Northward!

Prince John's stallion was the largest, so it was decided that Ceci would ride with him while Mary rode with Matt.

None of them really wanted to pack up and get back on the road. The initial shock of finding Ceci had worn off and the brothers were anxious to compare notes with her about the day she'd disappeared.

Ceci wasn't as anxious to talk about it as they were, though, since she was still having a hard time accepting the truth. So when John said, "We'll have to save the talking for tonight. We need to make the best time we can while it's daylight," she was relieved.

She didn't feel nearly as happy when it came time to mount the horse, though.

They'd decided to disguise themselves as much as possible for the race to the border. John put away his small crown, and he and the brothers donned their least elegant pieces of clothing and took some time to rub dirt into them.

Harry chuckled as he used his knife to cut the wide velvet hem off his cloak. "Mother will have a fit when she sees what we've done to our clothes."

Christopher shook his head. "No, she won't even notice, or if she does, she certainly won't care. She'll consider anything worth bringing Ceci home." He and the brothers turned to smile at their sister.

John said, "I think we'd better go back to calling you Cora until we reach the border."

She nodded, feeling slightly relieved. She wasn't quite ready to be fully Ceci.

Matthias asked curiously, "Why were you calling yourself Cora? You grew up as Cesily, right?"

Ceci nodded. "I changed it after my husband died. I changed Mary's name, too. My husband named her Martha, but I never liked that name. It seemed like a good time for a fresh start for both of us." She wrinkled her nose, trying to smile and hoping they wouldn't ask her anything else.

John and the brothers glanced at each other, but dropped the subject.

They dressed Ceci as a boy, stuffing her hair under one of Christopher's caps and giving her a pair of his pants. The waist was too big, but they solved that with a bit of rope. The pants were much too long, so Harry got out his knife again with a grin and cut seven inches off the bottom. "Well, the rough edges certainly lend them more of a peasant appearance," he joked, rubbing some dirt into the fine tweed and scuffing it briskly against a rough rock to make it appear old and worn.

The long pants came all the way down over Ceci's shoes, so the feminine cut of the boots wasn't visible, and her womanly shape was hidden under the bulk of a small blanket they'd thrown over her shoulders.

John mounted his stallion, which was tossing its head in annoyance at the mud that had been rubbed into its coat and shining hooves. He scooted back on the roomy saddle to make space for Ceci to sit in front of him. "You'll have to ride astride, like you used to when you were little," he reminded her, a faint twinkle in his eye.

Ceci, shaking all over, swallowed hard. Fortunately, she remembered the dreams where she'd been riding in front of PJ, his arms caging her in safety, so she took a deep breath and focused on how safe she'd felt in the dreams. She stepped onto the mounting block and John reached down to pull her up on the saddle, where he directed her to slide her right leg over to the other side. Now both her legs were resting alongside his, his chest warm against her back.

Ceci felt weird flutterings in her stomach and wondered if she was about to be sick. She didn't feel nervous anymore, though. As soon as John's arms, *PJ's* arms, had closed around her, her heart had calmed and she'd breathed easier.

The flutterings continued, though, so maybe she wasn't as calm as she'd thought. Or maybe it was just the strangeness of having a man's arms around her. She did feel very safe, though, and as long as she reminded herself that it was PJ holding her, not some prince she barely knew, she felt better.

A few more minutes, and they were off.

After they'd been on the road for an hour, John noticed that Ceci was weighing heavy in his arms, and glanced down to see that her head had fallen to the side. She was sound asleep.

He grinned to himself. No wonder. Last night had been emotional for all of them, and it was the first time Ceci and the brothers had released all the tension that had built up over the seventeen years she'd been gone. Her body was making up for all the nights she'd rested uneasily away from her family.

John breathed in deeply, feeling Ceci in his arms as she had been all those years ago on their rides, and breathed out slowly, allowing himself to focus on the triumphant end of their search. No matter what happened now, they'd found her. One part of the mystery was solved: she *had* lived. And, God willing, tonight they would be able to piece it all together.

As they rode, the horses alternately galloping and trotting so as not to wear them out, the brothers kept glancing over at Ceci. John understood their need, the compulsion to make sure she was still there, that she was real. From where he sat, he could see the line of blonde hair at the base of her neck, right where he'd seen the edge of the wig on the imposter, but the roots of the real Ceci's hair were the pale milk color of Christopher's, rather than the golden blonde of the imposter's wig.

John began to wonder what he would do with himself now that their quest was over. He would return to his father's castle, of course, and take over his duties as prince. But then what? It was high time for him to find a wife, but he hadn't had much luck with that. It was his unsuccessful attempt to get Princess Aurora to marry him that had led him to this quest in the first place.

John thought about Aurora. When she was younger, in her teens, she'd always been a bit too exuberant for him. She'd been laughing and joyful, like Ceci, but the teenage Princess Aurora was a little *too* full of life for him. Being around her wore him out.

That explained why he hadn't started falling in love with Aurora until she was out of her teens, he supposed, when she'd become much quieter, more solemn. But he wouldn't have been happy with that sad, solemn version of Aurora, either. He did dearly love to laugh, and needed someone to laugh with him.

He glanced down at Ceci. He'd barely seen her laugh, either, since they'd met her at Heighlawn. She was a solemn little thing, very much like Aurora, although he saw traces of the old Ceci when she was with Mary. Then, her face lit up and joy filled her eyes, a laugh even breaking out of that solemn mouth at times.

Maybe… maybe Ceci was sad, too, like Aurora. Maybe it was because she'd lost her family so long ago, lost her identity. But it seemed like it might go deeper. She'd mentioned her marriage a few times, as though it hadn't been happy. She'd even said she never wanted to get married again.

That thought made him sad. Part of the reason he'd wanted so much to bring Ceci home was because he wanted her to have the good life she should've had, with a husband and children if she wanted them, and valuable work in her father's village. King Rudolph valued the noble women of his kingdom as much as he valued the men, and expected them to do their part by taking leadership roles in their villages.

Ceci would most likely oversee the work of the women in her father's village if she stuck to her desire never to marry again. John knew the duke and duchess would be thrilled to have Ceci and Mary live with them for the rest of their lives, but John had hoped Ceci would go on to have a big, happy family of her own.

She wasn't the girl he'd grown up with. She had changed drastically and it would take her a while to become comfortable with her family again.

But she had all the time in the world, as much time as she needed.

John shifted her slightly in his arms and rode on.

After supper on the trail that night, the guards washed the dishes while John and the duke's family gathered around the fire, the men's eyes on the woman who sat with a child on her lap.

Ceci glanced around and gave a little laugh. "I think you're all expecting me to solve the mystery of what happened that night, but I really don't remember anything."

Harry said, "Do you remember David Lane, the undergardener you used to follow around?"

Ceci shook her head slowly. *David.* There was something there… but the thought skittered away as she tried to catch it.

Harry continued, "We're pretty sure you left willingly in his wagon. There was a boy at the first inn David stopped at that night who said he saw you peeking out from under the tarp that covered the back of the wagon. So we thought you probably hid in David's wagon like you used to do with Prince John."

Ceci frowned, confused.

Smiling, John explained, "You always wanted to come home with me, so you would hide somewhere in my carriage. There were a couple of times we drove right out the gates with you hidden in the struts under the carriage or curled into a ball under the luggage on the back. We only realized what had happened when a servant came running after the carriage, yelling for us to stop because Miss Ceci was inside."

Harry snorted. "What about the time she was in the trunk?"

John and Matthias gave a shout of laughter and John turned to Ceci and explained, "You'd snuck into my room while the servants were packing and pulled enough clothes out of one of the trunks so you could fit inside. After our carriage left, one of the maids found all the clothes bundled up under one of the beds and realized what had happened."

Ceci giggled.

Mary turned to look up at her. "Are they talking about you, Mummy?" she wondered.

"They're talking about Cesily, love. She was very naughty sometimes. You should never be that naughty," she admonished the girl, who nodded solemnly and turned back to face the fire.

The men were grinning at her. John's grin slowly faded, though, and he took up the story. "David was headed home to see his family that day, so the duke's men searched along the road to his village in Reimsland for years, never finding any trace of you. But after that boy at the inn told us you were hidden under the tarp, we realized David probably didn't know you were even in the wagon, and since he'd never made it to the next inn, something must have happened before he got there."

Ceci narrowed her eyes, but she had no memory of any of that.

John said, "Let's try this a different way. You say you don't remember that night, and that your past life only came to you in dreams. Tell us what your first memory is of your life with the tinkers."

"Ma telling me to hide," Ceci said immediately.

"Telling you to hide?" Matthias asked. "Why?"

Ceci's eyes looked through him, focusing on the past. "Because the bad men were looking for me," she said, her voice soft and a little bit higher than usual, like a child's.

John and the brothers frowned and glanced at each other. Christopher asked, "And where did you hide?"

"There was a secret compartment in the wagon behind the cupboard where Ma kept the dishes. It was just barely big enough for me to fit into."

"How many times did you hide in there?" Harry asked.

"Oh, several times that I remember. Then, Ma began dyeing my hair, and I didn't have to hide anymore. I never met people before she dyed my hair. I had to either stay hidden in the compartment, or stay in the back of the wagon with the curtains drawn."

"And did you ever peek out?" John asked, thinking of Agatha.

Ceci shrugged. "I don't remember." She paused, her mouth slightly open. "No, that's not true. If I heard children outside, I would pull the curtain back a little bit to see them."

John nodded, satisfied. "Agatha saw you one of those times. She was the maid who told us about the little blonde girl in the back of the tinker's wagon, the one she saw about a year before the tinker's daughter Cesily appeared."

Matthias said, "Alright, what we know is that the woman that Cesily called 'Ma' knew that some bad men were after her, and that they were specifically looking for a little girl with blonde hair. I'm surprised she didn't change your name to something less similar to your real name, though."

Ceci smiled. "I remember her calling me other names, but I wouldn't answer to anything else. I guess I was determined to hold onto my name because I'd lost everything else."

Christopher mused, "So you were trained to think that bad men were looking for you because of your blonde hair…"

Ceci nodded. "That's why I left Glastonheight Castle, actually. Lady Bucksbury did want me to marry one of her farmers, but I had decided to stay as long as I could to make more money… but then I saw the family portrait the day we arrived at Glastonheight, and one of the maids told us that there were men at the castle who were looking for the little blonde girl in the painting."

The prince and brothers gasped. "You ran because of us!" Matthias groaned.

Ceci nodded ruefully. "I thought you were the bad men."

John said quietly, "That's why you looked so scared when Henry brought you to us and you realized we were the men from Glastonheight."

She nodded.

John laughed suddenly. "So Henry and James were being truthful about seeing your blonde hair?"

Ceci nodded, a flush starting to rise up her neck.

"And you lied to us," John said, his tone a little more serious.

Ceci looked down at Mary, then took a deep breath and nodded. "I did. I'm sorry about that, but I was scared. I still thought you were the bad men."

John shrugged. "I completely understand. I would've done the same thing. You weren't only protecting yourself; you were protecting your child." He looked at them for a moment, then his mouth quirked. "But now I have to revise my opinion of Henry. He doesn't deserve all the mean thoughts I had about him, at least not that second time. And, actually…" the smile dropped from his face. "If Henry hadn't brought you to us that day, we probably never would've found you. You were actively hiding from us, and had changed your name, so the people we had talked to in Yaegertown would have no idea you were the girl we were looking for. We actually owe a debt to Henry."

That didn't sit well with John, so he grinned when Harry reminded him, "I'm pretty sure any debt we owe is canceled out by the debt Henry owes us for not having him thrown in jail the first time!"

"Very true," said the prince, shaking his head in remembered annoyance.

Christopher turned back to Ceci. "So you grew up living the life of a tinker? How did you meet your husband?"

Ceci shook her head and said with a quick smile, "Enough about me. Tell me about our parents. Mummy and Diddy," she said, a laugh coming into her voice.

Mary laughed, too, and turned to look at her. "Diddy? That's a funny name!"

Harry said, affection in his voice, "It is a funny name, but little Ceci Leigh couldn't say 'Daddy' properly, so it came out 'Diddy.'"

Christopher interposed, "I think she just *liked* saying it that way! She was always calling us silly nicknames."

Ceci laughed, their affection warming her.

Matthias leaned toward her, elbows on his knees, his eyes serious. "You did always call us silly names. It's one of the things that annoyed me, that made me avoid you." His mouth twisted. "I'm so sorry, Ceci, *so sorry* that I wasn't a good brother to you."

Ceci was embarrassed that he thought he needed to apologize to her. "Don't worry about it. Brothers and sisters fight sometimes; it's normal."

"No, Ceci," he said, his eyes intent on hers. "It was because *we* wouldn't play with you that you clung to other people, like Prince John and David Lane. It was our fault that you always wanted to go home with John instead of staying with us." His voice broke. "It was our fault that you climbed into David's wagon."

Ceci stared at him as her hand stroked Mary's hair. She hated the pain in his eyes.

But he was right.

Ceci couldn't remember that fateful night, and couldn't remember much of her old life, but she'd felt the pain of Cesily in those dreams when the brothers ran off and left her. The pain of a little girl wanting to be loved.

She stared at the brothers as they stared back, the words they all needed to say stuck in their throats.

Then Matthias stood up and walked over to her, kneeling down on one knee. "Lady Ceci, I pledge to you my fealty and brotherly love for the rest of my life. I swear to make up for my neglect years ago, and fill your heart to overflowing with love." He kissed her hand.

Harry leapt from his seat and knelt before Ceci. "And I, too, Lady Ceci."

Christopher knelt before her in turn. "And I, Lady Ceci. You have my heart and love, as long as I live."

Tears welled up in Ceci's eyes and she lifted her arms, encircling the necks of her brothers as they leaned in, their tears mingling with hers.

John pulled his handkerchief from his pocket and wiped his own cheeks, giving a reassuring smile to Mary, who was looking a little squashed on Ceci's lap as she peered at him from under Matthias' arm.

Fleeing from Uriah

Prince John and Section Captain Arne had earlier worked out a list of villages on their route north, so that the guards they sent off to lay the false trail could inform them via pigeon if anything went awry.

John had cause to be grateful for Arne's foresight when his guards returned from one of the villages on the second day with a pigeon message tube.

John broke the seal and unrolled the small paper Arne presented to him, reading the coded message in a low voice. "The village we were supposed to arrive at yesterday is overrun with the king's men. Uriah sent them to escort us for the remainder of the search." He looked up with narrowed eyes. "He must have decided we wouldn't bring Ceci back to him. What do you bet his men were watching the pigeons being sent out, and have already alerted their men in this area to search for us?"

"Wouldn't take that bet if my life depended on it," Arne answered. "They're probably watching us right now."

"Right," John said, nodding. He gave a hand signal to Arne, who turned and repeated it to his men.

John turned to Ceci, who was looking at him with wide eyes. Her mouth barely moved as she spoke, fear locking her muscles. "They're going to try to stop us?"

He smiled. "Probably. But we'll make it." His voice was full of confidence.

She nodded, but her throat was too tight to speak. She'd thought the long nightmare was at an end, so this new fear was a double blow. She concentrated on breathing deeply, but was distracted by the feel of strong arms encircling her. She glanced around and saw that Harry was standing behind her. She smiled wanly and leaned against him.

"Don't worry, love," he whispered, kissing her hair. "They won't take you again."

Ceci firmed her lips and nodded, breathing out heavily. She wasn't alone anymore. She and Mary had family now, men who would fight for her when she felt overwhelmed. Ceci didn't want to rely on anyone, especially a man…

But it felt so good to have people in her life she could trust, people who would help when she was worn out and scared. Everyone needed someone, and now, after years of having no one, she and Mary had *several* someones.

Over the next half-hour, the guards moved around the clearing where they had stopped, their movements casual and apparently focused on setting up camp for the night. Ceci was a bit nervous, though, because it felt like the guards were moving away from the camp area, leaving them unprotected.

John walked over and sat down beside where she and Mary were huddled. Mary didn't know what was going on, but she'd picked up on Ceci's tension and was clinging to her mother.

John said quietly, "My men are spreading out into the woods to create a perimeter. They'll make sure none of the king's men are close enough to see when we leave and which way we're headed. They probably know we're headed north, but Arne knows a slightly longer route that we can take to avoid the main road, and if we can get a headstart we should be able to avoid pursuit. We'll let the horses rest here until the wee hours of the night, and then make a run for it.

I know you're sore from riding so far, but can you get back on a horse in a few hours?"

Cora hesitated. Sore didn't begin to touch the way she felt.

Before she could come up with an answer that was honest but didn't sound weak, John motioned to SC Arne. "Do we have anything we can use to pad my saddle?"

"I'll find something, Your Highness," he replied, striding off.

"I'm sorry," Ceci began.

"No, no," John interrupted. "Don't apologize. It's easily remedied. I'm just sorry I didn't think of it earlier." Truth was, he'd been too distracted by her closeness, the fragrance of her hair, and hadn't been thinking straight. Usually he was able to focus fully on any situation, but Ceci was an unexpected distraction.

John was firmly keeping his mind away from why that might be. His goal was to get her home, and his emotions had no place in that plan. Of course his feelings would be in an uproar now that they'd finally found her. That's all it was.

"You and Mary had better try to get some sleep," John said, smiling at them before turning away to see to his men.

Ceci kept her eyes firmly shut, but she was sure she didn't sleep a wink that night. It was a relief when she felt someone shaking her shoulder and heard the whisper, "It's time."

Mary came awake instantly, already prepped by Ceci to expect a nighttime ride during which she would need to be a Quiet Little Mouse. Ceci and Mary gathered their things together and slipped away into the woods, where they found Prince John and the brothers already mounted on their horses. One of the guards handed Mary up to Matt, and another guard helped Ceci mount John's stallion, where she sank into the padding he'd devised for her comfort.

"Are you ready?" he breathed in her ear.

His soft voice so close raised goosebumps on her arms, and Ceci felt a tremor go through her. Unable to speak, she just nodded.

And they were off.

They had been riding for hours and the sun was high in the sky. They'd stopped twice to water the horses and stretch their legs, taking the time to grab some food and water as well, but otherwise they'd kept moving. The new padding on John's saddle had helped somewhat, but Ceci was still determined she would never get on another horse as long as she lived, *if* she survived *this* trip.

Prince John and SC Arne were talking in low voices on the edge of the group, looking over an unrolled map of the area. Ceci heard the section captain say, "We're not far from the border. We'll have to cut back to the main road now so we can make for the Bagginsland border gate."

John nodded and said, "I want all the guards on me and Matthias. All that matters is that we get Lady Ceci and Mary across that border. If we should be attacked, I want your full focus on them. Don't worry about the duke's sons or even about me. I'm commanding you to get Lady Ceci and her daughter to Bagginsland. Understood?"

The section captain nodded, his eyes troubled. Abandoning the prince in an attack went against everything he'd been trained to do, but he couldn't disobey a direct command.

Ceci's mouth was dry. She was just as determined as the prince was to get Mary to safety, no matter what happened to herself.

When John came to her, she asked, "How dangerous is it?"

He hesitated, then admitted, "Pretty dangerous. They'll have discovered by now that we left the campsite under cover of night. I'm sure King Uriah will be pulling out everything he's got to stop us."

Cora stared at him. "Are you risking war to get me home?" she asked, frowning.

John was silent a moment, then said, "Possibly. King Uriah is unpredictable. But we might never get you home if he got you inside his castle. I have no doubt that my father would support this plan."

John was worried about the consequences of their actions, but he couldn't see another way. Uriah was too much of an unknown factor to be able to predict how he'd take their duplicity.

John said, "When we're safely home, we'll send a message to Uriah that we feared the men who had kidnapped you were tracking us. I'll say we wanted to avoid an open confrontation with any of Uriah's citizens, and that's why we fled for the border."

Cora nodded, but she was still afraid.

When they began to hear the noise from wagons on the main road over the sound of their horses, SC Arne, who was at the front of the group, motioned one of the guards forward to reconnoiter.

The guard returned in a moment, looking uneasy. He shook his head.

The section captain rode back to Prince John. "No sign of the king's men."

"Which means they're hiding somewhere nearby," John said grimly.

Arne nodded.

"Alright. It's only a mile to the border. We can make it," John said, straightening in his saddle, his face tense.

Arne signaled to his men. The majority of the guards got in front of the section captain where he sat on his horse beside Prince John and Ceci. Matthias, with Mary huddled inside his arms, positioned his horse just behind them. Harry and Christopher rode up behind Matthias, and the rest of the guards backed them. Arne surveyed the group, then signaled to the guards in front.

"Hold on," John breathed in Ceci's ear, his grip tightening on the reins.

Ceci tensed.

The three front guards spurred their horses and burst from the woods, riding south on the main road to block it from pursuers. The other guards in front of Arne and Prince John broke cover to ride full speed north, spreading out to form a tight circle around the prince and Matthias' horses as they burst in turn from the woods.

As they pounded down the dirt road, Ceci's eyes darted from side to side. Nothing. No movement of any kind.

Then she felt John tense behind her. He leaned forward, pressing her toward the horse's neck, and his legs tightened, urging the horse forward.

Ceci had thought they were going as fast as they possibly could, but the horse stretched its neck out into a smooth gallop that made her breathless, the wind rushing past too fast for her gasping mouth to take it in.

And then she saw what John had already spotted.

Riders in common clothing were pouring from the trees ahead of them, aiming to cut them off before the border gate.

"C'mon, c'mon, only half a mile," John whispered to the horse, his breath hot on Ceci's cheek before it was snatched away by the wind.

All of Ceci's attention was on King Uriah's men ahead of her, whose swords were now ringing against those of the front guards, but part of her mind also noticed the tired horse laboring beneath her. She unconsciously tightened all her muscles, trying to make herself lighter.

And then they were in the midst of the fight, guards clashing with King Uriah's men on either side. In front of them, SC Arne never slowed his horse, never moved his head to look at his men fighting courageously, never took his focus off the goal ahead.

As the swords clanged around her, Ceci flinched. The noise, the shouts, the fury in the air… it was overwhelming. Her heart was pounding, trying to escape its cage. Desperate, she closed her eyes.

The swords rang out and Prince John whispered, "Don't worry, Ceci. It'll be alright," and for a moment, she was transported to a dark night, stars glittering overhead as another man's voice, strained with fear, said, "Don't worry, Miss Ceci. It'll be alright."

Shivers wracked Ceci and sweat broke out all over her. For a moment, she thought she might be sick, but as she was fighting the nausea, she felt arms tighten around her and she opened her eyes…

And the night sky disappeared. She was on the back of Prince John's galloping horse, the sun hot on her head as they raced through the battle. Her heart still pounded, but the nausea began to recede as her attention was fully captured by the present.

Her eyes darted over the fighting men on either side as they fled toward the gate. The fierce conflict made the men sway toward Prince John's horse, but his guards held the battle, and John, like his section captain, never moved his face from its position next to her cheek. He only gripped her tighter between his arms, his elbows digging into her sides.

Ceci desperately wanted to twist in the saddle to make sure Mary was safe behind them, but all she could do was pray the most desperate prayer she'd ever summoned.

Ahead of her, the border gate with Bagginsland loomed. Set into a narrow opening of the rock cliff that formed the border between the kingdoms, the doors were wide, thick, and firmly closed.

In front of them, SC Arne had burst from the main group of fighting men. A few of King Uriah's men peeled off from the edges of the battle and set off after him. Arne switched both reins to one hand and reached into a pocket of his saddle, his hand emerging with a short stick. He held it up in the air and the Vallenland flag unfurled.

"Open the gate! Open the gate for Prince John of Vallenland!" he cried, and the gates cracked open.

On a walkway above the gates, the bows of archers appeared, aiming down at the approaching horses as the gates began to swing open. The section captain peeled off, leaving the gate clear for Prince John to race through while Arne turned to engage Uriah's men, who had almost caught up to them.

Ceci saw Arne swing his sword once, twice, and then her view was cut off by the border gate.

A final ring of the swords, and they were through the gate, sounds of the battle muffled by the rocks that now surrounded them.

John's horse galloped forward a few hundred yards before he managed to pull it to a halt. He turned the horse and Ceci could see her brothers riding through the gate toward them.

A cry of relief broke from Ceci, and she pushed against John's arms, desperate to get down. He let her go, and she slid off the saddle and rushed to Mary.

Holding the girl in her arms, she looked back at John and whispered, "Thank you."

Ceci Remembers

It was late in the day when they escaped King Uriah's men, and they were exhausted from riding through the night and day. The horses were completely blown as well, so John gave the order to make camp there at the Bagginsland gate.

Ceci, looking around at the narrow canyon where they stood, wondered how in the world they would all fit and where the horses could be watered, but then she saw SC Arne and the guards making their way toward a narrow cleft in the rock. Following the rest of the group, Mary's hand safe in hers, she hesitantly walked through a fissure that was barely wide enough for a wagon, followed the trail around a couple of curves in the canyon, and came out in a wide, grassy spot.

Mary cried aloud, for there was a small waterfall flowing down the face of the canyon on the other side of the open area. Matthias turned around from the horse he was leading in front of them. "Want to see it up close, little one?" he asked.

Mary looked up at her mother, who nodded, and Mary took off running. Matt caught her and swept her up in his arms to perch on his shoulder.

Ceci watched them with a smile for a moment, then looked around and found John and her other brothers talking to the Bagginsland guards. As she approached, she heard the Bagginsland section captain say, "Aye, we've been having a few minor problems here, but that's normal. We've certainly seen nothing lately like what we saw today. Hard to believe Uriah would order an attack on you, no matter the provocation. Those riders weren't wearing guard uniforms, but there's no doubt they were the king's men. Only his soldiers have such well-fed horses."

John noticed Ceci standing there and smiled. "Are you alright? That was a pretty exciting ride."

She nodded briefly, then glanced around at her brothers. "I know what happened the night I disappeared."

Ceci, her brothers and the prince were sitting around the table in the Bagginsland section captain's office. Mary was being watched over by John's guards.

"So you remembered?" Harry prompted.

Ceci nodded. "Yes, when we were riding for the gate. You," she looked at John, "whispered in my ear that everything would be alright, and all of a sudden I remembered David saying the same thing that night." She took a deep breath. "I *did* hide in the back of his wagon, and we *were* attacked."

The abrupt halt of the wagon woke young Ceci with a start.

She could hear David talking to someone, and the fear in his voice made her heart start pounding.

"Well, let's just see if you're being honest with us, good sir," a sneering voice said right above her, and suddenly the tarp was pulled up, revealing Ceci huddled against David's blue trunk. She blinked, holding up her hand to block the light from the lantern.

"Oh, ho! And what do we have here? You didn't mention your little girl was in the back, boyo!"

David said, "What?" and his head appeared over the man's shoulder. "Ceci!" he exclaimed. "What are you doing here?"

Ceci's lip trembled. She didn't like the man who stood leering at her in front of David. One of his front teeth was missing, and the others looked none too clean. Nanny had always told Ceci that only bad children had dirty teeth, so this must be a bad man.

The sneering man's eyes ran over everything in the back of the wagon and settled on Ceci again. He slid his eyes to David. "Bet you love your little girl, don't you, boyo?"

"She's not mine!" David said, shaking his head. "She's the duke's daughter! I don't know how she got into the wagon."

"Duke? What duke?" the man sneered.

"Lord Wallingford," David replied. "His castle is about ten miles back. They're probably already looking for Lady Ceci, so you'd be smart to leave us in peace."

The man motioned and another man stepped up to the wagon. The first man pointed at Ceci. "Here now, see this little one? Look like a duke's daughter to you?"

The other man grabbed the lantern from his hand and leaned in to peer at Ceci, who stared up at him in fright. He took hold of her arm and yanked her forward, making her bang her knee painfully in the process. She cried out.

"Nah, that ain't no little duchess! Them's old clothes she's wearing. She ain't no noble." He scowled at David.

"That's what I thought!" the sneering man sneered. "Well, this is your lucky day, boyo! Strike you a good bargain, I will! We'll take your horse, wagon, and all assorted items within, including the little duchess," he bowed grandly to Ceci, making his companion laugh, "and leave you with your life. Can't say fairer than that, now can you?"

Ceci's eyes flew to David, who was staring at her with horror on his face.

He said, panic in his voice, "I swear, I'm telling the truth! Please, I beg of you, take everything, but leave her with me! If you take her, you'll have the entire kingdom hunting you anyway, so just leave her with me!"

The men laughed.

"I'd almost believe that, if'n I were the kind of man who trusted people!" the sneering man cackled. "But sadly for you," he thrust his chin belligerently forward, "*I ain't!*" He started to reach for Ceci.

David yelled, "Ceci, run!" and threw himself at the sneering man.

Ceci was so startled that she didn't move for a minute, then she was over the side of the wagon and flying down the dark road, sobbing. She heard horrible sounds behind her, thuds and cries of pain, and then suddenly a long arm snaked around her and a voice whispered, "Gotcha!"

The man carried Ceci back to the wagon, where David lay in the dirt. "Wanna say goodbye to your pa, little girl?" he growled and dumped her on the ground.

Ceci crouched beside David, tears pouring down her face, and touched him fearfully. Blood covered his face and she couldn't tell if he was breathing.

As she crouched over him, calling his name softly, David managed to crack open one eye and whisper, his voice so faint she could barely hear it, "Don't worry, Miss Ceci. It'll be alright." His eye closed, head dropping to the side.

"Yep, he's done for. You shouldn't have knifed him, fool. We could've made him drive the wagon until we got to the Reimsland border." As he spoke, the sneering man was tying a rope round Ceci's hands and feet. "Now, trussed up just like a Christmas goose, yeh are! Lay there quiet now, little goose, or we might have to roast yeh!" He and the other man laughed, and he yanked the tarp down over Ceci.

"The next time they pulled the tarp off, it was daylight. They were talking about having crossed the border, but I had no idea where we were. I had no concept of distance or geography. I just knew we drove for what seemed like days."

Harry shook his head, his eyes remorseful. "So David was killed. Poor guy; he must've been terrified for you, and all these years I've blamed him."

Ceci felt tears welling up. She'd completely forgotten about David until Prince John had whispered those words in her ear. She supposed she'd blocked all memory of him, even from her dreams, because her last moments with him were so horrible.

And it was her fault he'd been killed.

"How did you manage to escape, Ceci?" asked Christopher.

She sighed. She remembered everything now. "Well, I didn't escape until after they sold me."

His eyebrows slammed together. "What?"

"They sold me along with some other kids at an auction, and the man who bought us was taking us home in a cart, but the cart overturned in a creek. While all the kids were screaming that they were drowning. I ducked down and floated away from the cart until it was out of sight, then I managed to grab hold of a rock on the side of the ditch and pull myself out, and ran off into the woods. That's where I met the tinkers." She looked around at her brothers, who were staring at her with wide eyes.

Matt shook his head as if in a daze. "Ceci… all these years, I've imagined all kinds of scenarios about your disappearance, but I have to admit I never imagined this!" What his baby sister had gone through! Tears started to his eyes, and he hung his head in shame, the burden of his guilt overwhelming him.

Harry reached out and patted him on the shoulder in commiseration, then put his arm around Ceci and pulled her in for a hug. "We thought you were too little for our adventures. Little did we know you were tougher than all of us put together," he said, his voice gruff.

Ceci felt tears start to her eyes. The only thing she'd wanted as a child was their respect. Now she had it.

"Anyway," she continued after a moment, "I ran off into the woods, and found the tinker's wagon in a clearing. They were just starting supper over a fire, and I didn't even hesitate, just ran right up to the fire. I was that cold."

Missus Robertson looked up as a child burst from the woods and ran over to their fire. Her mouth fell open as she surveyed the girl.

Wide eyes looked up from a tangle of white hair, making the child look like a dandelion gone to seed. The brown eyes were shadowed, dark circles highlighting the fear in them. She was filthy, covered in dirt and scratches, like she'd rolled in a mud pit and then run through the woods with no regard for the branches in her way.

The woman's stare traveled down the girl's clothing. A long green dress made of good material, but old and shabby. Probably a hand-me-down from a noble to a servant. Her shoes were good quality, but again old and worn.

Missus Robertson narrowed her eyes, scenting trouble. "And who might you be, eh?" she bit out, her head thrust forward belligerently. Tinkers were often accused of thievery, since they moved on from place to place, never staying anywhere long. Anything that went missing was blamed on them, so Missus Robertson didn't want anything to do with a child who looked like she came from one of the noble estates, even if she was one of the miserable children conscripted into service there.

"Ceci Leigh," Ceci breathed, dropping a curtsy.

Missus Robertson's mouth quirked in a sour smile. "Fancy manners for a dirty urchin!" she pronounced.

Ceci scowled. "I'm the daughter of the Duke of Wallingford!"

"Oh, the Duke of Wallingford?" Missus Robertson raised her eyebrows, looking impressed, then scowled ferociously. "*Never heard of him!* Now, go on about you! We don't want no trouble here, and that's one thing you do reek of! Along with mud!" She sniffed, turning away.

"The Robertsons weren't too pleased when I showed up, but I wouldn't leave. I noticed the woman had some problem with her back that made it hard for her to bend over, so I started picking up the things she couldn't reach while she was cooking, trying to make her like me, and managed to convince Ma that I could be a big help to her with cooking and cleaning," Ceci explained.

Harry was scowling. "So they just wanted to use you, too!"

Ceci was startled, then realized that her brothers, for all their experience and knowledge, didn't understand how the world worked for regular people. She said gently, "They were poor, Harry, and I wasn't their child. Even their own child would've been expected to help take care of the family. Only noble children can afford to play all day."

Harry hmphed a bit, but he recognized the validity of what she said. It irked him to think of his sister in such a situation, but at least the tinkers had fed and clothed her and kept her safe.

"Over the next few days, Ma slowly got the story out of me about the men who'd kidnapped me. Like them, she never believed I was the daughter of a duke, but at least she had no desire to turn me back over to them. She and Pa cleaned out that hidden cupboard for me to hide in, but I outgrew it pretty fast and that's when she came up with the idea to dye my hair.

"I begged them to take me home, but it wasn't to their benefit to let me go, of course, since they didn't believe me when I said they'd be rewarded for doing so. They just thought they'd lose a good helper. So they kept putting me off, saying they'd take me home later, and Ma told me to stop talking about home… and I guess I finally forgot." Ceci shrugged.

She thought of something else. "Oh! And I think it's possible that Henry and James, the men who took me to Heighlawn, were the same men who killed David and kidnapped me all those years ago! When I first met them in Yaegertown, I disliked them intensely and when I had that flashback to the men killing David, I had that same feeling in my stomach. I know one of the men was missing some teeth, just like Henry. Do you think it could've been the same men all those years ago?"

John and her brothers looked at each other.

John said, "That seems quite a coincidence, but I've always found that my gut reactions are usually accurate. We do know that robbers from Arlesland were operating in Vallenland around the time you disappeared, and the trail of things from David's wagon is what led us to Arlesland, so we're sure it was Arleslanders who attacked you. So, yes, it's possible the same men who kidnapped you were ultimately the ones who delivered you back to us."

"Poetic justice," Matt breathed, and the rest of them gave rueful laughs.

Bagginsland

They rested well that night, and set off in the morning for the Bagginsland king's southern estate.

They rode through the gate into King Alexander's castle as the late afternoon sun was setting. The golden light still touched the turrets of the castle, but the lower levels were in shadow. Lanterns had been lit in the windows and outside the doors, and Ceci thought she'd never seen a more cheerful sight.

Something that made the sight even more wonderful was that Ceci knew that she wouldn't be unpacking boxes long into the night, or standing on her feet for hours serving guests at a welcome banquet. From now on, she'd be one of the pampered guests.

The thought made her feel a bit queasy as she remembered the harsh treatment she'd suffered at the hands of guests in the past, and she resolved to do her best to show King Alexander's servants how much she appreciated their hard work.

The king's sons were waiting to greet them. The oldest one came to assist Ceci from the horse, while his brother helped Mary.

As he lifted Mary from the horse, the younger prince said, "Well, hello, young lady! I'm Prince Aaron. And what is your name?"

"Mary," she said, looking up at him and then darting a glance at her mother for reassurance. Ceci smiled and nodded, then curtsied to both princes, Mary imitating her a little awkwardly.

"What a big girl you are!" Prince Aaron said admiringly. "Why, you must be… eighteen years old?"

Mary giggled. "No! I'm only this many!" and held up five chubby fingers.

"Well, who would've thought it! I was sure you were fully grown!" Aaron shook his head in amazement.

John grinned at Ceci and introduced her to the prince beside them. "Lady Ceci, this Prince Alex, the king's oldest son."

Prince Alex's eyes twinkled at her. He was an older man, in his fifties or late forties, but had a full head of dark hair above his smiling eyes. When he spoke, his voice was deep and reassuring. "Welcome, my friends. I hope your trip has been pleasant. We were surprised to get your pigeon this morning."

"We were surprised to have to send it," John said cryptically.

Prince Alex raised his eyebrows. "Interesting. I look forward to hearing the story over supper. Now, let's get you settled into your rooms."

They were necessarily traveling with only the bare essentials, and the rest of their things wouldn't arrive until the next day when the rest of John's guards, who had stayed behind as decoys, caught up with them. Thus Ceci and Mary only had one small satchel of belongings between them to be unpacked, which Ceci took care of before the maid assigned to them even arrived.

Ceci was listening to Mary chattering about their room, which was even more grand than the one they'd had at Heighlawn, and wondering how in the world to make herself presentable for the supper that evening since all her clothes were stained from the road, when a maid came in with hot water.

The girl saw Ceci frowning at her clothes and said, "Oh, miss, I mean milady, Queen Louisa is sending garments for you and Miss Mary."

"Oh, thank goodness! I wasn't sure what we were going to wear. Even the clothes that will arrive tomorrow aren't grand enough to eat with a king and queen, I'm afraid," Ceci said ruefully, starting to unbutton the back of Mary's long gown, which was grubby with trail dust.

Mary had had her bath, and Ceci had just stepped behind the screen for her own when she heard the door open and a woman's voice say, "Well, hello little love! That's a very pretty dolly you have!"

Mary said, "Her name is Cesily."

"Oh, that's a lovely name! And what a pretty dress you've made for her."

"Mummy made it from one of *my* old dresses!"

Ceci stuck her head around the screen and saw a woman about her own age sitting on the sofa next to where Mary was playing on the floor. She had golden hair with a slight reddish tint that was twisted up in an elegant knot, and fair skin liberally sprinkled with freckles. Sensing Ceci's gaze, she looked up, her large green eyes dipping down at the corners as she smiled.

"I'm Lady Margaret. King Alexander is my uncle, and the queen sent me along with some clothes for you and Mary!" She waved at the bed, where several dresses were laying.

"Oh, how wonderful! I was just stepping into the bath…"

"No hurry. Take your time. Mary and I will get acquainted." Margaret smiled and looked back down at Mary, who was pulling on her skirt.

Ceci stepped into the bath and scrubbed herself well, then toweled off and put on a robe. She wished she had time to wash her hair, but it would never dry in time for supper.

As she stepped from behind the screen, Lady Margaret stood up with a smile, saying, "Now, let's look at these gorgeous dresses Queen Louisa found for you! They're years out of date, of course, but the fabric is still in wonderful shape."

Margaret held up a yellow and green gown to Ceci's shoulders, squinted as she looked her up and down and said, "No. How about…" and she held up a pink and ecru gown. "Hmm.. that's better. But this is my favorite..."

It was a velvet sapphire-blue gown, with a wide midnight blue ribbon banding the bottom of the skirt and the bottom of the quarter-length sleeves. The same color ribbon had been pleated around the square collar, and a long swath of it formed a wide belt.

Margaret held it up to Ceci and smiled in delight. "Perfect!"

Ceci turned to the mirror and saw a stranger: a high-born lady in a fine gown. How would she ever live up to this new life?

Trying not to let her apprehension show, Ceci laid the dress down carefully on the bed.

Mary had crawled up on the bed to see what they were looking at. Now she picked up one of the larger children's dresses, her mouth opening in a silent O. "Mummy, look!"

"Yes, Mary. It's beautiful, isn't it?" Ceci took it from her and examined it closely. The dress was pale cream velvet heavily covered with gold embroidery in a pattern of twining vines, leaves, and flowers. Small jewels were sewn to the cuffs of the long tight sleeves and around the neckline.

"There's a tunic for it as well," Lady Margaret said, handing Ceci a cream-colored sleeveless tunic with golden fastenings down the front.

"Ooo!" said Mary, eyes wide.

"My goodness, you will look like quite the fancy lady, won't you? Just like your friend Lady Ana," Ceci said, eyes twinkling.

Mary nodded solemnly, eyes wide, making Ceci and Margaret laugh.

As Ceci followed Lady Margaret and an excited Mary down to the drawing room, she felt rather shy. The maids had twisted her hair into an elaborate style, and all the pulling and pinning had made her scalp a bit raw. She loved the sapphire dress and kept running her hands over the velvet, amazed that she was wearing such a thing, but she had to admit it was very heavy and restricted her movements much more than her servant clothing did.

Mary was chattering away to Lady Margaret as they walked hand-in-hand. She would only stay in the drawing room for a little while, then go back upstairs to have supper in the nursery.

When Mary walked into the drawing room, moving rather stiffly for fear of disturbing the complicated arrangement of curls on her head, which she was *very* proud of, Matthias spotted her first. "My

Lords and Your Majesties! A noble Lady has entered our presence!" He swept into a low bow, and Mary's uncles did the same, Harry trying to suppress a chuckle and failing.

Mary curtsied, wobbling a little because she was trying to hold her fancy skirt up but it *would* get caught on the buckle of her new shoe. "Oh, dear," she said, ruining the curtsey completely by squatting down to unhook the skirt.

John laughed with the others, but then he looked up and saw Ceci in the doorway, and his laugh caught in his throat.

She glowed in the light from the lanterns, the deep blue of her gown highlighting her creamy skin. Her dark hair had been woven into intricate braids and looped around her head, with the pale color of her real hair concealed under a wide beaded headband. The bodice of her gown was fitted, but the skirt belled out so she seemed to float into the room.

Harry gave a low growl of approval when he saw his sister, while Christopher said quietly, "How lovely you are, my dear."

Matthias didn't say a word, but when Prince John glanced at him, he saw tears standing in the man's eyes above his trembling smile.

As one, the brothers reached out to the nearest solid surface, be it table or mantle, and pounded on it in approval, with the three princes joining in and even raising their voices in a cheer while the king and queen laughed in delight.

Lady Ceci had returned.

The Lady's Staircase

Now that they were safely in Bagginsland, Harry was urging Prince John to make for the Vallenland border immediately.

"Mother and Father need to see Ceci as soon as possible," he argued at breakfast the next morning.

John said, "They don't even know we've found her yet. I'm sure the pigeon has reached my father, but he'll want to tell them himself and it will take a couple of days for him to get to Wallingford. Our horses are exhausted from that last push to get us out of Arlesland. It would be smart to rest them here for a day or two."

Harry said, "We can borrow horses from King Alexander! I'm sure he would be glad to lend them, and our own horses can follow later."

Ceci listened in silence. She was certainly anxious to get home… but a part of her was uneasy. She still hadn't fully accepted that she was the missing daughter of the duke, so she was scared that this beautiful dream she was living would come crashing down when they reached the end of the journey. She was also scared about the role she was expected to step into. Noblewomen in Arlesland weren't expected to do much, but she'd realized from things Prince John and her brothers had let drop that it was different in Vallenland. Her mother seemed to be very involved in the lives of the people who lived on the duke's land, and Ceci would be expected to take on some of those duties.

It was all she could do to take care of herself and Mary. How could she possibly be responsible for taking care of scores of people she'd never met? Ceci couldn't imagine such responsibility, and dreaded disappointing her parents when they realized she was unprepared for it.

She finally broke into John and Harry's argument. "Harry, everything has been a little overwhelming for me. Would you mind very much if we rested here for a day or two?"

Harry, mouth still open to argue with John, turned to stare at her. After a moment, his mouth shut with a snap. "Of course, my dear. Whatever you want, that's what we'll do."

John hadn't wanted to say it, but the reason he'd been arguing against starting for Vallenland immediately had been because he'd seen the fear in Ceci's eyes and thought she might need a few days to get acclimated to the idea of her new life. They'd figured out who she was and immediately made the rush for the border, giving her no time to assimilate the news.

Staying with the Bagginsland royals would afford her that opportunity, as well as giving her the chance to observe noblemen and women in a way that she hadn't seen before, as an equal, without the pressure of doing so under the eyes of her parents.

John clapped Harry on the shoulder and said, "We'll rest here two days. This will also give your parents time to get used to the idea of Ceci's return, and for their emotions to settle down a bit before she arrives."

Harry sighed. "I hadn't thought of that, but you're right." He nodded, content with the plan now.

After breakfast, Lady Margaret invited Ceci to join her for a walk through the gardens while the men went to the stables to admire the princes' horses.

Ceci was indebted to Margaret that morning, for the other woman carried the conversation easily, leaving Ceci to respond as needed, but not demanding that she contribute more than she was comfortable with.

As Margaret chattered on, Ceci slowly relaxed. Her only real experience of talking with a noblewoman was when she'd worked for Lady Bucksbury, whose nonsensical monologues had required no response other than "Yes, milady," when she infrequently paused for breath.

But talking to Margaret was very similar to chatting with the other maids she'd worked with. Granted, Margaret's stories about the men who'd caught her eye took place at noble banquets instead of at village dances, and instead of gushing about a new cotton dress, she told Ceci about her new silk gown, but it was much the same.

Finally, Margaret seemed to run out of things to say. Squeezing Ceci's hand, which she had looped through her arm, she asked, "And how about you, my dear? Any plans to remarry?"

Ceci shook her head firmly. "No. Mary and I are perfectly happy as we are, and now that I have a whole new family," she laughed shakily, "I can't imagine we'll ever be lonely again!"

Margaret laughed. "That's true! And your father's estate does very well, so you don't need a husband to provide for you, which is the main reason women marry anyway!" She glanced at Ceci saucily.

Ceci laughed and changed the subject. "Oh, what beautiful flowers!"

Margaret glanced at her, seeming to want to continue the previous subject, but allowed herself to be diverted, and the women wound their way through the gardens until they heard the far-off sound of the dinner gong calling them to the noon meal.

"Oh, fiddlesticks!" exclaimed Margaret. "And *of course* we're on the far side of the castle! Oh, well." She picked up her voluminous skirts and began to run toward the front entrance.

Ceci, surprised but laughing at Margaret's lack of decorum, picked up her skirts and ran, too, but as they reached the castle, they heard a "Yoo hoo!" and turned to see Queen Louisa smiling at them from a window on the second floor.

Stopping her headlong run, Lady Margaret shaded her eyes with her hand and looked up at her aunt.

Queen Louisa called down in a loud whisper, a smile on her face, "You can tell Ceci. I trust her."

Puzzled, Ceci looked from the queen to Margaret, who was now wearing a big grin. Margaret grabbed Ceci's hand and pulled her toward a door in the castle. They passed through it and Margaret kept Ceci's hand in hers, raising her other hand to lay a finger on her lips, adjuring Ceci to silence.

Eyebrows raised and mouth closed, Ceci stumbled a little as Margaret abruptly halted in front of a featureless section of the stone corridor and glanced around to make sure they were alone. Margaret squeezed Ceci's hand and directed her eyes down to the floor. Ceci looked down and saw the toe of Margaret's shoe nudge the base of the wall, where there was a small indentation in a bottom stone. Soundlessly, part of the wall in front of them opened like a door to reveal a stone staircase. Margaret pulled Ceci into the small room at the base of the staircase and eased the hidden door shut. Ceci heard her fumbling in the dark for a moment, then a match was struck and she saw Margaret's grinning face above the candle she was lighting.

Margaret whispered, "This, my dear, is the Lady's Staircase, and only the females of the royal family know about it, so you are sworn to utter secrecy." Margaret began ascending the stairs, whispering over her shoulder. "Apparently, there was once a queen who was unhappily married, and she had the Staircase built so she could sneak male 'friends' in. Being properly loyal to her gender, she passed the secret only to her oldest daughter, and the secret has gone down through the generations."

"So none of the male royals of Bagginsland know about it?" Ceci wondered.

"Not a one!" Margaret grinned. "Queen Louisa told *me* about it since she never had daughters of her own to pass the secret to. I'm glad she doesn't mind you knowing, because this is a much faster way to get to…" Margaret paused speaking long enough to open the door at the top of the staircase, then resumed, "… the guest rooms!"

They were in a small room full of women's clothing, and Ceci could hear the murmur of voices nearby. Margaret whispered, "This is an anteroom of Queen Louisa's chamber. The maids are never allowed in here, though, and there's another door here…" She stepped to the back of the chamber and opened a door, which led into... darkness.

Puzzled, Ceci followed Margaret through, and then realized the door was located behind a large tapestry in an alcove of the upper hallway. Margaret carefully peered out from the alcove, checking to make sure no one was in the hallway, and then motioned Ceci out. The girls ran to their bedrooms, giggling, to wash up.

Ceci enjoyed getting to know the Bagginsland royals over the next two days, and found herself intrigued by the new life she was stepping into. She and Mary spent most of their time with either her brothers or Queen Louisa and Lady Margaret, while Prince John spent his time secreted away with King Alexander and the Bagginsland princes, discussing things important to their kingdoms. At the end of each day, though, the groups came together and the company became livelier.

John and the youngest Bagginsland prince, Aaron, were both of naturally sunny dispositions, and although Aaron was ten years older than John, they spent a lot of time laughing together and joking around. Matthias and Harry often joined in, Harry's roar of mirth rising above the rest, while Christopher sat smiling and occasionally inserting a devastatingly witty comment.

Lady Margaret was at ease with her royal cousins, casually joking with them and Prince John, whom she'd met on other occasions. It was her first time meeting the duke's sons, but she was soon conversing happily with them as well.

Ceci, watching the laughing group, sometimes found Prince Aaron's eyes on her. Like his brother Alex, Aaron was a handsome man, but while Alex had dark brown hair, Aaron's was lighter, cut short but with a crisp wave that hinted at curls rigidly controlled. His brown eyes were heavy-lidded, his mouth perpetually smiling except when open in the frequent bursts of laughter that followed him everywhere.

When her eyes inadvertently met his, Ceci usually smiled quickly and averted her gaze. But the second evening she was watching him, thinking idly that the lock of hair that fell over his left eye was charming, when his gaze suddenly swung around, catching her unaware. Their eyes held a moment and his lips began to curve in a smile, his gaze growing warm.

Ceci felt a blush rising and dropped her eyes in confusion, pretending to smooth away a nonexistent wrinkle on her gown. When she darted a cautious glance up at him a moment later, he was looking away, but the smile lingered on his lips.

Homeward Bound

The next morning, a servant brought a small pigeon tube to Prince John during breakfast.

John unrolled the message and glanced up at Ceci. "It's from Morgana. She reached Wallingford late last night and gave your parents the news." A grin broke on his face. "Morgana says she's already worn out because they were so excited they didn't go to bed until the early morning. She says, and I quote, 'I had no idea that middle-aged people could talk so much. They were as excited as children!'"

Her brothers all laughed, but Ceci was confused. "Who is Morgana?"

John stared at her, then smiled and said, "I'm so sorry... I forgot you didn't know. She's my adopted sister. There was an emergency in the north of Vallenland which precluded my parents from going to Wallingford with the news of your return, so they sent Morgana in their stead. She came to live with us after you disappeared. She's three years older than me and convinced that she's my superior in every other way as well." He grinned. "I love her dearly, nevertheless!" His eyes softened. "She was a great comfort to me after your disappearance. She will love you, and I think you'll love her, too."

Ceci smiled back and tried not to think that Morgana was one more person she'd need to impress.

The rest of Prince John's guards arrived just before lunch, and the company set out for Vallenland that afternoon. It would take them almost a week to make the journey. Ceci would be riding in a carriage lent to them by the Bagginsland royals, which meant they had to stick to the main roads rather than taking smaller trails that cut across country.

Prince Aaron would accompany them to the Vallenland border, which gave them the added protection of ten of King Alexander's guards as well. John didn't think Uriah would attempt any kind of retaliation against them in Bagginsland, but they would be traveling parallel to the Arlesland northern border for most of the next few days, so it was prudent to have extra guards.

"I appreciate you taking the time to go with us," he said in a low voice to Aaron as they rode along with the guards at the head of the company.

Aaron shrugged. "There's nothing much for me to do at home right now... no special events at which I need to make an appearance." He laughed. "And, I love my mother dearly, but she's taken to nagging me about getting married." He sighed heavily.

John laughed in delight. He and Aaron had always gotten along well, and here was another thing they had in common: mothers who had gotten tired of waiting for them to find a girl to settle down with. "I know what you mean. My mother is after me to marry Lady Maureen."

"Oh, really?" Aaron said, a note of surprise in his voice. "But I thought you and Aurora..."

John shook his head emphatically. "I made the mistake of asking if she had any feelings for me at her birthday ball and she said no." He laughed ruefully.

"Huh," Aaron said thoughtfully. "I really thought she was interested in you."

John shook his head. "No, I don't think she's ever gotten over..." He interrupted himself. "Wait, do you...?"

"Want to marry Aurora?" Aaron finished his sentence, slanting a wry glance at him. He shrugged. "We've been close for a long time, but you and she were close, too…"

John nodded. "We were, but you had more time to visit her than I did, and she always talked a lot about you to me."

Aaron was silent a moment. "I think we would be a good match, and Father would love to join our kingdoms, but I agree with you: I don't think she's ready to move on."

John smiled at him. "Well, maybe it's time to find out for sure. You should invite her to come stay with you for a while."

Aaron laughed. "Maybe. Or maybe it's time for *me* to move on." He glanced over his shoulder at the carriage trundling along behind them and smiled at Ceci.

John kept the smile on his face only through force of will, because his heart had just dropped into his stomach.

Aaron was his friend, a man he liked and respected. He should be glad for Ceci that Aaron was drawn to her.

But Ceci didn't want to marry. She'd run away rather than be forced into a marriage.

But maybe it was just the Arlesland men she didn't want to marry, which he could understand. Maybe she'd be interested in a handsome prince from a prosperous kingdom like Bagginsland.

John suddenly felt ill.

Ceci's commitment to staying single was tested sorely over the next few days as they traveled through Bagginsland.

She found Prince Aaron's eyes on her more than once as they sat around the campfire at night, and his slow smile brought forth little flutters in her stomach. He was a handsome man, no denying that, and she found him attractive even though he was so much older than she was.

But Aaron wasn't the one who tested her resolve. That honor belonged to Prince John, although she thought of him as PJ now.

That was probably what gave him the advantage over Aaron. Her memories of PJ and the comfort those memories had given her over the years made her watch him surreptitiously. She wanted to know if the man was as kind and worthy of respect as the boy of her dreams had been. Maybe she had exaggerated his good qualities over the years.

But everything she saw confirmed her memories, and gave her new reasons to appreciate him. One event in particular stood out.

Mary was completely in love with her uncle Matt, but after him she gravitated most naturally to John. John always had time for her, but Ceci had been slightly hurt on her daughter's behalf one day to see John refuse to play with Mary, until she saw him encourage her to ask her Uncle Harry to play instead.

Harry, who was a somewhat intimidating figure to Mary because of his size, wild beard, and booming voice, had been trying to make friends with the little girl, with no luck.

Despite John's urging, she'd hung back, looking uncertainly from Prince John to Harry, until John had bent down to whisper something in her ear. Mary had giggled and then hesitantly approached Harry, holding Cesily out to him and asking him to sing a lullaby to the doll.

Ceci's heart had melted as she watched Harry sit down on a nearby rock, cradle Cesily gently in his arms, and, in a deep bass voice, warble a lullaby to the best of his ability. Mary had slowly crept up to him, listening intently to the words, and had begun to giggle when he changed the real words to more comedic ones.

After that day, Ceci had watched John much more closely, and saw that even though he had his hands full as leader of the group, he always noticed when someone seemed to need some of his time. To see a man who was planning to lead an entire country one day be so focused on each person in his care was intriguing to Ceci, especially since she'd been raised in a country where the overarching theme was "every man for himself."

He truly seemed to be a man to admire. She knew her brothers valued his opinion from the way they sought his advice and waited for him to make the decisions about their journey, but they were also comfortable enough to speak up if they disagreed with him. John always heard them out thoughtfully, and was willing to change his mind based on what they said.

In her chats with Lady Margaret, the other woman had casually mentioned that John was well sought after, but had never shown a preference for any of the eligible women who tried to fix his attention.

"Except Princess Aurora, of course, but I don't think she's truly interested in John... or Aaron, either, for all the time *he's* spent with her," she'd mused. She'd glanced at Ceci and laughed. "But that's neither here nor there! You'll meet all the royals and nobles soon enough, and then we'll have a nice coze together about them!"

Ceci had laughed... but secretly wished Margaret had talked a little bit more about the princess who had caught John's eye.

Ceci had little understanding of relationships between men and women. She'd once had a dream that a man would love her and protect her. Looking back on her life now, she had to wonder where that dream had come from, because she'd certainly never seen anything in Arlesland like that. Ma and Pa had fought like cats and dogs, with Pa always winning with his fists if he couldn't do it with his words, and the marriages Ceci had observed as they traveled from town to town had been much the same.

But that dream of a relationship full of love... Ceci realized now that it must have been based on what she remembered of her parents' relationship. She'd asked her brothers hesitantly if their parents were happy together and they'd looked at her with a bit of surprise in their eyes.

"O' course!" Harry had exclaimed. "Hardly see one without the other, and still holding hands like they're courting!"

Christopher had nodded solemnly. "They're wonderful together, Ceci. You'll be proud to be their daughter."

Ceci's eyes had surprised her by prickling with tears. She'd lived such a long nightmare in Arlesland, full of hatred and selfishness of each man to the other. Her life now, the life she was riding toward, seemed like a dream.

Ceci was glad she and Mary would have somewhere safe to live out their lives, where they could watch the love of a man for his wife from a safe distance. She would never give another man the power to hurt her like her husband had. But it made her glad to think that men like her brothers and father, like Prince John, did exist in the world that Mary would grow up in. It was too late for her mother, whose heart had been beaten down until the thought of love brought more fear than longing, but it wasn't too late for Mary.

So, even though Ceci was determined not to marry, she allowed herself to enjoy time with Aaron and John, telling herself it was good for Mary to see examples of men who were worthy of love and respect.

They finally reached the Vallenland border, and Prince Aaron took his leave of them. As he bent over Ceci's hand, she tried to pay attention to what he was saying, all the nice things about what a pleasure it had been getting to know her, but all she really had attention for was how close she was to her home.

To Mummy and Diddy.

Aaron finally got on his horse and rode away, and Ceci turned to face her brothers, who were standing behind her. The grins on their faces matched her own and she was suddenly filled with joy.

Harry gave a sudden whoop and grabbed her up, spinning her around until they were both dizzy, then soundly kissed her and said, his big bear paws on her cheeks, "Almost there, little sister. You're almost home!"

She began to cry, and the warm arms of her brothers surrounded her and Mary, and over their shoulders she could see John smiling at her.

On this last leg of their journey, John became even more solicitous of Ceci. He was careful not to displace her brothers, who rode close beside her carriage, but at the end of the day, when her brothers were busy with other duties, John would always take some time to sit with her and Mary and make sure they were feeling alright, both physically and emotionally, the closer they got to Wallingford.

Ceci had been hesitant to spend much time with him, afraid she might discover something to tarnish her memories of PJ.

But he was unfailingly kind, just as PJ had been in her memories so, slowly, she'd begun to open up when John asked her how she was doing, even talking about her deepest fears of embarrassing her family because she no longer remembered the mannerisms of a noble lady. John had listened to her carefully, and instead of saying, "I'm sure you'll be fine… we'll help you through all of that," which is what her brothers tended to say, he'd made specific suggestions.

"You've worked for the past four or five years in noble households, haven't you? So you've observed how the nobility conducts themselves."

"Yes, and I've heard servants gossiping about nobles who don't behave well!" Ceci had retorted.

John had laughed. "Undoubtedly. But those are usually the nobles who don't care a lick about what anybody thinks, anyway, so they aren't even attempting to act respectably. You don't have that problem, obviously," he'd teased, making her smile reluctantly, then said, "It's not just your family and friends who can help you, you know. The servants can be your allies, too. They can make sure you use the right spoon for the soup, that you don't insist on wearing a completely unsuitable dress to dinner, and that you don't make the unforgivable mistake of showing up late for breakfast when you're a guest in someone's home!"

That did make Ceci laugh, and she felt much better. She was nervous about asking for help from the nobles, but she was comfortable with servants, especially ones like the Bagginsland servants, who had been so helpful and kind.

"It's not just your family and friends who are going to be thrilled to have you home, Ceci Leigh," John had said softly, reaching out to squeeze her hand. "It's your *people,* the people of Wallingford, who have grieved with your family all these years. They will extend you every grace, every bit of help, that they can. Don't forget that."

Tears sprang to Ceci's eyes. She had been alone for so long, having to thrust her way through the world, fighting to take care of her child. To be taken care of was an overwhelming thought.

The *luxury* of it!

"Thank you," she whispered, her throat too tight to speak. "I'll remember."

Homecoming

Ceci's heart beat faster as they rode up the hill to Wallingford Castle, the cheers of the people lining the road from the village fading into a background roar. Her face was aching, so hard had she been smiling ever since they crossed the border into Vallenland. She hadn't done much smiling in Arlesland, except with Mary, so those muscles weren't used to so much effort.

People from the villages had turned out in droves to celebrate the return of their lady. They shouted that they loved her, had never forgotten her. Their love was such that she thought they wouldn't have noticed if she'd still been wearing her old rags instead of the luxurious clothing loaned to her by the Bagginsland queen.

But now she was approaching the only people whose opinion mattered. Her parents would see through her finery, see the real Ceci. They would be expecting the same connection they'd felt to the child who'd been stolen from them, but Ceci wasn't that child anymore.

No matter how hard she tried, she still felt like Cesily, the tinker's daughter, or Cora, the downtrodden maid. What if (horrible thought) they were all wrong and Cesily *wasn't* the missing Ceci Leigh? What if the real Lady Ceci showed up?

As Ceci's thoughts spun round and round, she felt a hand take hers. Startled, she turned to see Prince John riding beside the carriage, leaning in to squeeze her hand.

"It'll be alright. Just breathe. You don't have to be anything but yourself." John gave her hand one last squeeze as they turned in through the gates of Wallingford.

Ceci nodded, forcing herself to forget her doubts. A small burst of joy broke through the anxiety and she began to smile. She was going to see Mummy and Diddy!

When they were close enough to the house that Ceci could see the people standing in front of it, Christopher, Harry, Matthias and Mary dismounted and walked back to Ceci's carriage.

Prince John swung down from his horse and opened the door of the carriage as her brothers walked back to Ceci. Christopher, smiling, held out a hand and she took it hesitantly and stepped down. Instead of letting go, Christopher tucked Ceci's hand into the crook of his elbow as Matthias picked Mary up and put her on Ceci's hip, which immediately made Ceci feel calmer. Matthias wrapped an arm around Ceci's waist, and Harry wrapped one of his long arms around both Matt and Ceci, and in that fashion they proceeded to walk the remaining distance to the duke and duchess.

Ceci had thought her parents might run to her, or that she and Mary might run to them, as soon as they were close enough, but instead she felt very shy and uncertain. Her parents, arms wrapped around each other, tears streaming down their faces, in turn seemed content to feast their eyes upon the sight of their family reunited.

Ceci and her brothers stopped in front of the duke and duchess and there was a small silence as eyes that hadn't seen each other in seventeen years looked their fill.

Then Harry said softly, "Ceci, I present to you the Duke and Duchess of Wallingford, your loving parents. Father, Mother, I present to you the Lady Ceci Leigh, who was lost but now is found."

That broke the spell and the tears flowed from Ceci's eyes, blurring her parents' faces, but it didn't matter because now they were clutching her to them, burying their faces in her hair and neck, wrapping her so tightly she couldn't breathe, but she didn't care, nothing mattered except their arms around her.

The smell of her father's hair oil. The scent of her mother's perfume. It was the same and it made Ceci's knees go weak. Matthias's arm was still around her, though, and he held her firm as she sagged.

Now she always had someone to lean on.

That first day at Wallingford was exhausting. Ceci, used to being deprived of love, was shocked to find out how draining feeling happy could be.

Her mother had swapped her sodden handkerchief for a dry one when she came to fetch Ceci and Mary for luncheon, but the tears started leaking again when Mary held her arms up to her grandmother and gave her a rather wet kiss on the cheek. Lady Coraline lifted the child into her arms and hugged her for a long moment, the tears flowing freely. Then she put Mary down, wiped her eyes and said, "We have many, many years of those to make up for, so expect to be hugged to death, young lady!"

While Mary giggled, the duchess put her arms around Ceci and hugged her as well, whispering, "My arms will never get tired of this feeling, my dearest love," and then pulled back to look at her with her heart in her eyes.

The well of longing inside Ceci, the one that had been empty for so long, had begun filling up ever since her brothers convinced her of who she was. But that one long look from her mother, and the memory of the tears in her father's eyes earlier, did more to fill Ceci's need than her brothers could.

Her mother pulled her against her again, and Ceci breathed in her scent, and heard a small voice in her head whisper, *"Mummy."*

She was home.

Ceci had glimpsed Prince John's sister Morgana when they arrived that morning, just enough to notice that she was a striking golden-eyed woman with long dark hair, but the excitement of her reunion with her family made her forget Morgana almost as soon as she saw her. At luncheon, she'd talked with the princess briefly about their trip and the Bagginsland royals, but after the first pleasantries, John and Morgana had seemed content to listen to the reunited family's chatter, much of which came from Mary, who was telling her grandparents about every day of their journey in detail, even though much of it was the same each day. Her grandparents were listening avidly to each repetition as if it were the very first time Mary had mentioned it, drawing much suppressed laughter from the others.

After lunch, which was full of all the food her family insisted were her favorites, Ceci's parents had announced it was time for a tour of the estate. Prince John had said it was time for him to take a nap after their long trip, and Morgana had immediately chimed in, "And I need to send a pigeon to my parents, so you'll have to do without me as well."

But Ceci knew they were just being very, very kind, and giving her time alone with her family. She wanted to get to know Morgana, hoping to feel a similar connection to PJ's sister as she'd felt to Lady Margaret… but now wasn't the time.

So Ceci and Mary went off with their new family, with the duke's arm around Ceci's shoulders and the duchess' arm around her waist, and Mary proudly riding on top of Christopher's shoulders and giggling as she looked down at Harry, who was standing on tiptoe to try to be as tall as she was.

The next few days were just as anxiety-ridden and exhausting as she'd feared, but they were also full of a joy she couldn't remember ever feeling except with Mary.

All her worries were gone, as far as taking care of Mary. She could have Mary with her all day every day if she wanted, but she also had multiple people begging to take care of the child, from her parents down to the kitchen maids. Ceci didn't have to worry during the day that Mary might be getting hungry or tired. She was always in good hands.

Her worries about not knowing things like which utensils to use at fancy dinners had been allayed by time spent with her mother, who had invited her and Mary to a tea party in honor of Mary's doll Cesily. When they arrived, Mary had been intrigued to see that the small dining table in the duchess's sitting area had been laid out with all the china, crystal and utensils of a royal dinner. The tea turned into a four-course meal, although the portions were very small, and through it the duchess taught Mary which spoon to use for the soup and which goblet to drink from during the main course, and all the steps in between.

Ceci, listening to her mother instruct Mary, realized that she instinctively knew which utensils to use, and was sure the duchess must have taught her just this way many years ago. She hadn't forgotten.

Ceci Leigh wasn't dead.

She'd just been sleeping.

One evening in the drawing room, while they were quietly talking after supper, John turned to Ceci.

"There's something I've been meaning to ask you. When we were at Glastonheight, Christopher told the story of your disappearance to Lord and Lady Bucksbury, and she seemed to recognize the name 'Cesily.' When I asked her about it, she denied knowing anyone by that name, though."

Ceci stared at him for a moment, thinking, then her face cleared and she gave a small laugh. "Oh, of course! Mary and I traveled in the carriage with Lady Bucksbury and her daughter Ana, and Mary wanted me to tell Ana a story about her doll, so Lady Bucksbury knew Mary's doll was named Cesily."

John said, "Ah! I wonder why she didn't mention it?"

Ceci grimaced. "Lord Bucksbury always seemed very kind, but his wife was a schemer, always looking out for herself. I wouldn't be surprised if she wanted to think things over first and see if there was any advantage for herself in telling you about the doll. She may have wanted to question me and find out if there was any kind of connection beyond the name of the doll, too."

Matthias was listening to them. He said, "It's probably best that Lady Bucksbury didn't speak up. If we'd tried to approach you that day, you probably would've been terrified." He reached out for Ceci's hand and kissed it gently, his eyes sad.

Matthias had become an unexpected source of support for her. As the memories had slowly returned, Ceci had remembered that young 'Tias had been her most constant tormenter, the brother who had derided her abilities at every turn and played the most tricks on her. Being the closest to her in age, he'd been determined to prove he wasn't a baby like her.

But the adult 'Tias was heartbreakingly anxious to please her, to include her at every opportunity. He sought her out whenever she was missing from the group, asked her opinion on every topic of conversation. Ceci was gratified and made sure to respond to all his overtures, even when she didn't have much of an opinion to share.

Even more than her family, though, Ceci had come to rely on PJ. They'd spent enough time talking one-on-one by now that Ceci rarely thought of him as Prince John anymore. He'd become the bosom companion of her youth once again.

One day, after a rather nerve-wracking visit by an earl from a neighboring estate, who had called on them with his somewhat intimidating lady to welcome Lady Ceci home, Matthias realized Ceci had disappeared and sent John out to look for her. John checked all of the young Ceci Leigh's favorite hiding spots, and finally found her weeping in the walled garden.

The first she knew of his presence was a strong arm wrapping around her shoulders, drawing her into his warm chest, while a soft voice whispered, "Ceci, Ceci… please don't cry. You need never cry again. I know it's hard and confusing right now. Your whole world has been destroyed for a second time. But your family will never leave you, never let anyone take you from them again, and they will *always* take care of you and Mary."

He rocked her until the tears subsided. Sitting enfolded in his arms, his soaked handkerchief clutched in her hand, Ceci tried to focus on the peace she found there.

Her family loved her. She knew that without a doubt. But…

There was a huge stone blocking Ceci's throat, making her feel like she couldn't talk to him, couldn't share herself with him, but she forced herself to speak past it. "I'm still scared, PJ," she whispered.

John smiled at the nickname. "Scared of what, dear?" He rubbed her arms gently.

"Scared that I'll shame my family. I love them so much, and I don't want to embarrass them, but just when I think I understand everything I'm supposed to do, it goes right out of my head at the most inopportune time." She forced a laugh.

"Oh, dear, that is a problem." He clicked his tongue reproachfully. "But, fortunately, they don't *want* a grand lady. They just want their daughter, their sister, whose absence left such a big hole in their lives." His arms tightened and he whispered, "They... *we* just want you, Ceci Leigh. All you have to be is *you*, whoever that is."

She nodded against his chest... but the doubts lingered.

After a silence, John mused, "You know, that very first day we met you, met *Cora*, we were convinced you weren't the woman we were looking for. But even then, Matthias and I both saw something special in you, something that drew us to you. Blood calls to blood, and hearts call to hearts. We *knew* you somehow." He thought a moment, then went on. "You've already made so much progress. I have no doubt that your mother is proud of you and Mary both, and that nothing you could do would embarrass her. Your mother is a much higher stickler for etiquette than your father or brothers, so as long as you please *her*... And I know for a fact that you impressed Morgana, because she told me so." John smiled down at her.

Ceci laughed. "Morgana is a treasure!" The princess had insisted that Ceci spend as much time with her family as possible... but she'd taken to sneaking into Ceci's room at night, after Mary was asleep, and sliding into bed with them, where she would sit whispering with Ceci until long after midnight about anything and everything.

Ceci had been surprised the first time Morgana's smiling face had appeared at her door, but now she looked forward to the nighttime visits. Like PJ, Morgana was the recipient of Ceci's fears about etiquette or dressing properly, and she always managed to soothe Ceci's mind.

"Morgana told me that I could show up at a royal ball wearing a burlap sack and it would be sure to be all the rage because the nobles are so fascinated by my disappearance," Ceci said a bit wryly.

John gave a shout of laughter. "I think we should test that theory," he teased, giving her a gentle poke in the side to make her laugh.

Ceci turned toward him with a laugh and saw his smiling face so close to hers, the laughter in his eyes, and felt a twinge of regret. But she forced herself to ignore it and focus on the joy of his friendship.

Ceci's Fear

Princess Morgana left Wallingford a few days later amidst the protestations of all in the duke's family, especially Ceci. But Morgana had insisted with a twinkle in her eye that she had satisfied her curiosity about Ceci, and now it was better for Ceci to settle in without outsiders distracting her from her family.

She'd excepted her brother from that, however, by saying, "John should stay a bit longer, though, I think. He's worried about you for so long, Ceci, that it would be cruel to tear him away now that you're finally here." She'd laughed as she said it, but Ceci had thought there was an underlying worry there that Morgana hadn't given voice to, and she'd wondered if John had been more concerned about her absence than she'd realized.

Ceci had felt an odd swooping feeling in her stomach at the thought. It confused her, and for some reason she'd avoided John's eyes for the rest of the day.

She'd grown to depend on him so much. She could pour all her thoughts and fears into his ear. She relied on him, felt like her truest self with him.

And that terrified her because those were the things that made her vulnerable and easy to hurt.

Those were the things that brought *pain.*

That afternoon, Ceci was sitting in her mother's solarium while Lady Coraline sat on the sofa beside her, both watching the water falling from the fountain in the middle of the room.

"Darling," Lady Coraline said slowly, not sure whether she was overstepping her bounds, "I wonder… I've seen the way you look at John, and I wonder if you might… have feelings for him."

Ceci was silent for a long moment, staring down at her hands, which twisted in her lap.

Lady Coraline finally spoke again. "We love John, you know, and would be thrilled if you… care for him."

Ceci nodded. "I know. But," Ceci took a deep breath. "I can't marry him. I can't marry *anyone.*"

"But why, darling? Was your first marriage unhappy?" Lady Coraline had wanted to ask Ceci all kinds of questions about her life away from them, but didn't want to cause her beloved daughter any pain, so she'd relied on Ceci to talk about things as she was ready. One subject Ceci had never broached was her marriage, though.

Ceci didn't look up, just kept staring at her hands. Finally, she nodded. "It was horrible," she whispered. "He hated me."

"Oh darling, surely not!" her mother said, putting her arm around Ceci and drawing her near.

Ceci nodded, her head on her mother's shoulder. "He did. He told me so almost every day after the wedding. He didn't want to get married, but he owed some gambling debts, and Pa said he'd pay them off it he would marry me. I didn't know he was a drunk until after the wedding; he kept it well hidden. But he used to come home and beat me after he'd been drinking."

Lady Coraline was horrified. She knew such men existed, of course, but the thought that her daughter had been in such a relationship… it was devastating. Lady Coraline had vowed not to spend the rest of her life regretting the mistakes that had kept them from finding Ceci years ago, but at times like this it was hard not to drown in the remorse.

"Oh, my darling," she whispered. "I'm so sorry."

Ceci said, "It was so bad that I couldn't even stand to keep using the name 'Cesily' after my husband died, because I seemed to hear it in his sneering voice. The same for 'Martha,' which is the name he insisted we give to Mary. I decided to change my name to 'Cora…'"

Lady Coraline exclaimed, a smile breaking on her face.

Ceci gave a small laugh. "That name brought me such comfort and I had no idea why." She leaned into her mother's embrace for a moment, then straightened up and continued, "My husband changed overnight. I know now that he was a weak man who took his frustrations out on me, and I don't think John is like that…"

"Oh, no, darling! He's not!"

"… but I'm so scared that he will turn out to not be the man I think he is now. I… depend on John as a friend. I can't bear to lose that, let alone find out that I'm in another terrible marriage. I just can't do it. Mary was so young when her father died, she doesn't remember anything of that time and my husband put all his rage on me anyway, thankfully, but I can't risk putting her into danger." She pulled away from her mother. "So I've decided I will never marry again," she said, her mouth firm.

Lady Coraline was silent a long while, merely rubbing Ceci's hand and staring at the fountain. Finally she said, "I've known Prince John since he was a little boy. I know his parents well. There is absolutely nothing that I know about any of them that would make me think he would ever hurt you or mistreat you, no matter how angry he got. John is a rare man, one who has always been able to control himself. Even as a little boy, he never threw temper tantrums. Honestly, I used to worry about him when he would come to play with your brothers," Lady Coraline laughed. "He was so good-natured that they took terrible advantage of him! I was quite ashamed of them sometimes, but he never seemed to care. He would just give up whatever toy they wanted with a smile, and turn his attention to something else. I don't think he has a selfish bone in his body."

She stroked Ceci's hair, which had grown out so that now it was an odd blend of brown and white-blonde. "I think he would make a wonderful husband, and I think you would make him a wonderful wife. I know you're scared to love again, and I think you should always listen to your instincts. But I think, if you give it time, that you'll come to feel safe with John. Don't rush yourself, and don't rush him." She paused. "Did you know that he's the one who organized this last search for you?"

Surprised, Ceci shook her head.

"He showed up one day, and I took one look at the determination on his face, and said, 'You've come to find her, haven't you?' and John said he'd come to try. I'd never seen John fail at anything, although it might take him a few tries to succeed, so I knew he would find you. Your poor father was so exhausted, so disheartened after all those searches, but as soon as John took over, things started falling into place, clues started coming to light, things we'd never learned in all those years."

She squeezed her daughter's hands. "*He* found you, Ceci. He never gave up on you, and I'm convinced he would never hurt you. True love is beautiful, and rare, and should never, *never* be denied."

Ceci's hand went to her neck, where PJ's locket rested. She slid the secret panel aside, and felt the shape of the butterfly wings under her fingers.

Maybe her heart was like the locket. Maybe it could be unlocked by someone who knew how to make her open up and trust again.

Part of her wanted to believe that. But it was a part of her that was used to being ignored, because her faint optimism, her desire to see the good in others, had been wrong so many times.

Her joy and optimism had returned as Ceci settled into the love of her family and home, but her decision to never marry again was a strong one, forged in the battle of her marriage and beaten into implacability by her experiences with men like Henry and James. She couldn't trust her instincts.

The love of her brothers and the friendship of PJ had restored some of her faith in men, but she couldn't bear it if she married PJ and he changed like so many men seemed to. It was better not to love him than to risking losing him completely.

A Surprising Question

Prince John drew out his time at Wallingford as long as he could, but eventually he had to go home to take up his princely duties. After a few weeks at King Rudolph's castle, though, he found a reason to go back to Wallingford, and thereafter spent more time at the duke's estate than he did his father's estate.

His parents made no comments about his absence, but each time they received a letter with an excuse about why he was remaining at Wallingford, they raised their eyebrows and smiled at each other, hoping.

Ceci's parents also kept their speculations to themselves while telegraphing their secret hopes with glances and smiles. Ceci noticed their odd behavior and prayed PJ wouldn't.

But John only had eyes for her.

John had been intrigued to get to know the woman who had grown from the little girl he'd adored. He'd rejoiced as he saw her blossom in the light of her family's love, and worried because she had trouble understanding and trusting the good intentions of the people around her.

John helped her work through all of that, breaking down the walls she'd been forced to build in Arlesland to protect herself and Mary, and slowly, she'd come to be more open. Her parents' love, the affection and support of her brothers, had all worked its magic. Now there were moments when John thought he saw glimmers of the joy and love for everyone that had been the young Ceci's defining qualities. He wanted so much for her to feel that freedom, that security again.

He was overjoyed to see his dear friend regain her love of life… and a little surprised to find that his interest went deeper.

Watching her change day-by-day, grow in confidence and openness, John had found himself thinking about her constantly when they were apart. When he retired to his room at night, he found himself lying awake, smiling over something she'd said that day, or thinking about a particularly fetching hat she'd worn.

Then came the night he overheard Christopher talking to the duke.

Christopher had said, "… still don't think you should allow him to pay court to Ceci without talking to her first. She was adamant about not marrying, and it's disrespectful for you to think you know better than she does about what will make her happy."

The duke had been silent a moment, then said a bit sadly, "I'm just so thrilled to have her home again, and Mary is such a delight! It doesn't seem like you boys are going to marry and give your mother and me any more grandchildren to fill our old age with joy, so I wish Ceci would!" He'd sighed. "I can't believe she's going to be happy staying here with us the rest of her life. She deserves so much more!"

John had been stunned to realize that men were already starting to approach the duke about courting Ceci. She hadn't even made a public debut yet; she'd just paid a few calls with her mother on particular friends of the family. A few of the bolder neighbors had stopped by to call on her, and reports from those visits must have spread amongst the nobility. All they needed to know was that Ceci looked in a fair way to have inherited her mother's quiet beauty, and the men would swarm.

But John had been positive that Ceci wasn't interested in marriage. He'd had that small worry when Prince Aaron had indicated his interest, but Ceci, although blushing a bit around Aaron, hadn't seemed to return his regard, so John had unconsciously breathed a sigh of relief.

But now…

John found himself terrified he was going to lose her just as he realized he wanted more than friendship.

The next day, John left Wallingford and headed home. He found Morgana in the library and interrupted her reading with hardly an apology before launching into the topic that was consuming him.

He told Morgana how his relationship with Ceci had changed, how he could share all his thoughts with her and she never judged him for his flaws.

Morgana had listened to him with a grin, reveling in this new side of him, until he'd finally wound down enough for her to ask a question.

"Alright, so you know that Ceci has become very special to you, but is she up to the task of being a future queen? I think she's resilient, intelligent, strong-minded… all the things a king needs in a good partner. But she's still learning how to be a noblewoman, so is it fair to ask her to take on a much larger role?"

John had stared at her for a moment, appalled, then blurted out, "Can you believe I never even considered how well she would do as Queen?"

Morgana had gone into peals of laughter. "Yes, I can believe it, and I'm thrilled for you, brother! That, more than anything, shows me how much you care for Ceci, because you've been trained from birth to consider the well-being of your people before considering your own happiness, so the fact that Ceci's ability to be a good royal consort never entered your mind means you are head-over-heels for her!"

John hadn't quite been able to see the humor in it, though, and had spent a few agonizing hours wondering what he would do if she had no desire to be queen. He loved his kingdom and couldn't imagine giving up the kingship, so any woman who married him would *have* to take on that role.

What if he had to face a choice of loving Ceci or leaving her to fulfill his destiny?

John broke out in a cold sweat just thinking about it, and spent the night staring at his bed curtains, his mind racing with doubt.

After a couple of days at home, talking to Morgana and his parents, he'd realized that it was all moot if Ceci stuck to her plan to remain single.

Morgana had been confident that he could convince Ceci to change her mind, though. "I think she loves you," she'd said smugly. "She may not have admitted it to herself, but I think if you ask her to marry you, she'll realize that's what she truly wants."

John's heart soared and immediately demanded that he go back to Wallingford and put Morgana's theory to the test. As he rode along with his guards, though, he began to get nervous again and decided to first find out whether Ceci would make a good royal consort. Before he made her face the question of whether she wanted to marry him and eventually become Queen, he had to make sure his love for Ceci wasn't blinding him if she didn't have the right skills to *be* Queen.

So, when he arrived at Wallingford, he made sure that whenever he was with Ceci, he discussed issues with her that were important to their kingdom.

To his delight, she asked questions that were insightful and helped him consider things from a different angle. She also had ideas, based on the abysmal conditions she'd grown up in, of how to make the lives of the common people of Vallenland even better than they already were.

Listening to her, John realized that her unique upbringing, her life as a commoner, had prepared her to help his people in ways no other noblewoman could claim. She truly understood their struggles, knew how to connect with them.

Finally, there was only one small thing keeping John from asking her to marry him: she hadn't yet learned how to laugh uninhibitedly again. John knew he needed someone to laugh with, someone to lighten his load when being a ruler became overwhelming, so he was waiting to see if Ceci could manage to overthrow the darkness she'd grown up in.

Then one day, as he was walking with her in the Wallingford gardens, she broke off a lily and breathed in the heavy scent, then held it up for him to smell. As he leaned forward, she suddenly shoved the flower against his nose, making him jerk back in surprise. John put his hand up to brush off the yellow pollen, then frowned in mock anger at Ceci, whose eyes were laughing above gently curved lips.

As he watched, the smile became a laugh, and she said, eyes dancing, "Oh, dear… I'm afraid you didn't get it all off, Prince John," and turned away unconcernedly to pluck another flower.

John, scrubbing furiously at his nose, said, "That's no way to treat a future king, Lady Ceci!"

Ceci kept walking and threw back over her shoulder, "I think you need something to keep you humble, PJ." As she said his nickname, she glanced back and he saw the girl who had adored him, and whom he'd adored in turn, looking out of her eyes.

Ceci Leigh. His little friend.

His grown-up love.

It was time. He cleared his throat. "Lady Ceci, a moment, please!"

She turned, eyes still dancing. "Are you going to punish me, Your Highness?"

John laughed. "Well, I guess you might think of it that way," he said, grinning. "Please sit down for a moment." He motioned toward a nearby bench under an arbor of white roses.

Ceci settled down on the bench, her arm brushing the roses and releasing their scent so it drifted in the air.

She looked perfect, smiling up at him with the sun dappling her face. Her hair was caught back in a loose bun, so from this angle all he could see was the fair hair that was slowly overtaking the brown. She was an angel with hair the color of clouds against her sky-blue dress. The breath caught in his chest and for a moment he couldn't speak.

Then he slowly lowered himself onto one knee, never taking his eyes off her face. He saw puzzlement there for a moment, then realization began to dawn.

And then… he wasn't sure what emotion he saw.

"Lady Ceci, I wasn't sure I would ever find a woman who could make me feel certain I wanted to marry her. But I finally have. You take my breath away. Your joy, your mind, your heart… I don't ever want to live without them. Even having you a day's ride away is too far, so I must ask you, my darling friend, if you would consider becoming my wife."

John had hoped at this point that she would smile and accept, maybe with a few of those tears women always seemed to shed when they were very happy, and then he could take her in his arms and kiss her.

But she was just staring at him, a blank look on her face.

And then, slowly, hesitantly…

…she shook her head, chin trembling. She whispered, "I can't! I'm so sorry, but I can't!" and *then* the tears came as she leapt to her feet and ran toward the castle, her blue skirt trailing behind her.

John stared after her, stunned. He supposed he'd been unbearably arrogant, but he'd been sure she would say yes… or at least that she wouldn't say no.

Ceci ran into the castle and straight up the stairs to her mother's chambers, where Lady Coraline was embroidering. As Ceci burst through the door, Coraline looked up in surprise and set her sewing aside just in time to catch her daughter as she collapsed on her mother's shoulder, weeping bitterly.

Lady Coraline tried in vain to get Ceci to tell her what was wrong, but the girl would only shake her head and sob louder, so the duchess finally stopped trying and just rubbed her daughter's back and spoke soothing words, sure she knew what the problem was anyway.

That level of grief could only be love.

An Unexpected Summons

That evening, a message arrived via pigeon for Prince John after supper. He broke the royal seal on the note and read it with a frown.

Ceci's heart started pounding. Such a late message could only mean some kind of emergency, one that would call the prince away from Wallingford. She wasn't ready for him to go… especially after the traumatic scene in the garden.

She'd known things would be awkward between them, but the evening had been agony. She'd felt as if she were going to burst into tears at any moment. Ceci had almost begged off supper, sent down word that she had a headache, but time with her family was so precious that she didn't want to give up even a second of it.

So she pulled on her dress and let her maid powder her face a bit to hide the ravages of tears, and went downstairs with a smile pasted on her face.

She and John had avoided each other's eyes, but she could tell that he glanced at her often during the meal. She kept her eyes firmly on Matthias and her mother, who were seated at the opposite end of the table from Prince John and her father… but she was aware of every move John made.

When the servant brought in the note, Ceci turned her eyes to him for the first time that evening.

John looked up, straight at her. "I must leave," he said abruptly.

Her heart dropped and the tears that had threatened all evening filled her eyes.

"Is everything alright?" Christopher asked.

"I'm not sure," John replied, his eyes going back to the message. "My father doesn't say why he's calling me back. The message is vague… I'm not sure what it means, honestly. Something about an urgent matter he must discuss with me in person. He says I must set out as soon as I receive the message. I can be home in one day if I ride hard, so I suppose I must just wait until then."

They glanced around at each other, then Christopher hesitantly asked, "You're sure it's from your father?"

John glanced at him and then back down at the message. There was a long pause before he spoke. "No… no, I'm not. But it has the royal seal and uses our code words. It seems unlikely someone could've gotten our code words, even if they managed to replicate the seal. But the arrangement of the words is… unusual," he admitted.

"It's dark already. You surely aren't going to start out now?" Harry asked.

John's mouth twisted and he shrugged. "I think I have to. I'll just be on my guard, in case this is some kind of ploy."

Ceci's heart began to pound at the word "ploy." Her fear for him overwhelmed everything that had happened earlier, and she spoke impulsively. "PJ… send a pigeon to your father, asking for confirmation of this message. That will only take a few hours."

He frowned at her for a moment, considering. "I'll send a message letting him know I'm on my way, but I can't sit around waiting if there is indeed some urgent need for me to be at home. There have been no reports that would lead me to believe someone is targeting me. It's just rather confusing." He read the message again, the frown reappearing.

Unease was growing in Ceci, making her positive he shouldn't go. "What about King Uriah?" she asked, her mind going back to the man who had created such fear in the world where she'd grown up.

John looked up, puzzled. "Uriah? What do you mean?"

Ceci said, "He must be angry that we managed to escape. Maybe he's seeking revenge on you."

His eyes narrowed as he mulled the idea over. "Uriah is certainly unpredictable, but he's been king for a long time. He knows what would be at stake if he attacked me openly. I think his anger would be more likely to come out during our yearly trade negotiations. He'll probably punish us then by raising the prices of his exports. That's the way kings usually get their revenge. He would have to be seriously unhinged to risk war by attacking me in my own kingdom over something so small. If he were that upset, it's more likely that he would've done something immediately after we escaped, like refusing to let the rest of my guards leave Arlesland."

Ceci saw the logic in that, and her father and brothers were nodding agreement. They were much more conversant with political machinations than she, so surely they were right.

But Ceci remembered the rumors of Uriah's petty revenges against his own nobles, when he had sometimes bided his time for years before exacting revenge. But those instances had been against men whose livelihood he controlled, not against the monarchy of another kingdom as powerful as his own.

Prince John was smart and wary. He wouldn't fall into a trap easily, and it was unlikely Uriah would launch a surprise attack in Vallenland. It was much more likely to be a trap if someone were trying to lure him out of Vallenland, but to send him a message to go home to King Rudolph didn't make sense.

Ceci didn't attempt to argue further.

But the unease continued to grow.

John was uneasy as well. Something about the wording of the message nagged at him. However, the right code words had been used for an emergency, so he couldn't afford to linger.

John knew that five miles up the road there was a canyon with high walls, the perfect place for an ambush, so he would have to make a plan with SC Arne to spring any hidden traps without John or his men actually putting themselves in mortal danger.

The main thing on his mind as he directed the Wallingford servants to pack his things was that he was leaving Ceci much sooner than he'd prefer, because he knew they needed to talk over what had happened. He had planned to keep silent this evening so she could think about what he'd said, and then speak to her alone tomorrow. He was convinced that she was the only woman who could become the queen he needed, as well as the wife he wanted, and he was willing to wait if she needed time to think about it.

John sighed. He would go home, do what his father wanted, and then return to Ceci as soon as he could.

'Tias Atones

John set off within the hour with all his guards, and Ceci went to her room soon afterward. She felt on the verge of tears, so she was glad to crawl into bed, where she could pull the curtains and mull everything over in peace.

She'd thought she wouldn't fall asleep quickly, but the strain of the past hours had been more than she realized. Her heavy eyelids soon closed and she began to dream almost immediately.

She was riding through a dark forest on a horse that she was driving relentlessly forward, all her focus on the goal ahead. Her heart pounded and fear curdled in her stomach. She rode and rode, trying to find the thing she sought, but it was out of reach somewhere ahead of her.

Ceci woke up drenched in sweat. Pushing off the heavy covers, she struggled with the bed curtains and finally burst forth. She shoved her feet into slippers and grabbed her dressing gown, yanking it on as she ran down the hallway.

Ceci heard voices coming from her father's study and burst in to find her father and brothers gathered around the desk at the back of the room. They looked up in amazement as she ran up to them.

Her father was holding a pigeon message. Ceci gasped, breathless, "What is it?"

Harry glanced at her father and started to say, "It's nothing, Ceci, go back to bed…" but Matthias interrupted.

"No, she has a right to know. Tell her."

Ceci's heart was pounding so she could hardly hear.

The duke said, "It's a message from King Rudolph. He says he didn't send any summons to John tonight."

Ceci felt all the blood drain from her face. She spoke through lips that had gone numb. "We have to go after John," she said, frantic with fear. She couldn't lose him. *She couldn't lose him.*

Not PJ.

Please, God… not PJ.

Harry stepped forward quickly, his arm going around her shoulders. "We'll take care of it. Now, you go on back to bed."

"But I have to go with you!" she cried, pushing against him as he tried to walk her to the door.

Christopher said, "Ceci, we'll have to ride hard to catch up with John and warn him. You hate horses. You wouldn't be able to keep up, even if you could ride alone."

"I can!" she insisted. Right now, fear for John made her fear of horses seem ridiculous.

Harry motioned to the youngest brother. "Matt, take her. You'll need to stay here with Mother and Father anyway. Christopher and I will go after John."

Matt came at once, and put his arms around Ceci. She continued to fight him until he whispered in her ear, "Shh. Let them believe you've given in."

Startled, she stopped resisting. His jaw was set and he didn't meet her eyes as he bundled her out the door. They walked quickly to the other end of the hall where there was an alcove.

Matt stopped and turned to face her. "Ceci, you can't go. Harry was right; you wouldn't be able to keep up."

Ceci pulled her wrist from his grasp. She was so frantic that for a moment she forgot how close she'd become to Matthias in the past few weeks. Belligerently, she thrust her head forward and glared at him. "I could tame the wildest stallion right now without breaking a sweat!" she snarled.

Matt drew back and stared at her. Amazement broke on his face. "You're in love with him. You're in love with John!" he said, his tense face lightening into a smile.

Ceci stared at him, refusing to admit it even to herself. She wasn't in love with John. He was just her good friend.

Her best friend.

And she would be destroyed if he were killed.

A sudden sob surprised her and her face crumpled for a moment, but she refused to be distracted. "Are you going to get me on a horse or not?" she snarled again.

Matthias was in a quandary. He wanted to help her, especially now that he understood how important it was, but she was his little sister and he couldn't put her in danger, not after they'd just gotten her back.

Ceci saw the "no" forming on his face and her face crumpled completely, tears welling up and rolling down her cheeks. "Please, 'Tias, *please! I have* to go after him!"

And Matthias was ten years old again, watching his baby sister cry because he thought she was too young, too silly, to join him and his brothers on their adventures.

He'd been a lunkhead then, and he was being a lunkhead now.

He pulled her out of the alcove and up the stairs. "Go change into something you can ride in. I'll meet you at the stables. Keep to the shadows, though. If Harry and Christopher see us, we'll waste valuable time arguing."

Ceci rubbed the tears from her eyes and took off running.

When Ceci, clad in the same pair of Christopher's cut-down pants that she'd worn on their frantic flight to the border of Arlesland, ran out to the stables, she saw Harry and Christopher in the yard. They were mounted and giving instructions to the duke's men who surrounded them.

Ceci slipped through the open barn door without them seeing her and ran to the back of the stable. Matthias heard her coming and stuck his head out from the last stall. "Back here!" he hissed.

Ceci ran in to see him getting ready to saddle her chestnut mare. She stared for a moment, then shook her head. "I can't take Fire Dancer tonight. She's not fast enough."

Matthias frowned. "What?"

Ceci grabbed the saddle and headed two stalls down to the big black horse John sometimes rode. "I'm taking Black Diamond."

Matthias gaped. "Are you crazy? You've never ridden Diamond alone! Just because Prince John lets you hold the reins when you ride double with him…"

Ceci interrupted through gritted teeth, "I can do it." It was true that she wasn't completely comfortable on John's big stallion, but he'd been letting her do all the work on their last few rides. She could do it. For PJ, she could do it.

Matthias stared at her hard face and clenched jaw… And he believed her. Right now, he believed she could do anything she set her mind to.

Except put the saddle on a horse whose back was over her head. She *did* need some help with that.

Ceci Leads the Way

Finally seated on Black Diamond's back, Ceci refused to give into the panic she felt welling inside her. She forced herself to pretend that she was John, sitting astride a horse she could easily handle. She tensed her legs and arms and nudged Diamond with her heels so he walked out of the stall and toward the door. Matt ran ahead of her and peered out, turning back to hiss, "They're gone!" before running to bring out his own horse.

They rode down the drive at a gallop at first, then slowed down so they wouldn't run up on the other group. When they broke from the trees at the end of the drive, they could see Harry, Christopher and the duke's guards riding north, the way John had gone.

Ceci made a sound of dismay.

Matthias turned to her. "What?"

"They're going the wrong way!" she exclaimed.

He frowned. "No, that's the way John went."

"Well, that may have been the way he intended to go, but it's not the way he went," she said bluntly. She was too frantic to couch her words politely. "King Uriah never would've let him go north. He would've attacked him as soon as he came out of the estate."

"King Uriah?" Matthias frowned. "Why are you so sure this was him?"

"Because I am," she replied, her mind too focused on the danger to John to explain.

But Matt was determined to argue. "Even if it were him, this is a lousy place to attack someone. You want to attack from a high vantage point, at a place where the people you're attacking are trapped, so a canyon like the one five miles north would be optimal. That's why Harry and Christopher went that way."

"We're talking about Uriah. You can't predict what he would do."

Matt opened his mouth to argue again, so Ceci rolled her eyes and said, "If John and his guards knew this was a lousy place for an attack, they wouldn't have been expecting one, so it's actually the *perfect* place for an attack."

Matthias frowned. It made a kind of sense. To a madman.

Ceci couldn't stand to delay longer. "If they were attacked here, we should be able to find John's guards. Uriah's men wouldn't have taken *them,* just John."

Matthias thought it over. They could take five minutes to look, and if they didn't find anything, Ceci would probably go north without further argument. He nodded.

Ceci rode to the other side of the road and walked Diamond into the woods. "Hello! Is there anyone here?" she called, her voice slightly muffled by the thick trees.

Nothing. She rode a little further and called again. Still nothing.

After a few more minutes without finding anything, Matthias was just getting ready to insist that her theory was wrong when they both heard a faint cry. Their heads snapped around to the right. It came again, muffled as if someone were trying to yell through a gag.

Matt slipped his foot from the stirrup and slid to the ground, looping the reins over a tree branch, then set off toward the sound. Ceci, unable to dismount from Black Diamond without help, directed the horse to follow him.

And there they were. Hands and feet tied, bound to trees, Prince John's guards were spread around a small clearing. All but one appeared to be unconscious, their heads lolling forward onto their chests.

Matt removed the gag of the one who had called out and set about freeing his hands and feet. "What happened?"

The man spit out fibers from the gag and said, "Attacked as soon as we came out the gate. They took Prince John and headed south."

Ceci gave a cry. "I knew it! Was it King Uriah's men?"

The guard shook his head. "Don't know, milady. Dressed in common clothing and they didn't speak. Don't know if they had an Arlesland accent."

Matthias helped the man stand and glanced at Ceci.

She didn't wait for him to make a suggestion. Time was too important to worry about his male ego, and she'd been right so far. "Send this guard to warn Father so he can send a pigeon to tell Harry and Christopher to go south. We need to follow John and mark a clear trail for them to follow."

Matthias said, "Maybe *you* should go warn Father and let the guard come with me."

Ceci looked at the guard, who had been beaten badly and was favoring one leg as he stood. "He's in no shape for a hard ride." She asked the guard, "Where are your horses?"

He gave a shrill whistle, and they heard an answering whinny and the sound of hooves coming toward them.

"There," Ceci said to her brother, already turning Diamond to go back to the road. "He can ride to the castle so we won't lose more time. C'mon!" and she spurred the stallion, trying not to bounce too much as he leapt forward.

Matt ran to swing into his saddle and follow.

Riding behind Ceci as they raced south, Matthias marveled. What a girl she was! Not a sign of fear as she leaned forward over Diamond's neck, and after an admittedly rough start, she'd settled down into Diamond's gallop and looked like she'd been riding for years.

A stab of guilt hit him as he realized that if she'd stayed safely at home all these years, he and his brothers wouldn't have given her opportunities to find her strength, so she would never have had the courage to make this midnight ride into danger.

But then again… Ceci didn't need their permission to be herself. Her brothers might not have helped her become the amazing woman she was, but she would've managed to do it.

Pride in his heart, Matt was happy to be the one following *her* this time.

Ceci galloped until she came to a curve in the road, one small part of her mind marveling that she was handling the stallion so easily. John was right; all she'd needed was more confidence. She slowed and walked Diamond around the curve, then came to an abrupt halt. Far ahead in the moonlight, a wagon was faintly outlined as it left the road and trundled slowly into the trees.

Ceci walked Diamond to the edge of the trees to make them less visible. She heard Matt pull up behind her and do the same.

"Do you see?" she whispered over her shoulder.

"No lights," came the faint reply.

She nodded. The wagon was unlit, the lantern that hung from the driver's seat darkened. The night was cloudy, so most wagons would certainly be using a lantern for the moments when the moon was hidden behind clouds. But this one wasn't. It was pure luck the moon had come out long enough for them to see the wagon as it left the road.

Another clue that this was no farm wagon was the ten mounted men in the roadway behind it, their heads swiveling this way and that as they scanned the road.

"You think John's in that wagon?" Matt whispered.

Ceci nodded. "Where could they be taking him?"

Matt thought for a moment. "There are some cabins back there that were part of an old mining camp, but it's been defunct for years. The cabins are still in good shape, though."

Ceci said, "If they're taking him off the road, they aren't trying to sneak him back to Arlesland." She couldn't say what she was thinking.

Matt breathed, "You think they're going to *kill* him? That would be completely insane! Surely Uriah wouldn't do that."

Ceci said grimly, "You didn't grow up hearing the stories about Uriah that I heard. They would make your blood run cold. I think we would be wise to assume the worst." She was silent for a moment, pondering alternatives. "C'mon. We have to follow. We'll leave a trail for Harry and Christopher."

Matthias followed as she rode forward, but when she started to direct Diamond off the road, Matt said, "Stop."

Ceci turned to him, ready to press her argument.

He held up a hand. "I think you're right, but we're close to the border. Some of John's guards are there. It would take us half an hour to get there by the main road, but there's a shortcut through the woods that will only take half as long. There's no way we can take on all those men alone; we need the guards."

Ceci thought for a moment. "*You* go get the guards. There's no point in both of us going. I'll stay here and watch to make sure they don't take John somewhere else, and I'll leave a trail if they do."

Matt was furiously shaking his head. "I'm not leaving you alone here! Anything could happen and I'd never forgive myself if you were hurt." Or worse.

Ceci put a hand on his sleeve. "I won't change my mind and we're wasting time arguing. You're the only one who knows the shortcut, so you *have* to go." Without another word, she rode into the woods. She knew she wasn't acting like a younger sister who respected her older brother… but all her focus was on getting John back safely. She would order around the king and queen if she had to.

Matt ground his teeth and clenched the reins furiously, wishing he could follow her, protect her… but knowing she was right. He couldn't even hope that she'd be smart enough not to do anything foolish. All she was thinking about right now was keeping John from harm, and he knew she'd try to take on all the kidnappers alone if she had to. Even if he were with her, he doubted he could stop her, so the best thing, the *only* thing, he could do to help her was to ride like the wind for the guards.

He spurred his horse and raced for the border.

PJ's Savior

Ceci walked Black Diamond into the woods, reaching out every once in a while to quietly break a branch, leaving a clear trail for her brothers.

After several minutes, during which she wondered more than once if she'd lost the trail of the men ahead, she heard voices ahead and saw flickering lights. She slowed Diamond down, moving forward cautiously.

Ahead was a clearing where three small log cabins stood in a semicircle. The wagon she'd followed had pulled up in front of the cabin on the left, while a group of men stood smoking on the steps of the middle cabin. Inside it, she could see men moving about with lanterns. As she watched, a man threw something over the front window, blocking out the light of the lanterns completely.

"I hope Whistler won't drag this out," she heard one of the smoking men say.

Ceci's heart dropped. She turned Diamond and walked him back toward the road, pulling him away from the trail they'd made through the woods. If any of the kidnappers came back the way they'd come, she didn't want them to find a strange horse.

Sliding awkwardly from the saddle, Ceci tied the reins to a branch and patted Diamond's neck and leaned against him a moment, so grateful that he'd allowed her to ride him. Then she sternly took hold of herself and walked back toward the cabins.

The men who were smoking had moved to the right side of the clearing, where they were talking in low voices. As she watched, the driver of the wagon lifted the oil lantern from the hook on the driver's seat and slid open the blackout panel, revealing a steadily burning flame within. He used the flame to light a cigarette, drew the blackout panel back across to hide the light, and walked over to join the others. Ceci watched a few more moments, but saw no signs of any other men. There were fifteen men in the clearing, but she didn't know how many were in the cabin.

Suddenly, Ceci's head snapped around.

A cry of pain had come from the middle cabin, sending fear churning through her.

One of the men in the clearing snickered. "Ah, the beautiful sound of money!" The others laughed.

Ceci felt bile rising in her throat and fought it down. Heart pounding, she made her way as quickly and quietly as she could through the woods around the clearing until she was at the back of the cabins.

Looking around carefully, Ceci saw no signs of any men. The windows on the back of the middle cabin had been covered, but there was a small gap at the bottom of one of the curtains, through which Ceci could see light.

Taking a deep breath, her eyes still searching for hidden watchers, Ceci stepped toward the window, shoving her way through the thick bushes around it.

She peeked through the gap in the curtain and at first wasn't sure what she was looking at. Slowly it resolved into the fabric of a man's coat. The man was sitting in a chair against the back wall, right beside the gap in the curtain. Ceci tilted her head down and saw that the man's hands were stretched behind the chair. Tilting her head to another angle, Ceci felt a sob well in her throat.

She could see John's signet ring on the hand closest to her, and six inches above it she saw a rough rope, stained red with blood, cruelly cutting into his wrists.

Ceci turned from the window for a moment, forcing herself to breathe deeply. She had to focus on how to help John, not on how he was hurting. She heard a thud and another cry of pain and frantically put her eye back to the curtain to see blood dripping onto John's shirt.

"Not so handsome with a broken nose, Your Highness," a voice sneered, and several other voices chuckled, adding some insults of their own.

"Who sent you?" John gasped.

Ceci almost cried aloud when she heard the pain in his voice.

"Oh, aye, you'd like to know, wouldn't you? Well, I'll tell ya, because it won't do ya no good. You're gonna be dead before that candle gutters out."

Ceci slid around until she could see the candle in the lantern on the table in front of John. There was only a little nub of it left.

She dropped her head and prayed for Matthias to fly like the wind. They couldn't wait for Harry and Chris to arrive with her father's guards.

The kidnapper continued, "King Uriah's the one what sent us to get ya."

"Take me to him," John gasped, spitting out the blood that had dripped onto his mouth. "I'm sure he'd enjoy doing this himself more than just hearing about it from you."

"Oh, aye! Indeed I believe he would!" the man laughed along with the others in the room. "However, our king is a planning man, he is. Always looking for a way to lay the blame on someone else. So he's got it in mind to lay your death at the feet of Reimsland."

Ceci's blood went cold. This plot was more intricate than she'd thought.

"He's trying to make a scapegoat of King Albert of Reimsland?" John said thickly. "No one would believe he'd attack me. He's too ill to plan anything like this. Prince Bertie is in charge now, and he *wouldn't* attack me, so Uriah's plan doesn't make any sense."

"Have some faith in our beloved king! Uriah is a cunning lad, he is, and he can't have Reimsland becoming friendly with the other kingdoms when Albert dies. Thusly," the kidnapper said formally, "we come to tonight's grand play, wherein we kill a noble prince with a gen-u-wine Reimsland knife and dump the body just over the border, along with a scrap torn from a note about Bertie's plot to kill you, coded in the gen-u-wine Reimsland royal language."

The men roared with laughter.

"But King Uriah wanted to make sure you were roughed up good while you were still alive to enjoy it, and I'm happy to oblige him by doing such," the man continued.

There came some more sickening thuds and grunts of pain. John seemed to be past the point of being able to even cry out.

"Think, think!" Ceci thought frantically. *"How can you help him?"*

She heard one of the men give a loud yawn. "C'mon, Whistler. Wrap this up. He's too far gone for you to get any more enjoyment. Kill 'em and let's go."

"Nah, he's still conscious," Whistler said. "Just a few more minutes. Wanna give the king his money's worth."

Ceci began to hyperventilate. She had to stop this man herself. Matt wasn't going to make it in time.

Into her panicking mind came all the times in her life when people told her she was useless.

Her brothers, jeering at her for being a baby.

Pa, the man she'd thought was her father, telling her she couldn't do anything right.

Her husband, kicking her in fury until she lay sobbing on the floor, holding her pregnant belly and thinking about killing herself.

Ceci felt all that old fear, that certainty of her own uselessness, overwhelm her. Her body shook from head to toe and she felt bile rise in her throat. She was worthless. How could she possibly think she could save John from those men?

And then, into the maelstrom inside her head, came a boy's soft voice.

"You're stronger than you know, Ceci Leigh." PJ's eyes, *shining with confidence in her.*

Ceci bent over, hands on her knees, and took three deep breaths. She was John's only hope. She had ridden Black Diamond, and she could do this, too.

She *had* to do it.

Ceci stood up and walked around the cabins, keeping to the shadows, until she stood at the back of the wagon parked to the left of the clearing. The horse that had been pulling the wagon had been unharnessed and was cropping grass at the edge of the wood.

Ceci peeked out and counted the men on the other side of the clearing. They were all still there. She reached up to slip the oil lantern from its hook over the driver's seat, glanced over at the men to make sure no one was watching, then swiftly smashed the lantern against the tarpaulin that covered the back of the wagon.

Ceci didn't stay to watch what happened. She was off and running before the flames took hold, but she heard the *whoosh* as the fire raced across the oil dripping down the tarp. Seconds later came the first cry as the men spotted the fire.

Ceci darted to the back of the middle cabin in time to hear one of the men inside say, "Something's happening out front!" Running footsteps inside, then someone hollered, "Whistler! Come quick! The wagon's on fire!"

Heart pounding, Ceci ran to the wall of the middle cabin that was farthest from the fiery wagon. She saw a man come running out of the cabin and go after the others, who were beating at the flames. She waited a minute to see if anyone else was going to follow him, then she slipped up the steps, refusing to think about what would happen if Whistler were still inside.

The cabin was empty, though, except for the broken figure she could see through the door ahead of her. She took a moment to bolt the door behind her, then ran to the back of the cabin.

John was slouched in a chair, his wrists still tied behind him, head flopping forward like a dead weight.

"Oh, please! Please, please, please!" Ceci prayed as she lifted his head and felt frantically for a pulse.

There! It beat strongly under her fingers. He was just unconscious.

She glanced around and saw a wickedly curved knife on the table, the Reimsland royal crest carved into the bone handle. Trying not to think about what Whistler had planned to use it for, Ceci cut John free, then slid open the window beside him.

Sliding his arm over her shoulder, she tried to heave him from the chair. Panting, she took a moment to wish he hadn't eaten so well at Wallingford for the past week. "You could stand to lose some weight, PJ," she grunted, hauling him up by sheer willpower. She hesitated a moment, not wanting to hurt him, but knowing they didn't have time for her to be nice, and then tipped him head first out the window into the bushes. Then she slid out the window after him and pulled it closed. John had landed almost upright on the dense bushes, so she was able to drape him over her shoulders and stagger across the short clearing, refusing to give up although it felt like she was barely moving him an inch at a time. Somehow she made it, though, and pulled him into the woods, where the adrenaline pumping in her system abruptly gave out and she collapsed beside him.

The Hollow Tree

Ceci could hear the men shouting as they tried to put out the fire, and knew it would not be much longer before they discovered John was gone. She had to find somewhere to hide him.

But he was too heavy. It would take all her energy to move him a few feet when they needed to move a hundred yards.

Steeling herself, she leaned over John and slapped his cheek lightly. "John! John! Wake up! You have to wake up!"

His jaw sagged and eyes remained closed. She tried for a few more seconds, but no luck.

The volume of the shouts was lessening as the men got the fire under control, making the stress rise in Ceci. "John! John!" She slapped him hard this time, not worrying about hurting him, but there was no response.

Desperate, she finally whispered, "PJ! PJ, please! You have to try to wake up! I can't do this alone!"

John's eyes fluttered open and she almost wept.

"Oh, thank goodness! You have to stand up! I have to get you deeper into the woods."

"Ceci?" came his wondering voice. "What are you doing here? It's dangerous; there are men…"

"I know, I know," she said, fear making her impatient as she tugged at him. "Now stand up. They're coming for you."

John obediently lurched to his feet, but it was a much slower process than Ceci needed it to be. She pulled and pushed and finally got him standing with his arm around her shoulders and hers around his waist.

He was wobbly, but they were moving.

"Where are we?" he asked faintly.

Ceci didn't have much breath to spare for talking, but she managed to say, "Some old mining camp with three cabins. We're in the woods behind them."

John was silent a moment as he began to stagger with her up the hill behind the cabins, then he said suddenly, "The Carter mine!"

"What?" Ceci asked, not really caring but wanting to keep him talking so he wouldn't fall unconscious again.

"The Carter mine! Don't you remember? We used to play here sometimes. There was an old mine shaft where we used to look for diamonds."

A vague memory swam in Ceci's thoughts, but she couldn't quite grasp it. She grunted, "Is there somewhere we can hide?"

He was silent and she was about to repeat her question when he finally said, "Up the hill. The hollow tree."

Ceci had no idea what he was talking about, but as long as he knew, that's all that mattered.

John was making little huffing wheezes now, painful noises, and seemed to be slowing down. "Just a little farther now," she gasped, praying his strength would hold.

And it did… just barely.

As Ceci felt the ground leveling out beneath her feet, John became a dead weight and slowly began to fall over on her. Ceci fell to her knees, unable to stop his momentum, and managed to stop him before he hit the ground.

He was out cold again. Ceci laid him down and looked around them. She couldn't see much in the dim moonlight, but she thought they were in a fairly thick part of the woods. There were a lot of low bushes around them.

She didn't have the strength to move John much farther, and he couldn't move himself, so the best thing she could do was lay a false trail for the men who were no doubt already searching for them.

She rolled John farther under the bushes, and quickly piled some leaves over him, then swiftly went down the hill the way they had come. After a few hundred yards, she stopped to listen.

The men's voices were calling in the distance, frantic tones evident even though she couldn't make out the words. Good. They were still trying to figure out how John had escaped and where he'd gone.

She grabbed a small tree near her and broke off one of the branches, leaving it dangling by just a few strands of wood, and then moved up the hill, going the opposite way from where she'd left John. When she reached the top of the hill, she broke off a few more branches in the wrong direction and then doubled back to where John was lying under the leaves.

Ceci smoothed out the ground around him, erasing any signs that they'd been there, then crouched under the bushes, thinking about what he'd said about a tree. The false trail would buy them some time, but wouldn't fool the kidnappers for long. She had at least five minutes, though, hopefully ten or fifteen.

Ceci dropped her head, blocked out the faint sounds of the men in the camp below, and forced herself to concentrate.

The Carter Mine. The hollow tree. Looking for diamonds.

Ceci breathed in and out slowly, dredging for memories.

And into her mind swam a faint shimmer, the softest whisper. *Diamonds…*

Ceci had been excited when she set out with her brothers and PJ that morning, because they'd told her they were going to the diamond mines. When she slid down from where she'd been seated in front of PJ on his horse, though, all she saw was some old cabins.

"Where are the diamonds?" she'd asked, and her brothers had broken into raucous laughter.

"Diamonds!" Harry had shouted, flapping his hand at her derisively. "There haven't been diamonds here for years!"

PJ had taken her hand. "It's ok, Ceci Leigh. There aren't any diamonds… but there are some excellent hiding spots! I'll bet *you* can find a better one than *Harry* can!"

Ceci's eyes had lit up and she'd run up the hill behind her brothers as fast as she could, determined to prove PJ right.

Christopher had agreed to be "it" for their game of hide and seek, and the rest of them had scattered as he counted out loud. Harry and 'Tias had climbed trees, getting as high off the ground as they could. PJ had started to climb to the top of a huge rock, but then looked down to see little Ceci standing at the bottom, lip quivering. She was too small to climb like the boys.

PJ had smiled at her and slid back down the rock. "Why don't *you* pick a spot for both of us?" he'd asked, taking her hand. Ceci had beamed and looked around for something on her level.

And there, at the base of a tree growing next to the mighty rock, she'd seen it: a great hole in the trunk. Ceci pointed, but PJ looked puzzled. He couldn't see the fissure from his taller vantage point.

Ceci pulled him down to her level and he gasped, then ran to the back of the tree and gazed in amazement. The whole back of the tree was hollowed out, and the hole inside was big enough for three grown men. "Perfect!" PJ said, eyes shining like Ceci's. "All we need is…" He looked around and grabbed a fallen branch, then motioned for Ceci to proceed him into the hollow of the tree. She stepped into the dimness and turned around to see him follow her in, pulling the branch up to cover the small crack in the tree that could be seen from the front.

"Now they'll never find us!" Ceci whispered, jumping up and down in excitement.

PJ laughed softly. "You are brilliant at hide-n-seek, Ceci Leigh!"

Ceci hugged herself, his praise warming her from the inside.

Grinning, PJ put his finger to his lips and whispered, "Now be a quiet little mouse so they won't find us."

"The hollow tree," Ceci breathed, her eyes screwed shut as she tried to remember where it was. It had been next to a huge rock, with the tree almost seeming to grow out of the base of the rock.

Lifting her head, she listened hard for a moment. She heard movement in the woods, but it sounded like the kidnappers were still at the bottom of the hill. Standing up, she peered down the hill.

There. The glow from the burning wagon clearly backlit men moving at the edge of the woods behind the cabins. They were walking back and forth, staring at the ground, looking for signs of where John had gone.

Ceci jumped up, extricated herself from the bushes with care, and swiftly walked to the right. They'd been playing on the ridge that day, and she remembered going to the right as they came out of the woods.

She walked around for several minutes before she finally found the rock and tree, and only saw it then because the moon had finally broken free of the clouds. Her heart was pounding with fear over the time she'd wasted as she raced back to John, but as she peered down toward the camp, she could see that the men were just starting up the false trail.

Ceci pulled the leaves off John and rolled him out of the bushes carefully, then patted his face. "PJ! PJ! Wake up! We have to move," she whispered.

His eyes slid open and he stared at her.

"We have to move. I need you to stand up."

He groaned and closed his eyes. Ceci's heart sank. She couldn't get him up by herself. She dropped her head for a moment, then put her mouth close to his ear.

"I know you're tired. I'm tired, too. I know you're in so much pain, but I need you to try very hard for a moment, and then you can rest." She paused, raising her hand to stroke his cheek. Her heart surged with love for him, and she tried to give him the courage he'd given her. "You're stronger than you know, PJ darling," she said softly. "You can do this."

A pause, and then his eyes opened. His arm slowly moved to brace himself and he pushed his torso off the ground.

"Good work, PJ," Ceci breathed, standing so she could pull him up.

It took a few agonizing minutes to guide John to the tree, settle him inside, and race back to the bushes to hide the evidence of where they'd been, but when she was done she could still see the men moving through the woods away from her.

Ceci raced back to the tree and slipped through the crack in the trunk. She'd found a good sturdy branch to block the gap, and now she pulled it up, closing them in.

Ceci couldn't see anything, but she crouched down and found John's foot. Crawling across the open space, she sat down beside him and pulled him against her. His body was limp, so he must have passed out again.

"Poor love," she whispered. "Rest now. Help will come."

They were together. All was well.

PJ and Ceci Leigh

Ceci started awake, appalled to realize she'd dozed off. John was leaning on her shoulder inside the hollow tree, his breathing deep and even. Outside she could hear the shouts of the men who were hunting John.

Gently pushing John so his head rolled off her shoulder and she could lean him back against the inside of the tree, Ceci crawled to the opening and peered out. The dead branch did a good job of blocking her view, but she could see flashes of light. The men had lanterns or torches with them, and were searching the undergrowth and woods.

As she watched, she saw an arm holding a torch approach the hollow tree. The man swung the torch back and forth across the face of the rock for a few moments, then called, "Nothing here, nowhere they could hide!"

Ceci sighed in relief and crawled back to John, pulling his head back down to her shoulder and sliding her arms around him. He was still out cold.

Ceci wasn't as terrified as she had been. She thought there was a good chance now that they could remain hidden until her brothers arrived to rescue them, so she stopped worrying about the men outside and turned her thoughts to the one beside her.

Holding him close enough to smell the soap on his skin, Ceci allowed herself to dream.

What if she could hold him like this forever? What if she were the one he woke up to every morning?

Sometimes, when Ceci's husband had been on a bad bender the night before, he would sleep half the day away afterward. And sometimes, when she was very, very lonely, she would wake up beside him as he lay snoring, and she would pretend that he would wake up and kiss her gently, stroke her cheek and tell her that he loved her, and give her sweet kisses as he held her in his arms.

Lying beside her husband, the dreams had inevitably ended in tears as she faced reality, but now, holding John in her arms, she allowed herself to dream again.

Maybe… maybe she would be safe with John. Maybe her dreams weren't so unrealistic after all.

But…

John stirred against her, murmuring words into her neck. She shifted him so his mouth was against her ear and whispered, "What, PJ? Did you say something?"

"I love you, Ceci Leigh," he murmured.

She felt an odd trembling inside, a crumbling.

She whispered back, "I love you, too, PJ," as a tear rolled down her cheek. She'd never dreamed love, real love, could hurt so much.

He subsided against her and his breathing deepened again.

Awhile later, Ceci realized the voices of the men outside were growing fainter, as if they were moving away. She crawled to the opening again and realized there were no flashes of light anymore. The men had either moved to another area of the hillside or had given up altogether.

There was still no sign of her brothers or the duke's guards.

When Ceci crawled back to John and tried to pull his head back to her shoulder, he awakened and pulled away to sit up straight.

"Where are we?" he asked in a low voice.

"Inside the hollow tree," Ceci whispered back.

There was a small silence. "What happened?" he asked.

"We got a pigeon from your father that said he hadn't summoned you, so Harry and Christopher rode north to find you with some of the guards, while Matt and I rode south." Ceci thought it would be easier to stick to the basics, rather than telling him she and Matt had snuck out against her father's wishes. "We tracked the men to the mining camp, and I snuck you out of the cabin while Matt rode to the border for your guards."

There was silence for a moment while John absorbed her words. His thinking must have been a little muzzy, though, because he didn't question how she'd gotten him out by herself, or why she and Matt didn't have guards with them already.

All he said was, "I think your virtue will be compromised by being alone in a hollow tree with me, Lady Ceci, so you'd better accept my offer of marriage."

Ceci almost burst into laughter, managing to muffle it only at the last moment. She huffed, "That's an unfair advantage, Your Highness! And I'm not sure you have your priorities straight. Maybe you should wait until we're out of danger to press your suit!"

She heard a low rumble of laughter in John's chest, and he lifted her hand to his lips. "Maybe I'll just press a kiss, then," and he did so on the palm of her hand, closing her fingers around it, then laid his head back down on her shoulder and fell asleep.

The love swelling in her almost overwhelmed Ceci. This was what she'd dreamed of! This was the love she'd always wanted.

But...

Pulling his beloved face into her neck, Ceci pressed a kiss on John's head, then laid her own against it and, despite the turmoil in her heart, fell asleep again.

Much later that day, Ceci was sitting outside with John under the apple tree that overlooked the valley below the castle. John had a broken nose, two broken ribs, and a very sore jaw, but insisted he didn't want to be stuck inside in bed, so they had compromised on sitting quietly under the apple tree.

The night before, as the kidnappers made their way back down the hill after their unsuccessful search, Matt had burst upon the mining camp with some of King Rudolph's royal guards just as Harry and Christopher arrived on the main road with the duke's men. The combined troops had captured the kidnappers handily.

Ceci hadn't heard the hullabaloo, though, since she and John were still fast asleep inside the hollow tree. The first hint she'd had was Matt's voice calling her name.

Now, many hours after their rescue, she could hear the faint sound of her parents and brothers talking behind them, but under the old tree the loudest noise was the buzzing of bees in the clover around them.

John had received a letter from Princess Aurora of Archenland and he was reading it to Ceci.

"'After we were attacked in Rock Valley, my parents arrived to make sure I was alright, and that's when my mother told me that you've found your darling Ceci again! I hope your life will be much happier now.'" John looked up at Ceci, thinking how much his life had changed since the last time he'd talked to Aurora.

Ceci smiled, although her heart was a little sad because she remembered that Aurora was the name of the princess Lady Margaret said John had been interested in. "She sounds lovely." She paused, then asked diffidently, "Are you very good friends?"

"I thought I wanted to marry her at one time," John said, then slanted a smile at her. "Before we found you again."

"Oh." Ceci didn't know what to say. She was glad he was no longer interested in Aurora… but now she was afraid he might ask *her* to marry him again.

In the hollow tree, things had seemed so simple. John loved her and she loved him, so they should be together forever. The end. Just like in the fairy tales she read to Mary at night.

But, in the cold light of day, all of Ceci's fears had come flooding back. Her mind continued to rebel against the idea of being that close to a man, *any* man, even PJ.

She just *couldn't*. And she didn't know how to tell him that, because last night she'd been sure that she *could*.

Well, almost sure.

Watching her, John felt his heart sink. The downturned corners of her mouth, the way she refused to meet his eyes today… He'd thought he'd won her over last night, but today it was clear he'd been wrong.

But he kept talking, hoping his honesty would win her over. "I can't believe I ever thought about marrying someone else, because what I feel for you is so much stronger. I don't doubt my love for you one bit, Ceci. No one else could ever make me as happy as you do just by sitting quietly beside me." He reached out to take her hands in his. "Don't you think you could be happy with me, too?"

Ceci stared at their hands, unable to meet his eyes. She was so ashamed of toying with the emotions of this man who meant so much to her, who had never shown her anything but kindness. She hated that she'd given him hope last night only to snatch it away today.

But when she thought about marrying again, she felt sick to her stomach and her heart started to race.

John saw it all on her face, and said in desperation, "I can't bear the thought of leaving you, of not talking to you every day, of not seeing your face at breakfast, hearing your laughter, sharing jokes with you. I'm more comfortable with you than I've ever been with anyone else. I can talk to you like I've never been able to talk to anyone, even Morgana, and she's my best friend."

Hearing his pain broke something inside her, something that cried out for her to help him. Ceci looked up then, into his eyes, and saw her pain mirrored there.

She said, trying not to cry, "I feel the same way. I've always felt alone, and a lot of that abated when I came home. My parents and brothers have been so good to me, and I love them so much… but I can't talk to any of them, even 'Tias, the way I talk to you. I feel like I have to explain things to them, but you just understand. It's so *easy* with you."

John turned around in his seat, grimacing against the pain in his ribs, and leaned toward her to take her hands. "Then Ceci, my darling, won't you please trust me enough to marry me?"

The tears fell then, but not the happy tears he'd wanted to see when she accepted his proposal. These tears poured like pain from her eyes.

"I'm so sorry," she whispered, squeezing his hands once, and fled.

Ceci, lying in her bed with the curtains pulled, faintly heard the door open and close, but the sound of her crying muffled the footsteps so that the cool hand that slid her hair back from her wet face was a bit of a shock. Ceci opened swollen eyes to see her mother's face.

Lady Coraline's eyes mirrored Ceci's pain, her lips drawn with sadness. For a moment, Ceci realized her mother must have looked like that while she'd been missing, and her heart ached to think she was bringing that kind of pain to her mother again.

"I'm sorry, Mummy!" she whispered, the tears flowing freely.

"Oh, darling! Don't be sorry! We just love you so much and hate to see you in so much pain."

Ceci sobbed harder as Coraline rubbed her back.

"Darling… did John ask you to marry him?"

Ceci nodded, her sobs not abating.

"And you said no?"

The sobs increased, answering her mother without words.

"But why, darling, if it makes you so unhappy?"

Ceci didn't know how to explain, couldn't even explain it to herself, but she tried. "I love PJ so much. He's my *best friend!* I can't risk that relationship, and I'm terrified something will happen after we get married. I can't risk it! *I can't!*" she wailed, curling up in a tight ball.

Lady Coraline sighed. She didn't understand why Ceci was so determined to make herself miserable. Maybe it was time for some hard truths.

"Darling, I know that you think you're protecting yourself… but how will you feel when John marries someone else? He'll have to, you know. He has to provide a heir for the throne. He may not marry for love, but even if the marriage is only a political one, how will you feel knowing he's holding someone else in his arms?"

Ceci wailed and tightened herself even further into a ball. Her fingers grabbed at her hair and pulled, the agony inside her needing a physical expression of pain.

But still she shook her head. All she could think of was the joy she'd felt on her wedding day, rejoicing that she would finally be with someone who loved her, and the horror when she'd realized even a kind, quiet man like she'd thought her husband was could turn into a monster.

In the beginning, she'd tried to fight him off. Then she'd tried to flee from him. Eventually, she'd just frozen emotionally, retreating inside herself where she was alone and safe. Safety meant not feeling anything.

So even though John made her so happy, she knew his love would also bring her pain. And she just _couldn't_.

A little later, Lady Coraline stepped into the hall where John waited with anxious eyes. She shook her head sadly. "I'm so sorry, John, but whatever she went through has too tight a hold on her. You might be able to break through it, but it will take a lot of patience… and I honestly don't know if you'll ever be able to convince her that marrying you is worth the risk of losing you as a friend. I think she _knows_ she's being illogical, but she's incapable of overcoming that."

John felt his heart crack in two.

When he'd made the decision that fateful day to find Ceci, he'd thought that when it was done he would finally be able to start living a full, happy life. He'd never dreamed it would bring so much heartache.

He remembered how sorry he'd felt for the duke's family back then, how secretly grateful he'd been that he hadn't had the day-to-day agony Ceci's loss had brought them. Now they were happy and he…

He was the one in torment.

Ceci Leigh's Heart's Desire

A week later, John looked around at Ceci's family as they stood on the steps in front of Wallingford Castle. Ceci and Mary were in the middle, with her parents on either side, and her brothers around them. John's wounds had healed enough to travel, and since Ceci was still adamant in her refusal to marry him, he'd made the difficult decision to return home. He'd done what he'd vowed to do, he'd found Ceci, and now it was time to start living his life, no matter how empty that life might be.

He and Ceci had said their goodbyes privately the night before, promising they'd always be first in each other's hearts, even though the specter of John marrying someone else was in the forefront of their thoughts. Ceci's tears had flowed freely and she'd clung to him while he held her in silence, wishing he could find the words to persuade her, but unable to think past the agony in his heart. He didn't know how he'd manage to go on without her, and could only pray that he could lose himself in working for his people.

Firmly turning his thoughts from the sadness of that last goodbye, John gave a final nod to them all, his eyes lingering sadly on Ceci and Mary a moment, then mounted his horse and followed his guards down the driveway.

Puzzled, Mary watched her friend PJ ride away. She had just realized something important.

"Mummy," she said, "PJ really, really doesn't want to leave. Why does he have to?"

Ceci, unable to talk through the tears she was fighting against, turned in desperation to Matthias, who immediately kneeled down beside Mary.

"PJ is sad to leave your mum and you, but he belongs with his family."

Mary knew that wasn't right. "No!" she shook her head emphatically. "I heard him telling Mummy that me and her were the family he wanted!"

A sob burst from Ceci and she turned to cling to her mother, weeping like a child.

Matthias hugged Mary and spoke words he knew were false. "PJ will be alright once he gets home." Squeezing her again, he stood up and put his arm around Ceci, one hand still on Mary's head.

Mary looked up at them, frowning. Her mother was crying. She didn't want PJ to leave, either. Why did Uncle Matt say it was alright? Adults were so confusing.

Mary turned and watched PJ ride down the drive. Her mother had her parents and her brothers to take care of her, but PJ had told Mummy that no one else loved him like she did. Mary had heard the tears in his voice when he'd said it. He was so sad, and he'd be so lonely on the ride home. That wasn't right.

Mary slid out from under Uncle Matt's hand and pelted down the driveway, the ribbons of her dress flying behind her. "PJ!" she called. "PJ! Wait for me! I want to go with you! Wait for me!"

Ceci's head jerked up. Through swimming eyes, she saw a little girl running along behind a handsome boy on a horse, and her heart thudded in her chest. All the times she'd begged PJ to let her go with him flashed through her head.

What was she thinking? How could she let PJ leave without her? He *wanted* her to go with him and she'd said *no*.

The child inside her rebelled and Ceci finally stopped thinking and let herself *feel*.

PJ was her true love. True love was beautiful and rare; her mother had told her so.

And it should never, *never* be denied.

"PJ!" she whispered, and slipped from the arms of her family to go flying down the drive behind Mary.

Prince John heard Mary's cry and turned to look, the despair in his eyes changing to surprise as he saw her running toward him. He dismounted in time to catch her and swing her into the air, a smile banishing the shadows on his face. As he opened his mouth to ask what she was doing, her eyes darted to something over his shoulder and he turned to see Ceci running down the hill toward him, skirts clasped in her hand and her hair, cut short now so it was completely blonde, flying around her face like it had when she was little.

As she closed the distance, he could see tears streaming from her eyes and hear her calling his name. He slid Mary to the ground, giving the child a quick, reassuring smile, and held out his arms in time for Ceci to crash into them.

"Don't leave me!" she sobbed. "I'll marry you!"

Delight burst in his heart, along with relief that overwhelmed him. He swung her around in a circle, her feet flying up and making Mary crow with laughter.

He set her down and clasped her face in his hands. "Do you mean it? You'll marry me?"

She was still sobbing a bit. "Yes! Yes! I'll marry you! I was stupid to think I could live without you!"

Mary giggled. "You were *very* stupid, Mummy!" and jumped around in excitement.

Ceci and John laughed, never taking their eyes off each other, and he leaned down to press his forehead against hers.

"I love you, PJ," she whispered against his lips.

"And I love you, Ceci Leigh, forevermore."

And he sealed it with a kiss.

Epilogue

A few weeks later…

King Uriah of Arlesland stared at the letter in his hand, which was stamped with the royal seal of Vallenland.

"… I would have written you sooner to give you the glad tidings of my engagement to Lady Ceci, but I was regrettably recovering from a vile attack. I fear that someone is again attempting to create a hostile environment between our kingdoms, because the attackers tried to convince me they were working at your behest. We were able to find a spy among my father's men who had been passing confidential information to our enemies, and he has been dealt with."

Uriah grunted. So that's what had happened to the man he'd established in King Rudolph's household all those years ago. He'd feared such, since the regular reports from the man had stopped abruptly soon after the failed attack on Prince John. Well, he'd been able to get a copy of the royal seal to Uriah and, amazingly, had even managed to find out some of the secret royal code words. Undoubtedly, the code had been changed again by now, but Uriah's men might be able to predict what the new code would be, based on the old one.

"We thank you again for your kind invitation to bring the Lady Ceci to meet you, and regret we were unable to do so. When we finally found Ceci, she remembered nothing of her past, so as you can imagine the revelation was a terrible shock to her. We believed the men who had taken her might attempt to kidnap her again for a ransom, so we believed it was in her best interests to get her home as quickly as possible. Before we could send you a message to that effect, we discovered we were being followed and made the decision to fly to the border immediately. Another attempt to place blame on your kingdom overtook us at the Bagginsland Gate, when brigands tried to keep us from passing through the gate.

My parents and I deeply regret these attempts to bring acrimony to our kingdoms. It is our most sincere wish to maintain the peace."

Uriah snarled. So that's how he was going to play it, eh? Still keeping to this farce of "other forces" attempting to start a war? Uriah screwed the letter into a ball and flung it into the fire, his brows heavy, rage boiling unchecked within him.

He stared at the fire, brooding over past sins done against him. He remembered the sniggers, the whispers from the nobles and royals at Queen Valeria's birthday ball all those years ago. He'd been excited about his foray into the wide world, but the snobbishness he'd been met with had made him vow to never again try to make friends with the leaders of the other kingdoms.

Uriah was alone, just him against all the other kings now that Albert of Reimsland was incapacitated and that twit of a son of his was ruling in his stead.

But he would make them pay. He'd been planning his revenge for decades, and it was almost time to bring it to fruition. He was a patient man, but he'd gotten a bit bored lately and begun amusing himself by targeting the royals in other kingdoms, such as Princess

Aurora of Archenland. Every incursion taught him something about their defenses, something he could use in the final attack.

A knock came on his door and a servant entered with another pigeon tube. Uriah unrolled it and scanned the short message.

Poison in his ring

A cruel smile lit the king's face.

The End

The World of Eoroe: Bryten series continues in book two, **The Guarded Heart**, which tells the story of Princess Aurora. It is available as an ebook (abridged version) or paperback (full version) at

AuthorJoCook.com

For a special peek of The Guarded Heart, turn the page!

Sneak Peek of The Guarded Heart

*And now, a sneak peek of book two in the
World of Evroe: Bryten series, The Guarded Heart...*

Awake after another restless night, Martin lay staring at the window as the light outside grew brighter. He wasn't particularly excited about starting another day. It was unlikely he'd see her, and even if he did, she'd be oblivious to him.

To keep from going crazy with longing, he allowed himself to think of her as much as he wanted, but only when he was alone. It was hard to find time alone in the Guards, so that kept his daydreaming to a minimum. Late at night and early in the morning were the only times he had, so his mind woke him up early, no matter how exhausted he was.

He thought her eyes were getting sadder lately. If she knew she was loved, she would look very different. He was positive of it. If they just had a chance, she could look that way with him.

Martin closed his eyes, and created a new life for them.

He could see her, lying in a meadow beside him, her fiery hair spread out around her head, making her look like a miniature sun, like the force of nature she was born to be. Her mouth would be wide open in a big laugh, her eyes full of delight, her lips full of kisses meant for only him.

He would kiss her softly and tell her he loved her. Her green cut-crystal eyes would be wide open to him, no screen hiding her thoughts. She would whisper, "Martin, I love you, only you. My heart is yours..."

"... forever," Aurora whispered, then jerked awake. She couldn't remember the dream, but she could remember the feeling of being exactly where she was supposed to be, with the only man she could truly love.

Then exhaustion from another restless night crept in, along with reality. Rolling over to face the window where the dawn was just breaking, Aurora felt the usual loneliness sweep over her.

The World of Eoroe: Bryten series continues in book two, **The Guarded Heart**, which tells the story of Princess Aurora. It is available as an ebook (abridged version) or paperback (full version) at

AuthorJoCook.com

Acknowledgements

I have a large support system of good friends and family who encourage me in many ways, but there are a few who deserve some extra kudos.

Firstly, my sister Carol, for buying a house with me where I have enough space to write, and various spaces to do it in (front porch, back porch, upstairs porch)! She went along with my insistence that we get a house with a creek nearby, and it has saved my sanity many days when figuring out plot points was driving me crazy!

Secondly, my parents, whose support is never-ending and invaluable. (Yes, Daddy… I would love for you to bring me supper tonight!)

And to the most important part of the book process: beta readers! Carolyn Lance, Jo Dawson, Ying Gao, and Nina Boaz, you rock! Your suggestions were invaluable, and I totally re-did the beginning of the book based on your feedback! Thank you for making it so much better.

I would be remiss if I didn't acknowledge my cats, Sunshine and Boris, because they were a huge part of the process. Sitting on my lap so I couldn't type comfortably, sitting on the keyboard so I couldn't type *at all,* fighting so I couldn't get any work done… I blame all mistakes on them!

And lastly, the friends and family who have had to listen to me yammer about my books until their eyes glaze over: Mama, Carol, Angela, Jason and Dr. Picklehead… Thank you.

-Jo-

About the Author

Jo Cook dabbled with writing her whole life, but it was only during the World Upheaval of 2020 that her writing angel deigned to dictate something more than a novella. The Guarded Heart is Jo's debut novel, and she hopes to be publishing stories for many years to come.

Jo has a bachelor's degree in psychology and a master's degree in conflict management. She's been a flight attendant, copy editor, and small-business owner, and she spent a couple of very hot months bouncing around in a Tigger costume at Walt Disney World.

Her favorite authors include Georgette Heyer, Dick Francis, Kate Morton, J.K. Rowling, Rosamunde Pilcher, Heather Frost, Tad Williams, Frank Herbert and Suzanne Collins.

Jo's perfect day would involve thrifting, a good book, movies, and lots of lemonade.

Visit Jo Cook's website and subscribe to her newsletter to receive a FREE novella, A Rose for Carter (starring Rosa the kitchen maid and Carter the yard boy, who are mentioned briefly in Book One of The Guarded Heart), as well as news about upcoming releases!

AuthorJoCook.com